UNFRIENDED

A TOP 8 NOVEL

Also by Katie Finn

Top 8

What's Your Status? A Top 8 Novel

UNFRIENDED

A TOP 8 NOVEL

KATIE FINN

Point

FOR AMALIA,
Best Friend Forever

Library of Congress Cataloging-in-Publication Data

Finn, Katie.
 Unfriended : a top 8 novel / Katie Finn.
  p. cm.
 Sequel to: What's your status?
 Summary: After months of upheaval, seventeen-year-old Madison MacDonald of Putnam, Connecticut, is glad when summer brings some normalcy, but soon her deepening relationship with Nate is putting a strain on her friendships.
 ISBN 978-0-545-21128-4
 [1. Best friends--Fiction. 2. Friendship--Fiction. 3. Dating (Social customs)--Fiction. 4. Summer--Fiction. 5. Online social networks--Fiction.] I. Title.
 PZ7.F4974Unf 2011
 [Fic]--dc22

                            2010046479

ISBN 978-0-545-21128-4

Text design by Steve Scott

12 11 10 9 8 7 6 5 4 3 2 1   11 12 13 14 15 16/0

Printed in the U.S.A.   40
First printing, July 2011

ACKNOWLEDGMENTS

*I owe huge thanks to all the wonderful people who
have done so much for the Top 8 series:*

Abby McAden, who took a chance on me as a first-time author.

Rosemary Stimola, WBA (world's best agent).

*Steve Scott and Kevin Callahan, who make these books
look so amazing.*

*Amalia Ellison, Sarah Milligan, Jane Finn, Jason Matson,
Alex MacDonald, Becky Amsel, and Becky Shapiro,
who are all made of awesome.*

*Et beaucoup, beaucoup mercis to Aimee Friedman, who has
edited these books with such amazing insight, humor, patience,
and grace.*

*And thank you SO MUCH to all my wonderful friends who lent
their gorgeous faces for the profile pictures:
Katharine Brandt, Zack Clark, J. Claude Deering,
Amalia Ellison, Ari Finkelstein, Stuart D. Friedel, Sneha Koorse,
David Luna, Chris Rowe, Greg Rutty, Becky Shapiro,
and Melissa Hatcher Sundaram. You guys rock.*

"I do mind. The Dude minds.
This will not stand, you know.
This aggression will not stand, man."
— *The Big Lebowski*

"If two wrongs don't make a right, try three."
—Laurence J. Peter

CONSTELLATION . . .
Navigate Your Friendverse!

M²/
Madison MacDonald

Song: School's Out/Alice Cooper
Quote: "In summer, the song sings itself." —William Carlos Williams

Age: 17
Permanent Location: Putnam, Connecticut
Current Location: Putnam Beach

Followers: 54
Following: 54

Favorite Locations: Stubbs Coffee, New Canaan Drive-In, On A Blender Smoothie Shop, Putnam Beach

Royalty: Stubbs Coffee Princess

About Me: I ♥ my boyfriend, my friends, movie musicals, the fact that the Pocono Mountains are 2+ hours away from Putnam, iced vanilla lattes, piña coladas, getting caught in the rain, and the fact that there is no more school for TWO WHOLE MONTHS.

Taken by: Nate/Nate Ellis

M² At the BEACH & very happy about it. Let the summer BEGIN.
Location: Putnam Beach. Putnam, CT.

Nate Tutoring. My young charge? Currently foiled by FOIL.
Location: Stanwich Library. Stanwich, CT.

La Lisa La plage. Le soleil. Mes amies. En anglais? Time to TAN!
Location: Putnam Beach. Putnam, CT.

Schuyler Wearing SPF 75 and I STILL think I'm getting burned. What is wrong with the sun and/or my skin??
Location: Putnam Beach. Putnam, CT.

Dave Gold → La Lisa Bonjour, you. 1-4-3.
Location: Hott Wheelz (PRINCE). Putnam, CT.

Queen Kittson Sun. Beach. New bikini. Diet Coke. Bliss.
Location: Amagansett Beach. East Hampton, NY.

La Lisa → Dave Gold 1-4-3 back, ma chere.♥
Location: Putnam Beach. Putnam, CT.

Sarah♥Zach Trying my best to give my campers a sense of the GRAVITY of the stage. They are not getting it. And the fact that they are 8 is NO EXCUSE.
Location: Reach4theStars! Theatre Camp. Catskill, NY.

Lord Rothschild Why does nobody come to my concession stand? Only had ONE customer all morning. And she just wanted to know how to get to the other concession stand. ☹
Location: Second Concession Stand, Putnam Beach. Putnam, CT.

Young MacDonald Being a CIT rocks! Kumba-YA!
Location: Camp Arrowhead. Pocono Pines, PA.

Jimmy+Liz Hi honey!! I can see you from my lifeguard chair if I use my binoculars! (Liz)
Location: North Putnam Beach. Putnam, CT.

Jimmy+Liz I see you from MY lifeguard chair, babe! Do you see me waving? (Jimmy)
Location: South Putnam Beach. Putnam, CT.

Jimmy+Liz I see you!! ☺ (Liz)
Location: North Putnam Beach. Putnam, CT.

M² Am I the only one who is worried that NOBODY IS WATCHING THE OCEAN FOR DROWNING CHILDREN?
Location: Putnam Beach. Putnam, CT.

Jimmy+Liz Oh. Right. Good call. (Jimmy)
Location: South Putnam Beach. Putnam, CT.

King Glen Fixing transmissions & trying to figure out a way to get to the Hamptons this weekend. Anyone going that I can hitch a ride with? And then crash at their place?
Location: Putnam Motors. Putnam, CT.

be_tricia I know it's afternoon and all, but I'm craving breakfast food! Think the diner will still serve me eggs benedict??
Location: Colonial Diner. Putnam, CT.

 Brian M AAAAAAGH. Summer school is just like regular school. Except worse. And hotter.
Location: Putnam High School Science Wing. Putnam, CT.

 Gingerly OMG. The textiles collection here has fabrics that go back to 1750! I can't touch them, of course. But just to be in their presence! Swoon . . .
Location: Putnam Historical Museum. Putnam, CT.

 Rue Such a gorgeous summer day. Can't even think of a con to go with this pro. ☺
Location: Putnam Beach. Putnam, CT.

Aligned: M², La Lisa, Schuyler, Rue, Jimmy+Liz, Lord Rothschild, Justin
Location: Putnam Beach. Putnam, CT.

CHAPTER 1

Song: Sunburn/Owl City
Quote: "What we call the beginning is often the end."—T. S. Eliot

I stretched my arms in front of me, past the point where my towel ended and the hot sand began. I was at Putnam Beach, lying on my stomach on my favorite striped beach towel, enjoying the feeling of the warm sun on my back. I turned my head to the side and closed my eyes, smelling the beach air, taking in the silence and calm and—

"Mad?" A voice to my right interrupted my reverie. A voice that belonged to my friend Schuyler Watson. "Could you pass me my sunblock?" she asked. Without opening my eyes, I patted around me until I felt her bottle of SPF 75 and heaved it in the general direction of the towel next to me.

"Ow!" I heard her yelp. A moment later, she added, "Thanks, Mad!"

"You're welks," I said. A groan came from the

towel to my left, and I had a feeling that my abbreviation hadn't been appreciated, but who cared? I let out a long breath and felt myself smile. It was summer. It was a Friday. I was with all my best friends, and we had nothing to do today or tonight except hang out with each other. Finally, at long last, vacation had arrived.

It felt like it had been a long time coming. Frankly, ever since this past April, it seemed like everything in my life had been in a constant state of upheaval. But now things were back to normal—in all the ways that mattered.

I opened my eyes and looked at the towel to my left. My once-BFF, now just FF, Ruth Miller, was sitting there, wearing a one-piece bathing suit and her prescription sunglasses, reading a thick science textbook, her phone resting next to her. She caught my eye and smiled at me. I smiled back before resting my chin on my arms and looking out at the water of Long Island Sound, feeling utterly at peace.

"Sérieusement?" I heard a French-accented voice to my right say. I pushed my sunglasses up on top of my head and turned to see Lisa Feldman, another FF, staring at Schuyler.

Lisa seemed determined, through force of will, to correct the mistake fate had made by allowing her to be born in New Jersey and not Paris. She used French whenever possible, despite the fact that none of the rest of us spoke or understood it. But to my surprise, I'd actually begun to pick some up. Last week, when I had seen

Jules et Jim with my cinephile boyfriend, Nate Ellis, I'd only needed the subtitles about half the time.

Lisa's dark curly hair was piled on top of her head, and she was wearing big Audrey Hepburn–style sunglasses and a tiny black bikini, the better to tan as much as possible. As soon as summer rolled around, Lisa began a tanning regimen that she took *très* seriously, and by the time school started in the fall, she was at least three shades darker than she had been that spring.

Schuyler was wearing a bikini as well—or so she claimed. It was impossible to tell, as she had covered it up with a T-shirt and shorts, and wore a huge floppy hat so oversized that she kept having to lift up the brim to see us. Her long red hair was pulled back in a braid, the better to prevent her from chewing on it, which she was wont to do when stressed. Right after her breakup with her boyfriend, Connor Atkins, the hair chewing had gotten completely out of hand, and Lisa finally resorted to threatening to make her watch the terrifying *Dateline* special again, about the woman with the twenty-pound ball of hair in her stomach. It was this threat alone that had scared Shy into braiding her hair.

"What?" Schuyler asked, looking at Lisa. She held up her bottle of sunscreen, which featured a picture of two very pale kids sitting under an umbrella, wearing hats like Schuyler's. *Ain't No Sunshine When It's On!* the bottle proclaimed. "This?"

"Oui," Lisa said, shaking her head. "You look *ridicule.*"

Schuyler just shrugged and began reapplying.

7

"Better than what happened last summer," she said, and I nodded emphatically. Schuyler was very fair skinned, and without lots and lots of sunblock (as she'd discovered the hard way) her face ended up the same color as her hair.

"Guys like it when you have a little bit of a tan," Lisa said knowledgeably. "*Trust* me."

Schuyler turned to me and frowned, her version of an eye roll, but I just shook my head and smiled. Lisa had been like this—very in-the-know and constantly dispensing advice—ever since she'd slept with her boyfriend, Dave Gold, for the first time after the prom. (She had also started holding forth about how her relationship with Dave was *très* mature. But this was slightly undermined by the fact that Dave had recently developed an obsession with motorized toy cars.) I had been doing my best to just ignore it, but for Schuyler—the only one of us currently without a boyfriend—Lisa seemed to be a little harder to tune out.

"You actually do have to be sure you get a little sun every day," Ruth said, looking up from her textbook. "Otherwise, you run the risk of Vitamin D deficiency."

"See?" Lisa said, looking triumphant. "*Voilà.* Ruth agrees with me."

"That's not exactly what I heard her say," I said as Ruth laughed and Schuyler joined in.

I took a second just to enjoy the moment. A few weeks ago, I wouldn't have believed this was possible—the four of us, hanging out again, with no weirdness or lingering tension. In April, when my Friendverse profile had been hacked and my world turned upside down, I'd done my best detective work to find the culprit. But when I'd discovered the truth, it had broken my heart—the hacker had been Ruth, my best friend of the last nine years. As she was pretty computer illiterate, she'd hired Frank "Dell" Dell to do the actual hacking. He had been expelled, and Ruth and I had settled into a polite acquaintanceship, but I'd had no hope that we'd ever get our best-friendship back. But that had all changed after the prom.

Lisa was opening her mouth, no doubt to defend herself, when all our phones beeped simultaneously. Ruth lifted hers up from her towel, Lisa grabbed hers from her purse, I dug in my Pilgrim Bank canvas beach bag for mine, and Schuyler picked up her iPhone (dubbed the ShyPhone by all of us) and stared at it quizzically. Schuyler was more often than not completely perplexed by her phone, and still occasionally baffled by things like how to unlock the screen.

My screen was flashing with a Constellation message directed to all four of us.

 Lord Rothschild → M², Rue, La Lisa, Schuyler Hey, guys! I see that you're at the beach, too! Come visit if you're hungry, or just want to hang. I'm at the second concession stand. Not the first one. The SECOND one. Come on by! Please?
Location: Second Concession Stand, Putnam Beach. Putnam, CT.

Mark Rothmann was a friend of mine from school and a fellow Thespian. He'd gotten to know the rest of my friends over the course of planning a complicated—and not entirely aboveboard—operation during our prom. The eleven of us who'd been involved had all agreed to simply call this operation "Promgate." Mark hadn't really known any of my friends before that, but there are just some things in life that bond you. And using a spotty English accent while pretending to be an earl and steal back a priceless school heirloom was apparently one of them.

"*Je ne sais* why Mark keeps complaining," Lisa said. "I would think that a job where you were alone all the time would be awesome. He could probably just stop showing up for work, and nobody would even notice."

Mark was working at the very undesirable Second Concession Stand, which was at the far end of the beach and perpetually deserted. But that might have had something to do with the fact that Justin Williamson, my ex-boyfriend and one of the most popular guys at school, was working at the *First* Concession Stand. I looked at Mark's location on the Constellation message and realized that one of us probably had to go and visit him now. That was the thing about Constellation—there was no pretending that you were somewhere else.

Constellation was a new feature that Friendverse had introduced a few weeks ago. It did what Status Q, Friendverse's status update program, did: you used it to tell people what was on your mind throughout the day. But unlike Status Q, Constellation was focused on your location, which showed up automatically as part of your update. And even if you didn't post a new status, you could set your Constellation so that your location would be updated throughout the day. (Mine, for example, was set to update every fifteen minutes.) Constellation was also really helpful in finding people, because if you were in the same location as someone on your friend list, you'd get a message that you had "aligned" with them. In your feed, you could also see which of your friends had aligned, and who was hanging out with who. And if you went to one place often enough, you could win points and be declared a Royal of that location. Last week, I had been declared Princess of Stubbs Coffee, the coffee chain that provided me with my daily iced latte, a summer necessity. Getting Stubbs Princess was pretty much my proudest achievement of the summer so far.

But even though I would have liked *everyone* to know about my Stubbs royalty status, I'd increased the security of my online accounts a lot since the spring. The only people who could follow me on Constellation were people I was friends with. Not everyone had these security measures in place, and if you didn't, anyone could see where you were and what you were doing. But after everything that had happened over the last few months, I'd come to realize that not everyone had your best interests at heart when it came to the information you posted.

"You're right," Ruth was saying to Lisa with a wistful sigh. "I'd like a job where nobody was keeping track of me. Mrs. Adamson docks my pay if I'm a minute late. Which is probably why the twins have started booby-trapping the driveway."

I nodded, and we all sat in silence for a moment, reflecting on the state of our summer employment—such as it was.

I had hoped to get hired by the Putnam Players, the local community theater group. But the only positions they were filling were the ushers—*volunteer* ushers. So I'd settled for working at On A Blender, the smoothie shop on Putnam's main street. It was fine, except that none of my coworkers seemed to want to actually do any work. In addition, I was worried that some of my fingers were in danger of becoming permanently frozen from scooping ridiculous amounts of ice.

Ruth was working as a mother's helper, babysitting six-year-old twins. Apparently, the kids had seemed great in the interview. It was only when she'd started full-time that they'd revealed themselves to be demonic, scheming creatures. Because of this, and the fact that their names were Jane and Alec, we had taken to calling them the Volturi.

Lisa had scored the most impressive job of all—she was interning at the Putnam Hyatt, occasionally handling translations for any French-speaking guests and staying out of the way of the terrifying head concierge, Mr. Patrick.

Shy had been the first of us to secure a job, since she knew that otherwise she would have to spend the summer at home getting private tutoring alongside her stepsister, Peyton, who terrified her. Peyton was finishing her junior year (or "sixth form," as she referred to it) at home via private tutor, a necessity after she'd been kicked out of her Swiss boarding school for reasons Schuyler still wasn't clear on. So right after school let out, Schuyler had started working on the fuel dock of the Stanwich Yacht Club. But in the first three days, she'd fallen in the water twice and accidentally let a boat—or a ship, or whatever—drift out to sea, untethered. The vessel had eventually been recovered, but Schuyler had been moved to a less potentially damaging section of the yacht club, and was now working at the pool rental shop, signing out towels and water wings. She'd told us proudly that sunblock sales had increased ten percent since she'd started there.

Meanwhile, Nate had been hired for the summer to tutor Maxwell Avery, a seventh grader who had, impressively, flunked all of his classes this past year, including study hall. Maxwell's parents, dazzled by Nate's great grades and acceptance to Yale, had essentially put him on retainer, so that he could tutor Maxwell on call.

Occasionally, the situation was really frustrating, because it meant that Nate could be called away at a moment's notice. But it also meant that he sometimes had whole days free, which made me *very* happy. Ever since school had let out, Nate and I had been spending as much time together as possible. But even so, it still seemed like it was never enough. I was utterly smitten with my boyfriend.

I scrolled through the Constellation updates on my phone until I came to Nate's, and saw that he was still at the library. I touched the screen, zooming in on his über-adorable profile picture, and felt myself smile involuntarily.

"How's Nate?" Ruth asked, and I glanced over at her, dropping my phone onto my towel in surprise. She gave me a knowing look, and I felt my cheeks get hot, realizing that I had probably been gazing dreamily down at my screen.

"He's good," I said, and Ruth shook her head, smiling.

"You two," she said. "So cute."

"So?" Lisa asked, leaning forward. "Have you said it yet?"

Schuyler frowned. "Said what?"

"One-four-three," Lisa said, raising an eyebrow at me. "Have you?"

Ruth turned to me and Schuyler hoisted up the brim of her hat, their expressions expectant.

One-four-three was Lisa's code for "I love you," derived from the number of letters in each word. We'd been using it a lot around six months ago, when Lisa became fixated on if Dave was going to say it to her, or if she should say it first, and what it would mean if she did, and what would happen if she said it and he didn't say it back. Finally, she and Dave had exchanged one-four-threes. Lisa still claimed that Dave said it to her first, but we disputed this, as technically she'd said it first to him—just in French.

I shook my head, wishing that Lisa hadn't brought this up. One-four-three had been on my mind altogether too much lately. When I'd initially asked Lisa how she had known that she loved Dave, she had just shrugged with one shoulder and told me that she just *knew*. At the time, I'd found it an entirely unsatisfactory answer, but now I finally understood what she meant.

It had happened a little over a week ago. Nate and I had just had dinner at The Good Person of Szechuan, my favorite Chinese restaurant. As we were heading out to his truck, he walked around to the passenger side and held my door open for me, then closed it after I got in. And as I watched him get behind the wheel, buckle his seat belt, and look over and smile at me, I realized that I loved him. It was that simple. Like the fact had just marched into my brain, waving a tiny YOU LOVE NATE sign, and was now refusing to be ignored. It turned out that Lisa had been right—when you felt it, you *did* just know.

"No," I said, as I realized all my friends were still looking at me, waiting for an answer. "We haven't said it."

"But do you?" Schuyler asked, batting her brim away.

I could feel my face heat up as I looked down at the blue-and-white stripes of my towel. "Yes," I muttered.

Schuyler clapped her hands together excitedly. "I knew it," she said, turning to Lisa. "Told you!"

Lisa sighed, rummaged around in her purse, and tossed a five-dollar bill onto Schuyler's towel. *"D'accord,"* she muttered.

"Wait," I said, staring down at the bill, "did you guys have a *wager* going?"

"So why haven't you said it yet?" Ruth interjected quickly, clearly trying to distract me. But it worked.

15

I brushed the sand off my hands, then brushed that sand off the towel. "I don't know," I murmured. I looked around at my friends and realized that if I could talk to anyone about this, it was them. "It's just . . . things are really great with us right now. And I don't want to rock the boat." I saw Schuyler flinch, as she had been doing recently whenever we mentioned anything vaguely nautical. "Sorry, Shy," I said quickly. "I mean . . . I don't want to do anything that might change things. And it's a big deal, right?"

We all looked at Lisa, the only one who had said it to someone who wasn't a family member. I braced myself for another *my-relationship-is*-beaucoup-*mature* lecture, but Lisa just nodded. "It is," she said softly.

"And also, what if he doesn't say it back?" I continued. "I totally understand now why Lisa was freaking out so much."

"I wasn't freaking out—" Lisa started, a little huffily.

"OMG," Schuyler said, eyes widening. "If you said it and he didn't say it back . . . what then? Is there any way to recover from that? Would you guys have to break up, or something?"

I felt my stomach clench. "Don't say that," I said quickly. There had been a moment, during the planning of Promgate, when I'd had to confront what it might be like to lose Nate. And the idea had shaken me so much that I tried as hard as I could never to think about it.

"I wouldn't worry about it," Ruth said soothingly. "I mean, you guys have only been together three months. There's no rush to say it."

"Right," I said, trying to smile. But ever since the fact that I loved Nate had taken up residence in my brain, it was getting harder and harder *not* to say it to him. Like every time we were together and I didn't tell him, it felt like a tiny lie. "But anyway," I said, trying to change the subject, "maybe I should go say hi to Mark. He's probably getting lonely."

"I'm sure there are other people on the beach who can visit him," Schuyler said, scrolling through her phone. "Like Jimmy or Liz, or—" Her face turned pale, which was saying something, considering she was already sporting a layer of thick white sunblock. "OMG," she whispered, and I noticed that the ShyPhone was shaking in her hand.

"What is it?" Lisa asked, leaning closer to her.

"Connor," Schuyler choked out. "He's at Stubbs." She looked at us, stricken, and I tried to approximate a suitably horrified expression.

"How dare he," I said. "Because that was . . . um . . . your special coffee shop?"

"It's not that," Schuyler said. "Roberta Briggs is there, too. And they've *aligned*."

I felt my expression shift to one of genuine concern. Roberta Briggs had been considered the hottest girl in school since approximately fourth grade. And because of this, most guys were much too intimidated to actually talk to her, so she was consistently, and worryingly, single.

"But maybe they're just both there," Lisa said, trying to take the phone away from Schuyler, who was still

17

holding a death grip on it. "It doesn't mean that they're there together. *Pas du tout.*"

"But it *might* mean they're there together," Schuyler said, still holding on to the ShyPhone as Lisa tugged harder. "It doesn't *not* mean that!"

As I watched Schuyler's stricken, pale face, I realized that this was the problem with Constellation. Because it just gave people's locations, without any context, it could lead to this kind of jumping to conclusions and worry when it probably didn't mean anything other than two people happening to be at the same place at the same time.

"Shy," I said, and as she looked over at me, Lisa took the opportunity to wrest Schuyler's phone away from her. "Don't you think that maybe you should talk to Connor? You clearly miss him. . . ."

I heard Ruth draw in a breath, and Lisa frowned at me. We had all tacitly agreed not to bring up this possibility anymore, as the last time we'd tried, it had culminated in a crying jag so intense we'd had to make a midnight run to CVS for tissues and Gatorade, to prevent Shy from getting dehydrated.

"I can't do that," Schuyler said, shaking her head hard enough that her braid whacked the side of her face and got stuck in the sunblock for a moment. "You know that, Mad. You know he'd never forgive what . . . what I did."

I felt Lisa's and Ruth's eyes slide over to me, and I found myself wishing, a moment too late, that I'd just brought this up with Schuyler privately. I kept forgetting that the Connor breakup had its roots in a secret that only Schuyler and I knew.

Promgate had started, in large part, because of something that Schuyler had done at Choate three years before, involving a cheating scandal. Since Connor prided himself on his "uncompromising ethics"—which he'd even put in his campaign literature when he ran against me for senior class secretary—Schuyler had refused to tell him about what had happened at Choate, knowing that they would break up if he found out. But they had broken up anyway, because he had gotten tired of Schuyler obviously keeping things from him. When I'd seen how miserable Schuyler was after their breakup, I'd begun to suggest that maybe she just tell him what had happened, since at this point it couldn't really hurt.

"What are you talking about?" Lisa asked, looking from Schuyler to me, eyebrows raised.

"Because of the prom," I said quickly, looking at Schuyler. "Right?"

"Right," she agreed a little too emphatically. "Because of the prom." I saw Lisa look between us again, clearly not convinced. If it had been up to me, I would have told both Lisa and Ruth what had happened. But it wasn't up to me, and Schuyler hadn't wanted any more people than necessary to know.

"Speaking of the prom," Ruth said, lowering her voice, causing all of us to move a little closer, "any . . . news?"

I knew what Ruth was really asking—if Isabel Ryan had surfaced again. Isabel, who went to Hartfield High, was connected with Schuyler and the drama at Choate. Promgate had been necessary because she'd blackmailed Schuyler into giving her our prom queen crown. We'd gotten it back, but along the way had realized that Isabel had been working in tandem with Dell—who, it turned out, was her cousin. Isabel had wanted to get revenge on Schuyler, Dell had wanted to get revenge on me—and for good measure, on Ruth as well. Although I'd previously had no issues with Isabel, after Promgate, it became clear that she blamed me not only for thwarting her revenge plans but for wrecking her prom.

Ever since then, I had been living with a kind of low-grade anxiety that Isabel would suddenly pop up at the least opportune moment—like when I was struggling through my AP History final, for example. But the school year had ended without incident. As a precaution, I'd added her to my Constellation list—it made me a little more comfortable to know where she was. Which, since school had let out, was Nantucket.

"No sign of her," I said, and it seemed like my three friends let out a collective sigh of relief. "I think she's finally gone back to her cabin of evil, or fortress of solitude, or wherever it is she normally spends her time."

My phone beeped with a text, and I grabbed for it, hoping it would be my boyfriend, and feeling myself smile when I saw it was.

INBOX 1 of 28
From: Nate
Date: 6/20, 4:45 P.M.

OMG! Double feature tonite at the drive-in. Want to go on a date with me, gf?

I shook my head and smiled again. Nate thought my love of TLAs and slang was ridiculous, and I knew this text was just his way of teasing me. I started to send back an OMG TOTES text, then paused, my hand hovering over my keypad. I had promised to hang out with my friends tonight. We hadn't planned anything specific, but since our work schedules were all different, it was harder during the summer to get together than it was during the year. But it's not like we'd had ironclad plans or anything. And I knew they'd understand.

OUTBOX 1 of 34
To: Nate
Date: 6/20, 4:47 P.M.

Sounds like a plan, bf. See u in an hour?

"Don't tell me," Lisa said, and I looked up from my phone. "Nate?"

"Nate," I said. I dropped my phone and sunglasses in my bag. "He wants to see a movie tonight, so I should probably head home to get ready."

Lisa's mouth dropped open, Schuyler bit her lip, and Ruth turned to me in surprise.

"I, um, thought we had plans to hang out tonight," Schuyler said tentatively.

"*Oui*," Lisa said, frowning. "We did."

"I know," I said. "But here's the thing: I'm always going to have you guys. We'll be together all of next year. But Nate is going to school in the fall." I felt a lump in my throat begin to form, but I pushed on past it. "We're going to be in an LDR." Schuyler frowned, and I clarified, "Long distance relationship."

"You'll still see Nate, though," Ruth said encouragingly. "Yale's only forty-five minutes away."

"But he'll be at *college*," Schuyler murmured, like she was only just now putting this together.

"With college girls who put out," Lisa added.

"Exactly," I said, but then a moment later, her words hit me. "Wait. What?"

"Go," Ruth said, smiling at me. "Have fun with Nate."

"Yes. Abandon us," Schuyler said dramatically. A second later, her forehead creased. "I didn't really mean that, Mad. I was just kidding. It's fine that you go."

Lisa sighed. *"Allons-y,"* she said. "But just don't turn into one of those girls, *d'accord*?"

I shook my head quickly. "Don't worry." We had great scorn in our group for "those girls," the ones who abandoned their friends whenever they got into a relationship. But I wasn't being one of those girls. I was just hanging out with my boyfriend while I still could. My friends were always going to be around, after all.

"And I'm going to get a water," Schuyler said, smoothing out her new five-dollar bill. "Or maybe French fries. So I'll go to Mark's stand and say hi for all of us."

"Bonne idée," Lisa said to her. "But I vote for French fries."

"Second," Ruth piped up.

I finished tossing things into my beach bag and was preparing to head out when Schuyler looked at me in alarm. "Mad," she said. "We were supposed to figure out a date that we could do the bonfire. Remember? We'd planned on figuring it out *today*."

I sighed inwardly. When Schuyler fixated on something, she didn't let it go easily. And this summer, that something was The Bonfire.

Putnam Beach closed at sunset every night. But once a month, it stayed open until midnight, and you could reserve your own little patch of beach and have a bonfire, or stargaze, or go night swimming. Because this was super popular, you had to reserve way in advance, and we'd never managed to get organized enough to pull it off. But Schuyler seemed determined that this would finally be the summer of the bonfire. However, organizing this was harder than it sounded, as our extended friend group was big and a little unwieldy, and it was very hard to figure out a date that everyone would be around for.

"Right," I said. I glanced down at the time on my phone, aware of how quickly it was ticking by. "Let's figure it out tomorrow, okay, Shy? I don't want to be late."

I saw Schuyler's pale face fall for a moment, but then she nodded. "Sure," she said. "But we *have* to do it this summer. Okay?"

"Absolutely," I said.

"We will," Ruth said, nodding at her.

"Bien sûr," Lisa said, tossing her sunglasses down

onto her Eiffel Tower towel. She pulled her copy of French *Vogue* out of her purse and opened it, pointing out a picture on the page. "Now. Opinions, *s'il vous plaît*. What do we think of this haircut?"

As Schuyler leaned over and squinted down at the picture, Ruth smiled at me. "Talk to you later," she said.

"Talk to you soon," I replied, completing our traditional goodbye. I stood, rolled up my towel, and stuffed it into my canvas bag. As I watched, Ruth edged her towel closer to Schuyler's, so that before long, the strip of white sand where my towel had been had totally disappeared. The sight of this bothered me for a moment, but then I told myself that I was being ridiculous. After all, these were my best friends. We had all been through so much, I knew nothing could damage our friendship now.

As I headed to the parking lot, my phone beeped with a Constellation update. I looked down at the screen and saw that Tricia Evans had just arrived at the beach.

CHAPTER 2

Song: If I Knew Then/Lady Antebellum
Quote: "Better never than late."—George Bernard
Shaw

I dropped my phone back into my bag and looked around for Tricia. She went to Hartfield High, so none of us had known her before this summer. Lisa had met Tricia at the beach a few weeks back, when they'd bonded over the fact that they'd both been wearing T-shirts with French phrases written on them. And ever since then, she'd been hanging out with us pretty regularly.

"Madness!" I heard a voice call across the parking lot.

I glanced to my left and saw Tricia hurrying toward me. Tricia was big on nicknames, and seemed to be constantly trying out a new one on me whenever I saw her. I had a feeling this one might not stick, though. At least, I hoped not.

"Hey," I called. When she reached me, she shoved her sunglasses on top of her head and pulled out a pack of strawberry-mint Orbit. Tricia was going into her senior year, like the rest of us, and she was pretty, with light brown hair and gray eyes. Today, she was wearing a T-shirt with a picture of a wooden horse, and the words *HHS Trojan POWER!* beneath it.

I couldn't help but feel a little bit relieved that she had shown up. Since I'd been spending so much of my time with Nate, the fact that Tricia was hanging out with us helped to alleviate any lingering guilt I might have had about ditching my friends.

"I saw on Constellation that you guys were all here," Tricia said. Her eyes traveled down to my beach bag and the keys in my hand, and she frowned. "But maybe I'm too late."

"No," I said, pointing to where my friends sat on their towels. "Everyone else is still there. I just had to leave early."

"Oh," Tricia said, raising an eyebrow at me. "Got a big date with the boyfriend?"

I smiled without even meaning to. It was just what happened when I thought of Nate—like Pavlov's dog, who had been trained to think that food was coming whenever he heard a bell ring. I nodded, then glanced over at the line of cars heading out of the beach. "I should actually get going. . . ."

She winked at me. "Gotcha," she said. "I totally understand. But I e-mailed you a link to this really awesome site. Let me know what you think, okay?"

"Sure," I said, already taking a few steps toward

my car—Judy, my Jetta (aka Judy Jetta-son). "See you around, Tricia."

"Not if I see you first!" she called back with a cheerful wave.

I smiled and hurried to my car. When I got there, I looked across the parking lot once more. Tricia was rolling out her towel as Lisa held out the magazine to her, and Schuyler was returning to the group, balancing two containers of French fries. I looked at my friends for just a moment, then put my sunglasses back on and opened the car door, squinting a little against the sinking sun.

****

When I got home, I slammed the door and dropped my beach bag by the stairs. I was running much later than anticipated, as the one-lane road that led from the beach to Putnam's main road had been totally jammed. And I now had only about twenty minutes to wash the sand out of my hair and try to make myself look like I hadn't spent the entire afternoon lying out in the sun. Luckily, no one was home to catch me in a conversation or distract me.

My mother, CFO of Pilgrim Bank, had left for the UK last week to sort out the details of the merger of her bank and some British bank. She had covered the fridge with to-do lists and reminders that were actually a pretty sad indication of what she thought of the competence level of my father and me. Most of them said things like TRASH NEEDS TO BE TAKEN OUT and IF YOU TURN ON STOVE, DON'T FORGET TO TURN IT OFF and DON'T DRINK MILK THAT'S EXPIRED.

She had thought she'd be gone only a few days, but apparently, negotiations were dragging on. I tried not to sound too happy about this when she called to tell me, but I actually was. Because my mother's absence meant that there was absolutely nobody paying attention to what I was doing.

My father, normally the head sportswriter for the *Putnam Post*, had taken a summer sabbatical to write a book about some famous old-timey baseball scandal. He now seemed to spend most of his waking hours writing in his study, at the library, or driving to and from Cooperstown, in upstate New York, where the Baseball Hall of Fame is located. When he was home, he seemed to be in some kind of a fugue baseball state, wandering around muttering statistics, and not noticing when I came home at night.

And since my Demon Spawn brother, Travis (though, admittedly, he hadn't been *quite* as bad lately), was away for the entire summer, there was nobody hanging around to tattle and remind my distracted father that normally I did have a curfew, and it actually wasn't three A.M. Travis was currently away at a camp in the Pocono Mountains, working as a counselor-in-training, and was then going to spend the second half of the summer at an art camp in South Carolina.

In my room, my pink laptop beckoned temptingly from my bed. But I kept my resolve strong, walked past it, and took the World's Fastest Shower. Then I got changed into that night's date outfit—a jean miniskirt and a flowy white top—and looked in the mirror. Despite

Schuyler's best efforts, I had managed to get a little bit of a tan, which was set off by the white top. I smoothed back my straight, light brown hair—my bangs had *finally* grown out, thank gawd—and leaned forward to examine my eye makeup. In the past, I hadn't worn much makeup at all, but recently I had gotten really into what I called "a slightly more defined eye" and Lisa called "far too much watching of Taylor Swift videos." It had taken a lot of trial and error—and eye makeup remover—but I'd finally gotten the hang of it, and I really liked the effect.

I was just looking for my lip gloss when my phone beeped with a text. Thinking it might be Nate, I picked it up from my dresser immediately.

INBOX 1 of 30
From: Kittson
Date: 6/20, 5:45 P.M.

MADISON. I can see you're at home. Go online—
I want to iChat with you.

My Constellation must have updated. Knowing from experience that resistance was futile, I crossed over to my bed and booted up my laptop.

Kittson Pearson had become one of my close friends, against all odds and my own expectations. She was one of the most popular girls in school, and had dated Justin after me. But in the wake of my hacking—and after we weathered Promgate together—she'd become a good friend. She was spending the summer in the Hamptons, much to the dismay of her boyfriend, semi-reformed class troublemaker Glen Turtell, and I found myself missing her more than I'd thought I would. I had a feeling she would have helped me with the eyeliner thing, for example.

Once my computer booted up, I clicked on my iChat. While I waited for it to load, I checked my Gmail and saw the e-mail that Tricia had mentioned. I clicked on the link, but it just led me to an ERROR screen. I tried again, and after a moment, the same screen loaded. Figuring that Tricia must have copied the link wrong, I shrugged and brought up iChat again.

"Finally!" Kittson said as she appeared on my screen, wearing a hot-pink bikini and sitting in a room that appeared to be mostly decorated with wicker.

"Hey," I started, but at that moment Kittson's image froze for a few seconds before coming back to life again.

"What's up with your iChat?" she asked, peering at me and wrinkling her nose. "You're all weird and jerky."

I sighed. A few weeks ago, my parents had decided to install a bunch of new parental online controls. From what I had gleaned, it was due to some of Travis's recent internet searches, but I had not wanted to learn any more about it than that. I figured the controls were probably what was slowing down my internet connection—making this just one more way that my brother was still managing to interfere in my life.

Kittson came back into focus. The connection seemed better now, and I hoped it wouldn't give me any more problems. "So what's up?" I asked, glancing involuntarily at the clock at the top of my screen, hoping that whatever it was, it could be summed up quickly. I didn't want to keep Nate waiting.

"Nothing," she said, leaning forward and looking closely at me. "But what is going on with your eyeliner? I *love* it."

From Kittson, this was high praise indeed, and in the small screen that reflected my own image, I could see that I was smiling. "Thanks," I said. "It's just something I'm trying."

"I approve," she said, nodding gravely. "I've been telling you forever that you should do something bolder with your look."

I couldn't exactly recall that, and was about to say as much, when from downstairs, I heard the doorbell ring. "I have to go," I said. "Nate's here."

Kittson shook her head. "Believe me, it's good to keep a guy waiting," she said.

"I'll keep that in mind," I said, trying to keep myself from smiling, "but is everything okay?"

Kittson looked like she was about to say something, but then shook her head. "Yeah," she said. "I was just bored and wanted to talk, that's all."

"I'll call you tomorrow?" I asked.

"Sure," Kittson said, examining her nails. "I might not be around, but if I am, I'll answer." Then she signed off without saying goodbye, something I'd grown used to by now from her.

The iChat screen froze once more before coming back to life again. I made a mental note to tell my father about it when he reappeared. Then I shut my computer off and headed downstairs to meet my boyfriend.

CHAPTER 3

Song: I And Love And You/The Avett Brothers
Quote: "Whatever our souls are made of, his and
mine are the same."—Emily Brontë

 La Lisa Wondering why it is taking SOME PEOPLE an hour to choose a movie.
Location: Putnam DVD. Putnam, CT.

 Justin Today was SO busy. Nonstop customers. Thrilled the beach is finally closing for the night.
Location: First Concession Stand, Putnam Beach. Putnam, CT.

 Lord Rothschild ☹
Location: Second Concession Stand, Putnam Beach. Putnam, CT.

 Schuyler Maybe because SOME PEOPLE only want to choose movies that are in French with subtitles.
Location: Putnam DVD. Putnam, CT.

 Rue I think I'm beginning to miss the Volturi.
Location: Putnam DVD. Putnam, CT.

King Glen Seriously, NOBODY is going to the Hamptons this weekend? What is wrong with you people?? **Location: Colonial Diner. Putnam, CT.**

 M² OMG. Is there a better movie than Moulin Rouge? **Location: New Canaan Drive-In. New Canaan, CT.**

 Dave Gold → M² Yes. There are many, many, many better movies. And very few of them involve Ewan McGregor singing and dancing. **Location: Putnam Pizza. Putnam, CT.**

 Dave Gold → Nate Dude. I see you're at the drive-in, too. Moulin Rouge? Lameness. **Location: Putnam Pizza. Putnam, CT.**

 Nate → Dave Gold Dude. We're seeing it with a double feature of Troy. Does that make it better? **Location: New Canaan Drive-In. New Canaan, CT.**

 Dave Gold → Nate Not really. **Location: Putnam Pizza. Putnam, CT.**

 Nate Starry night. Bag of popcorn. Very manly movie. My girl. All is good. **Location: New Canaan Drive-In. New Canaan, CT.**

"I'm just saying," I said, sliding closer to Nate as his truck took a corner, "that I don't buy it."

He laughed, and then glanced over at me with one of his slightly crooked smiles, and I felt my heart, as always, begin to pound a little faster. Jonathan Ellis—known to all except his parents as Nate—and I had been going out for three whole months now, but I still got butterflies in my stomach when he smiled at me. And that was to say nothing of what happened when he kissed me.

These days, it seemed like things were better than ever with us. Right after the prom, Nate and I had had a breakthrough conversation, when we'd both realized that we hadn't been talking enough about the things we needed to. And ever since then, we were opening up to each other more. It was really tough at first—much harder than I'd thought it would be. But as I'd told him more and he'd told me more, it got less scary. And now I felt even closer to him. It was strange—lately, he'd almost begun to feel like not only my boyfriend but my best friend. I was trying my very hardest not to think about the fact that, come September, he was going off to college. Because it was only June. We had the whole summer, filled with fireflies and ice cream dates and fireworks, still ahead of us.

We had just had a date at the New Canaan Drive-In movie theater, seeing a double feature of *Moulin Rouge* and, of all things, *Troy*. It was Nate's theory that the drive-in had been losing revenue of late, and so was trying to market to couples by showing a chick flick paired with a guy's film. Nate had suffered through *Moulin Rouge*, which I adored, and then I'd suffered through *Troy*, which I did not adore. I mean, parts of it were fine—like, um, Brad Pitt's triceps—but mostly, there seemed to be an excessive amount of funeral pyres.

Nate had loved it, though. And for some reason, when the huge wooden Trojan horse was wheeled inside the palace walls, he had unexpectedly let out a laugh.

"What?" I'd whispered to him.

"Nothing," he'd said. "It just reminded me of something." I was about to ask what, but then the Greeks had leapt out from the horse, shocking the Trojans, who hadn't realized that they'd just been tricked into bringing the enemy inside the gates, and my attention was drawn back to the movie.

And because Nate's truck had bench seats, we'd watched the movie sitting right next to each other, his arm around my shoulders. This had almost made up for having to watch sword fighting for two hours.

"Don't buy what, my Mad?" Nate asked me now as I adjusted the bag of takeout between my feet. Even though we'd finished off a big bag of buttery popcorn (movie #1) and split a box of Sno-Caps (movie #2), both of us were still hungry. So we'd just picked up takeout from Putnam's diner, the Colonial. Nate had gotten pancakes, and I'd gotten my current diner usual, grilled cheese with waffle fries, extra ketchup.

I had been complaining about *Troy*, which I knew was dangerous, as it left me open to *Moulin Rouge* mockage. "I guess I don't buy that that huge war would have started over one person," I said. "I mean, really, Menelaus couldn't have found another wife? He was the *king*. He had to throw all of Mesopotamia into disarray over Diane Kruger?" And, on that note, if Brad Pitt and Eric Bana are walking around with no sleeves, does any

36

girl in her right mind really choose Orlando Bloom in a tunic? I think not.

Nate was quiet as he paused at a stoplight. "I buy it," he said, and I looked at him, surprised. "I think . . ." He cleared his throat before continuing. "I think if someone is your true love, you have to go to any length to try and get them back." He gave me a quick smile, and I felt my heart begin to beat faster.

There was silence, nothing but the rumbling of the truck's engine, and I was suddenly seized with indecision. Was this the moment when I should tell Nate that I loved him? I could feel my pulse racing. But before I could decide, the light changed and Nate put the car into drive.

"I'll tell you what I don't buy," he said, arching an eyebrow at me. "I don't buy Nicole Kidman lying and pretending she doesn't love Ewan McGregor. What kind of way is that to treat someone?"

I smiled. "No, that makes total sense to me," I said. "She loves him *so* much that she is willing to risk him hating her to save him." Nate frowned and opened his mouth to argue, but I laughed. "I think they're actually the same thing," I said. "To sacrifice for love. But that's the girl version. Guys do it with wars, that's all." I looked out the truck window and realized that we were almost to our destination . . . the Bluff.

My father had come home from Cooperstown that evening (he'd sent me a text asking me if I knew how to work the stove), so my house was not an option as a place to, um, hang out. And unfortunately, Nate's parents were home, too. I'd met Nate when his family and mine had ended up on the same trip to the Galápagos Islands. And Mr. and Mrs. Ellis seemed to think that because we'd shared this experience, all Nate and I ever wanted to do when we were at their house was to watch videos of the trip. And apparently, Nate's father had just re-edited the footage of the tortoise.

I actually had a soft spot for tortoises, though. I'd given Nate one of a pair of carved tortoises when we'd first started going out, and kept the other for myself, since tortoises stay together for life. We hadn't really talked much about it, but I knew that Nate had understood the significance—after all, in the Galápagos, he'd had to sit through all the same lectures I had, all about "The Magnificent, Monogamous Tortoise." And the last time we'd been iChatting, I'd glimpsed his carved tortoise sitting on his bedside table—the exact spot where mine was.

So with both of our houses not options, we headed for what had become our go-to makeout spot. The Bluff was a place that Nate and I had discovered together, by accident. (I was actually really glad about this. I wouldn't have wanted to go someplace where he had possibly made out with other girls.) We had found it in late May, when we had been trying to get to an end-of-year party that Sarah Donner's boyfriend, Zach Baylor, had been throwing at his house in Hartfield, the town that was twenty minutes outside of Putnam and Stanwich.

Nate and I had driven through the unfamiliar streets of Hartfield, getting increasingly lost, until I conceded that we should just get directions on my phone—something Nate was gracious enough not to mention that he'd suggested half an hour before. Just as I'd taken out my phone, Nate had pulled down a deserted-looking driveway to turn around, but then had stopped. I paused in scrolling through my phone, which had suddenly lost all service, and saw where we were. "Wow," I'd murmured, just taking it in. Nate had nodded and smiled at me, then killed the engine, and we got out of the car to look at what was in front of us.

It was a large, empty plot of land. There was nothing on it—just an open expanse of overgrown grass. It was a huge piece of property—there were houses on either side, but far enough away that all you could really see of them were occasional lights through the trees. We had walked across it, as though an explanation for it would be found somewhere. But it was just empty—like a very rare New England tornado had swept through and picked up this one house, leaving everything else around it untouched.

"Check it out," Nate had called to me from the very edge of the property, and I walked to join him. In driving in circles around Hartfield, we must have been moving uphill, something I hadn't registered until now. We were pretty high up—and had a great view of Hartfield spread out in front of us.

"What is this place?" I'd asked, looking from the view to the open space behind us—a space so large that Nate's truck, at the end of it, looked impossibly small.

"I have no idea," Nate had said. He'd taken my hand

then and pulled me close to him. "But whatever it is, it's ours." Then he'd leaned down and kissed me.

Ever since then, we'd been coming back to the spot whenever we wanted some uninterrupted time together. Nate had named it the Bluff early on, even though technically, it probably didn't have enough of an overhang to qualify it as a true bluff. But whatever we called it, it was an ideal spot. We'd learned after the second time that it was located in some kind of strange dead zone. It was almost impossible to get cell service, and neither of our phones were able to connect to the internet—which meant, in terms of Constellation, that we dropped off the map entirely. When my friends had gotten concerned after this had happened, I'd told them about the Bluff, but vaguely: I didn't want Lisa and Dave—or Ruth and her boyfriend, Andy Lee—to start using it as *their* makeout spot. It was my place with Nate, the one spot that was entirely ours, and I loved it.

Nate killed the engine and we got out, taking the Colonial Diner bag, along with the blanket Nate always kept in his truck for our visits here. Nate left the doors open and kept the stereo on, so we'd be able to hear the music. We walked to the center of the property and spread out the blanket on the ground.

"So, I have a new theory," I said as I sat down cross-legged. Nate stretched out across the blanket and rested his head in my lap.

"Tell me," Nate prompted. We liked to put forward guesses as to why this land was just sitting here empty. They ran the gamut from the aforementioned tornado to a very large sinkhole that had somehow miraculously repaired itself, to a shoddy construction job.

"Really, really efficient termites," I replied, and Nate burst out laughing. I joined in, and then we both fell silent, soaking in the night air. I ran my fingers through his soft, curly brown hair and Nate turned his head and looked up at me.

"I think there was a house here," he said, taking one of my hands in his—the one that wasn't stroking his hair—and running his fingers across my palm, making me shiver. "I think that there was a really perfect, really beautiful house here once."

"And what happened to it?" I asked as Nate rested my hand on his chest, brushing his fingers across the back of it.

"I think that it got torn down," he said, his voice strangely thoughtful and sad. "I think that this was a home for two people who were really in love. And something happened."

"What happened?" I asked, feeling myself getting swept up in his story, as though there was a real answer, as though Nate wasn't just wildly speculating.

"What always happens," he said, glancing up at me. "Betrayal. Hurt. Misunderstandings. And I think the other person didn't want to be in the house without them. So they tore it down."

I looked at the land surrounding me and suddenly felt sad, even though Nate was just making all this up. I almost preferred his cursed-ancient-burial-ground theory to this one. "But maybe it was that *and* termites,"

I said, trying to lighten the mood, and was rewarded when Nate laughed and leaned up and kissed me.

What started as just a light kiss quickly turned more serious, and we stretched out on the blanket together, the takeout bag pushed to the side and forgotten.

Making out with Nate lately had been better than ever, and it was because I knew absolutely where we stood. Nate wasn't a virgin, like me; he'd slept with his ex-girlfriend Melissa when they were still together. (I had tried very, very, very hard after I'd learned this not to hate Melissa irrationally, as she actually was a really nice person.) We had decided that we weren't ready to sleep together yet, which took pressure I hadn't even realized had been there off our makeout sessions. Now, we would just make out for hours, and when we began to move a little closer to new bases, we always checked in with each other to make sure it was okay.

But lately when Nate and I were making out, I tended to get totally lost in him and in the moment, and often it was Nate who moved us back to more familiar territory. And frequently, as we were kissing, I'd be struck by how amazingly right it all felt — that this was Nate, who made me laugh and who I could talk to about anything — but it was also *Nate*, who could literally make my knees weak when he ran his lips over that one spot on my collar-bone, and whose kisses had the power to remove all rational thought from my head. It seemed too wonderful to me that both of these things could be found simultane-ously in the same person.

After we'd been kissing on the blanket for a while —

I had absolutely no idea how long it had been. Making out with Nate seemed to take place in some strange wormhole where I completely lost all sense of time passing—we paused and caught our breath.

"Wow," he murmured into my hair, kissing me on the forehead.

"Yeah," I agreed, opening my eyes, blinking at the surroundings, and trying to remember where I was. Things came slowly into focus. Nate and I weren't on a balcony in the South of France. We were at the Bluff. Nate smiled at me, and I sat up, straightening his shirt and my own. "Dinner?" I asked, reaching for the bag, and glad that while we'd been otherwise occupied, some hungry woodland creatures hadn't made off with our food.

"Absolutely," he said, sitting up as well. I reached for the takeout bag and unpacked our picnic. My grilled cheese was stone cold, but I'd actually come to enjoy the taste of them that way. Nate's pancakes were chocolate chip, with extra syrup, and looking at them, I felt my stomach rumble and hoped that he'd share.

"Fry?" I asked, angling the container closer to him.

"Why, thank you," he said, taking one. Then he opened his plastic container and poured syrup over his pancakes. I leaned over, looking at them hopefully. He smiled and held out his fork to me, and I cut off a piece of pancake. It was cold, but also chocolatey, and syrupy, and I cut off another piece before handing the container back to him.

"How are they?" he asked. Rather than answering, I leaned over and gave him a slightly sticky kiss. "Those *are* good," he said, and I gave him a smile before leaning back and picking up my own food. "Question," he said after a moment of both of us eating in silence. It was amazing what a good makeout session could do for the appetite.

"Shoot," I said, taking a bite of my grilled cheese.

"On Dave and Lisa's status updates," he said, swirling a piece of pancake in the syrup, "I've seen them leaving each other messages—like 'one-four-three,' I'm pretty sure." He raised one eyebrow at me, something I always loved, as it reminded me of the first time I saw him do this, when we first went to the drive-in together.

"Yeah," I said. "What about it?"

"I think it's some kind of code," he said excitedly. "And I think we should figure it out. I bet it's not that hard to crack."

I smiled, feeling like I should have been expecting this. Right as Stanwich High had let out for the summer, Nate had read a book called *Spy, Spy Again,* an anonymous memoir of a high-ranking former CIA agent. He had become obsessed with it, and with codes and clues and espionage in general. He was in the middle of three other books on spying, and his DVD picks all tended now toward things like the Bourne trilogy. And because "watching a DVD" had become our mutual code for "making out on the couch" I found it very hard to concentrate on kissing Nate when things kept exploding on the screen and Matt Damon kept beating people up in foreign locations. Nate had even started texting me in code (but then usually texting me the key to the code if we were pressed for time). I was trying to just roll with this, and even though he had insisted on giving me some of his spy books to read, I had yet to open any of them. But reading them myself actually didn't seem to be necessary, as Nate was perfectly happy to recap them all—in detail—for me.

"It's not hard to crack at all," I said. "I can tell you what it means right now."

"Oh," Nate said, looking a little crestfallen. He'd probably hoped that we could have found the key to the code together. This had become Nate's idea of fun.

"And it's not even that complicated," I said. "It's an alphanumeric cipher." I paused for a moment after saying that, not quite able to believe that Nate had gotten me using this terminology. "So each number stands for the number of letters in the word that they're saying to each other."

"Ah," Nate said, tucking that one lock of hair that always seemed to escape (the hazards of growing out your bangs) behind my ear. "Impressive. I wasn't sure you'd been listening."

"Always," I said, smiling at him. I had leaned forward for a kiss when Nate continued.

"So what are they saying?" he asked.

"Oh," I said, leaning back. "They're saying—" I stopped short when I realized what I'd be saying to him when I told him the meaning of this code. I'd be saying "I love you." Even though I'd just be explaining something to him, translating for someone else, I would still be saying those three words to Nate.

I could feel my pulse quicken as I tried to figure out how to handle this. I didn't want the first time I said these words to him not to be real. "Well," I said, my face getting hot. "Like I said, the code is the number of letters in each word. So *one* stands for *I*. And *three* stands for *you*. And so, *four* stands for . . ." I trailed off, hoping he would figure out the missing word without me having to tell him. After a moment, comprehension dawned and I thought I saw his own cheeks redden slightly.

"Ah," Nate said. "Gotcha." We both ate in silence for a minute before Nate put his pancake container down and turned to me. "But why the code?" he asked. "I mean, I've heard Dave and Lisa say that to each other. I've heard them yell it to each other across vast distances."

I smiled. It was true; even though there had been a lot of drama about saying it to begin with, Dave and Lisa were now not at all shy about telling each other—and anyone else in hearing distance—how they felt. "Lisa came up with it," I said with a shrug. "I guess sometimes it's nice to have something that's just between you." This was, I realized, probably the reason I liked the Bluff so much. "Something that's private."

"I can see that," Nate said. He leaned close to me, gave me a quick kiss, traced his finger down my cheek, then looked at me for a long moment.

I could feel my heart begin to beat quickly. Was this it? Was Nate going to say 1-4-3 to me? Did that mean—OMG, did that mean that *he* loved *me*?

My pulse was racing, and I looked into his eyes, searching his expression for a clue. I held my breath, my heart hammering, wondering if it was going to happen. Nate took a breath, looking right into my eyes. But at that very second, the music playing from Nate's stereo switched to something with thrashing guitars and a fairly tone-deaf singer who nonetheless sang very loudly. Nate looked over at the stereo and then back at me, smiling. I smiled back and tried not to let the disappointment I was feeling show on my face.

Nate pulled out his phone and checked the time, frowning (I knew that's what he was doing, since at the Bluff, our cell phones were reduced to being very expensive clocks).

"Time to go?" I asked, feeling my heart sink. Nate no longer had a curfew, so whenever we had to cut our makeout sessions short, it was because of me. And even though my father wasn't really aware of what I was doing, I knew that when he was home—and hungry, if the stove continued to baffle him—I couldn't push the curfew thing too far.

"Time to go," he confirmed, and we put our takeout containers in the white paper diner bag. We were always really careful about cleaning up after ourselves when we came to the Bluff. Not only because I'd paid attention in second grade and learned that nobody likes a litterbug, but also because we didn't want to leave evidence we'd been there—just in case this property did still belong to someone who might not have liked the fact that teenagers were hanging out there several nights a week. Not to mention we didn't want to attract ants or raccoons or bears. Even though Nate had assured me that bears were exceedingly rare in suburban Connecticut, I thought it better we not risk it.

Nate got to his feet, then offered me his hand to pull me up. I stood, and together we folded up the blanket and then got into the truck. Nate started the engine and backed out of the deserted driveway carefully, not turning his lights on until we were on the main road. I pulled on my seat belt to give it some slack, and then slid across Nate's bench seat (truly, my favorite feature of the truck) so that I was sitting close, leaning into him. Nate took one hand off the wheel and draped his arm across my shoulders.

He pulled up to a stoplight and we sat in front of the red, the truck rumbling beneath us. He bent down and kissed the top of my head. "I think it's going to be a great summer," he whispered to me.

Pete Townshend came on the stereo, singing our song, "Let My Love Open the Door." I smiled and kept time by tapping my fingers on Nate's arm.

"One thing that's been bothering me about our song," he said, shaking his head.

"And what's that?" I asked, smiling up at him, feeling utterly peaceful and relaxed.

"Well," said Nate, faux-seriously, "he keeps wanting his *love* to open the door. But really, wouldn't you think he'd have better luck with a key?"

I shook my head at that but wasn't quite able to stop myself from smiling. I leaned my head back against Nate's shoulder, and as the light changed to green, I turned up the volume and let Pete Townshend sing us home.

CHAPTER 4

Song: You Make My Dreams/Hall & Oates
Quote: "The past is never dead. It's not even past."—William Faulkner

 M² Making smoothies. Wondering if the whole "wheatgrass" thing was actually an elaborate practical joke that somehow caught on.
Location: On A Blender Smoothie Shop. Putnam, CT.

I rubbed my hands together to try and get some feeling back into them and shifted my weight from foot to foot. From the research I'd done on the internet, hypothermia could be prevented if you kept moving.

I was in the walk-in freezer of On A Blender, trying to locate an elusive box of frozen strawberries. The walk-in freezer was a tiny space stocked floor to ceiling with cardboard boxes of frozen fruit and vegetables, and bags upon bags of extra ice. I'd learned from my employee handbook that we—the "smoothie operators"—were discouraged from revealing to the customers that we didn't use fresh fruit. The handbook pointed out that it had been fresh at *some* point, and unless they asked exactly when that was, we weren't supposed to tell them.

I scanned the rows of boxes, but could not see strawberries anywhere. Which was a problem, as the Strawberry Jammin' was far and away our most popular smoothie. I let out a sigh of frustration and noticed with alarm that I could now see my breath. I was wearing the ugly, ancient gray OAB sweatshirt that we kept underneath the counter for trips to the walk-in, but it didn't seem to be helping very much.

I heard the door to the shop open, and the bell jangled loudly. But I didn't hear the one thing I was listening for, my coworker giving the trademarked OAB greeting, "Who wants to go On A Blender?" In fact, I didn't hear anything.

"Kavya?" I called, even though I knew that the freezer door was pretty much soundproof, so this was fruitless—much like me, at the moment.

I stood still, listening hard, hoping that someone wasn't robbing us because my coworker had spotted something shiny and wandered off. There had been a section in the handbook for dealing with "smoothie criminals," but I had just skimmed it in the hopes that I wouldn't actually have to put the information to use. And I had seen my other two coworkers, Daryl Oliver and John Reyes, slipping out to the alley to take a "tea break" five minutes before, so I knew they weren't inside. And that when they came back, they would have an irrepressible urge to giggle at inanimate objects.

I heaved open the heavy silver door and stepped out into the narrow hallway that led directly behind the counter, where the register and smoothie prep area were.

On A Blender had been in Putnam for a few years now, but after working there for a while, I was amazed that it had survived a week. There was a manager, allegedly named Gary, who signed our paychecks—but I'd never seen him, and this seemed to be the only managerial duty that he performed. He certainly wasn't making sure that his employees were doing any work.

Daryl and John spent the majority of the workday eating all the mangoes and watching *telenovela*s on the TV (it was suspended from the ceiling and, according to the handbook, was meant to face the customers and only play—on repeat—the corporate OAB promotional video, *The Wonderful Whirl-ed Of Smoothies!*). I hadn't really known Daryl or John before this summer, but I recognized them from school, where they were central fixtures in the stoner crowd that hung out by the vending machines behind the gym, rarely seeming to attend classes. It seemed like the two of them were keeping up their extracurricular activities in the summer. I'd seen John, on more than one occasion, just staring at a whirring blender, mesmerized, as the line of people waiting on smoothies got longer and longer.

The smoothie shop was small, with the walls painted bright, primary colors and hung with blown-up pictures of laughing people and cuddling couples, all holding smoothies and looking ecstatic about this. In front of the counter, there was a customer waiting, arms crossed, tapping her foot and making a big show of checking her watch. And completely unaware of this was Kavya, who was sitting on the back counter, scrolling through her phone.

I hadn't known Kavya Choudhury at all before we'd started working together. She was from Stanwich, but had only moved there this summer, from Los Angeles. She was very unimpressed with the East Coast in general, and with Connecticut in particular, and spent most of her time on her phone, talking or texting with her friends back in California. But even though she did less work than I would have believed possible, her looks alone were probably helping us make a profit. If she'd gone to Putnam, she would have undoubtedly given Kittson a run for her money as prom queen. She had perfect skin and long brown hair. Though she was around my height, she managed to be both willowy *and* curvy, something I hadn't even known was possible before meeting her. There was a steady stream of guys who seemed to come into the shop simply to gaze at her, and one particularly persistent, deluded middle schooler who asked for her number every time he came in. Last week I'd discovered, much to my distress, that she'd finally given him mine.

"Hi," I said a little more loudly than usual, for Kavya's benefit. She glanced up at me, looked over at the customer, then, apparently disinterested, turned her attention back to her phone. "May I take your order?"

"Yes," the woman said in a tone of voice designed to let me know how unhappy she was. "I'll have the Blender in the Grass. And *quickly*. I'm now running late."

"Right," I said, heading for the small refrigerator where we kept the wheatgrass. "Coming up." I gave her my best responsible-employee smile, then turned to the refrigerator, which was right next to where Kavya was sitting. "Kavya," I hissed.

Without looking up from her phone, she shook her head. "I can't handle vegetables, Madison. It's my enzyme thing. I've told you this before."

In fact, she had. After we'd been working together for about a week, she had told me that she had something called OAS, which meant she was totally allergic to vegetables and couldn't even handle them without getting "like, a rash. Ick." This was in addition to not being able to scoop ice ("I have the worst circulation *ever*. And it's so not good for me to let my hands get too cold.") or deal with any of the cleanup duties ("I wish I could. Really. But I have this back thing, and I think sweeping might really aggravate it."). Which basically meant, even when there were *four* of us working, I was sometimes the only one actually doing any work, with Kavya refusing to touch vegetables, and Daryl, when he hit his paranoid state, convinced that the blueberries were staring at him.

"I know," I said as I pulled open the fridge door. I took out two of the small wheatgrass plants, set them on the counter, and heaved over the weird metal wheatgrass juicer. "But can you ring her up while I do this?"

Kavya looked up from her phone, then gave a deep sigh. But she climbed down from the counter and walked over toward the register and our (most likely) non-repeat customer. I fed the wheatgrass through the machine—really, a ridiculously large amount of wheatgrass to produce such a small, foul-smelling dribble of juice. I poured the juice into a small cup, set it on a plate with an orange slice, and placed it on the counter. The woman took her change from Kavya, frowned at me, then downed her juice in one shot and hustled out the door, the bell above her head jangling.

"Bye, now! Return to Blender!" I called after her, even though I had a feeling that she would not be doing this. But according to the employee handbook, this was the required farewell. The door slammed behind her with window-rattling force. "Kavya," I said, trying my very best to sound calm and reasonable, but even I could hear, not really succeeding, "why weren't you waiting on the customer?"

"I can't touch vegetables," she said, shaking her head as she reached for her phone again. "I *told* you that."

I opened my mouth to respond when the bell jangled again. I looked up and saw, to my surprise, my ex-boyfriend standing in the doorway.

Justin Williamson, as ever, looked like he had just stepped out of the pages of an Abercrombie catalog. I always half expected to see a muddy golden retriever and a group of shirtless rugby-playing guys just to the left of him. He was undeniably cute, but after Nate, it was a kind of cute that no longer seemed all that interesting to me.

Justin's eyes scanned the store and rested on me. I gave him a tentative smile, trying to decipher his expression. After Justin and I had broken up, he'd remained on the fringes of my friend group, and we'd been cordial when we'd seen each other in school. Because of this, I'd felt like we could turn to him for a favor during Promgate. We'd asked him to distract Isabel by pretending to be romantically interested in her at a crucial moment. Isabel had taken the bait, and the plan had succeeded. But afterward, perplexed as to why I'd asked him to flirt with a total stranger, Justin had wanted to know the reason. At that moment, I had been exhausted and not sure how much I should reveal to him. So Justin had jumped to his own conclusion—that I'd been using him. Over the last remaining weeks of school, he had taken to avoiding me in the hallways. It's not like Justin and I ever talked that much—not even when we'd been going out—so it wasn't an enormous change. But it bothered me that he thought I'd just used, and then dismissed, him.

"Yum," Kavya breathed. I saw that she'd walked to the front of the counter, her eyes not leaving Justin—who, at this moment, was backlit in a golden haze from the late-afternoon sun. "Who is *that*?"

"Justin Williamson," I murmured as subtly as possible, since he was starting to walk toward us—and it's not like the shop was all that big. "My ex."

Kavya glanced at Justin, then back at me, and raised her eyebrows skeptically. "Really?" she asked, her voice heavy with disbelief. Which was actually fairly insulting.

"Really," I hissed at her as Justin reached the counter and smiled at me.

"Hey, Mad," he said easily. "How's it going?"

I blinked at him. He was acting utterly normal, as though he hadn't been turning away from me whenever we passed each other in the hall. But maybe this was his way of letting me know he was over it. "Fine," I said, recovering. "Good. Really good. How are you?"

"Can't complain," he said, giving me a lazy smile and leaning his elbows on the counter. I heard a strange bleating sound and realized after a second that it was coming from Kavya's phone, which was dangling, forgotten, at her side. Clearly, I'd never heard a message go unanswered before. Kavya was staring at Justin, all her L.A. cool gone, and it was the longest time I'd ever seen her focus on something other than her texting. Justin also glanced in Kavya's direction and just stared for a second. She tended to have that effect on people. This was generally followed by a temporary inability to speak English, and most of the male customers just ended up pointing silently at one of the happy-couple smoothie posters.

I could tell that Justin was not an exception to this. He blinked at Kavya, opening and then closing his mouth. It was the way that he used to look at me, and then the way he used to look at Kittson. It was the look of Justin becoming smitten. I felt myself give a half smile as I watched. But, unbelievably, with what seemed like an effort of will, Justin turned away from Kavya. He took a gulp of air, then smiled at me again. "I heard you were working here," he said.

I was about to point out that he probably hadn't *heard* this from anyone, but rather had seen it on Constellation, when Kavya nudged me out of the way to stand in front of him.

"Hi," she said, giving him a wide smile. "I'm Kavya Choudhury." She smoothed down her white employee T-shirt, the one with *Love Me Blender* written across the front in curly red script. I realized I was still wearing the enormous gray sweatshirt, and I unzipped it and shrugged it off, shoving it underneath the counter next to the lost and found basket.

"Hi," Justin said. He looked at her for a moment longer before, unbelievably, turning his attention back to me. Out of my peripheral vision, I saw Kavya's jaw drop. Her phone bleated again and I realized that this was probably the longest her friends had gone without getting a response from her. They probably assumed that she was in some kind of mortal peril. "So what's good here?" he asked me.

"Well," I said slowly, still trying to figure out what was going on. Justin had practically had cartoon hearts circling his head as he'd gazed at my esteemed coworker. And *no* guys ignored Kavya, especially when she was turning on the charm. She was even able to use it to get Daryl and John to do things that she refused to, like take out the trash or work on Saturdays.

I looked over at Kavya, who seemed as thrown by this as I was. I cleared my throat and looked back to Justin, hoping he wouldn't request anything with strawberries. "The Yes, We Have Some Bananas is good. And so are the Boyz N The Berry and the Vanilla Milk S-Moo-thie."

"I'll have whatever your favorite is, Mad," he said, his eyes not leaving mine. "I could use something sweet." He gave me a smile, the one that used to make my knees weak. It couldn't be that Justin was flirting with me—he knew I was going out with Nate—but he was definitely acting strange. Like maybe he'd spent too much time in the sun today or something.

"Okay," I said, grabbing one of the plastic blenders and heading to the prep area. "Coming right up." Kavya followed me, watching as I scooped frozen mangoes, peaches, blueberries, and ice into the plastic blender.

"I thought you said he was your *ex*-boyfriend," she hissed as I placed the blender on the black base and turned it to the right to lock it on there.

"He is," I whispered back.

"Not what it looked like to me," she said, frowning. "What*ever*," she huffed, turning on her heel and flouncing off in the direction of the employee restroom—no doubt to examine her hair for split ends, as she was wont to do in the afternoons.

I blended Justin's smoothie and shook it into a tall white Styrofoam OAB cup, snapped on the lid, and grabbed one of the long red straws to go with it. I placed them on the counter and rang him up.

"That looks great," he said. I glanced down at the cup and wondered what he was talking about, since all you could see was white Styrofoam. He pulled out his brown leather wallet and extracted a five from it. "Keep the change," he said, smiling at me.

"Thanks," I said, putting his change in our *Tips . . . Because We Blend Over Backward For You!* jar.

He picked up his smoothie cup and looked at me for another long moment before nodding. "Thank you, Mad," he said. "I'll see you soon."

"Sure," I said, even though I had no plans to see him soon—unless I ran into him at the beach, or something, but I just nodded back. He headed for the door and I skipped the mandated goodbye, on the grounds that it would make me sound incredibly dorky. I watched him go, then placed the used blender in the sink. I rinsed it out and turned back to the counter—and saw Justin's wallet, forgotten, still sitting there.

I grabbed it, pushed myself up to sitting on the counter, then swung my legs over it and hopped down. I ran across the shop, yanked open the door, and stepped out into the hot afternoon. Putnam Avenue was much less packed with shoppers than it normally was, and everyone who passed me seemed to be wilting in the incredibly humid air. I looked up and down the street for Justin, but he wasn't anywhere to be seen.

I stuck the wallet in the back pocket of my jean cutoffs—the nice thing about not really having a manager around was that there was no dress code whatsoever—and took out my phone from my other pocket.

Hey! You forgot your wallet. I'll hold on to it for safekeeping until you can pick it up.—Mad

I'd only added my name because I wasn't sure if I was still in his phone or not. I looked at the screen, waiting for a response, but none came.

I was about to head back in when I heard the distinct sound of two guys giggling. Hoping we wouldn't have any customers for the next few minutes, I walked to the back alley, where Daryl and John were perched on empty, overturned plastic fruit crates, both of them cracking up about something.

"Hey," I said, and they looked up at me. As was their habit, John waved amiably while Daryl frowned, as though he wasn't entirely sure who I was. While I always thought of them as a unit, they actually looked nothing alike. Daryl was very tall and gangly, with a shock of bright red hair, while John was probably six inches shorter than him, and compact, with thick black curly hair.

"Hey, Mad," John said. "Howzit going?"

"Mad," Daryl said, drawing out my name and nodding like I'd just cleared something up. "That's right."

"So we're working at the Stanwich Yacht Club tonight," John said. Daryl glanced over at him, looking surprised, as though this was the first he had heard of this. "Okay if we cut out early?"

Proving that there were lots of employers who didn't have mandatory drug testing, Daryl and John worked nights as valets at the Stanwich Yacht Club. After I'd found this out, I'd told Schuyler and Nate and anyone else I knew whose families were members—to never, ever, *ever* use the valet service. I wasn't sure if it was possible to misplace a car, but I wasn't going to put it past them. "It's fine by me," I said to John, who gave me a big, relieved smile. "But, you know," I continued, "I'm not actually your manager. So . . . it's really not up to me."

"Then who's it up to?" John asked, after a protracted pause.

"Gary," I said, and Daryl nodded.

"Gary," he repeated slowly. "That's right."

I realized I should probably head back to the store and make sure that we weren't being potentially robbed for the second time that day. "I'll see you guys in there," I said, turning and heading out of the alley. There was a back entrance to the store from the alley, but it required that you climb a set of unlit stairs that I never failed to stumble over.

John gave me a salute, and Daryl nodded. "Yeah," he said. "See you . . . Mad," he added triumphantly, after a long pause.

I hustled around to the front entrance, pulled open the door, and walked inside the blessedly air-conditioned smoothie shop, which, thankfully, appeared to be unburgled. As soon as I stepped inside, my phone beeped with a Constellation update.

 Dave Gold POOL. PARTY. Mi casa. Tonite. Someone bring chips!
Location: Hott Wheelz (PRINCE). Putnam, CT.

I smiled. Dave's parents were perpetually out of town, and so his pool parties were incredibly fun, as there was nobody telling you to observe water-safety rules or move the passed-out Ginger off the diving board.

As I put my phone back in my pocket, I felt Justin's wallet next to it. I thought about putting it in the lost and found basket, but then hesitated. This was his *wallet*, with his money and license in it. And I had a feeling that Daryl and John, if they were seeking the means to pick up some more herbal refreshment, were not to be trusted with a wallet that might have some cash in it. So I left the wallet in my pocket. Then I glanced toward the door, but there was still no sight of Justin coming back. Trying to push the oddness of our interaction from my mind, I headed over to the smoothie station and got back to work.

CHAPTER 5

 Nate All traffic on Putnam Avenue has slowed to a standstill while we wait for a duck to cross the road. I am not even kidding.
Location: Putnam Avenue. Putnam, CT.

 Dave Gold → Nate Methinks you shouldn't be typing and driving, dude.
Location: 84 Shoreline Road. Putnam, CT.

 Nate → Dave Gold I wish I was driving. But I'm sitting totally still. Considering getting out and walking.
Location: Putnam Avenue. Putnam, CT.

 Nate → M² Stuck in absurd, waterfowl-related traffic. Running 10 late.
Location: Putnam Avenue. Putnam, CT.

 M² → Nate Oh, really? Darn. Because I was totally all ready to go. Early, even.
Location: 76 Winthrop Road. Putnam, CT.

Nate ➔ M² You know, I can always tell when you're lying. Even over the internets.
Location: Putnam Avenue. Putnam, CT.

M² ➔ Nate ☺ You got me. See you soon!
Location: 76 Winthrop Road. Putnam, CT.

Queen Kittson Everything is great here! Nothing wrong at all! Hooray for Long Island!!
Location: Amagansett Beach. East Hampton, NY.

When Nate and I arrived at Dave's, we could hear that the pool party was already in full swing. And technically, we weren't even *at* Dave's yet, but parked about half a mile down the street. Putnam cops routinely broke up teenagers' parties whenever they saw a lot of cars with Putnam High parking tags around one driveway. So it was now totally normal to hike from a great distance to get to the party itself.

I got out of the truck, holding Nate's towel and my beach bag, and walked around to meet him. He took my free hand in his, kissed the back of it quickly, and then threaded his fingers through mine. We walked up to Dave's with our hands intertwined and swinging back and forth between us.

Maybe it was incredibly rude to Dave, since we hadn't even made it to his party yet, but I was already hoping that Nate and I might be able to leave a little early—especially since my father had left me a message that there was a crisis at the paper and he was needed late at the office. I was thrilled about this (well, not about the crisis, whatever it was, but that I might be able to get some uninterrupted Nate time).

We walked around to the back of the house, where an expanse of grass overlooked the water of Long Island Sound, bordered by a low rock wall. We rounded a curve and there was the pool—large, with a diving board and an extra-deep deep end. And sitting on lounge chairs that lined the edges, or swimming in the pool itself, were my friends.

Ginger Davis, the theater department's costume guru, was floating on a raft in the middle of the pool. She was leaning over the edge of it to talk to Jimmy and Liz, who were squeezed together onto a float that was clearly only meant for one.

Schuyler was sitting on the diving board, her mile-long legs hanging over the edge and her feet brushing the surface of the water. She was wearing a bikini—maybe because it was now night, and the chances of getting burned were significantly reduced. She was talking to Lisa and Tricia, who were standing by the side of the pool.

It appeared that once tanning hours were over, Lisa could go back to dressing for fashion, as she was wearing the most Parisian-looking bathing suit I'd ever seen, a vintage-looking strapless black one-piece paired with high black espadrilles.

Tricia was wearing a retro-looking sundress, and leaning over to better hear what Schuyler was saying. I just hoped that she wouldn't get too close to the edge. Last summer, Dave had shown absolutely no impulse control when it came to pushing people into the pool, whether or not they were fully clothed.

But luckily, Dave was busy steering a motorized toy car around the patio, causing Lisa to frown at it whenever it passed her. While Dave worked the remote, he was talking to Mark Rothmann, who was wearing a plaid bathing suit and had a pair of goggles perched on top of his head. Mark caught my eye and smiled at me, so he clearly had forgiven me for not visiting him more frequently at the Second Concession Stand.

Glen Turtell was sitting on one of the pool's lounge chairs, fully dressed, talking to Brian McMahon, both of them watching the progress of the car as it careened around the patio. I was glad to see Brian, since it meant that his incarceration must have been lifted, and he was now allowed out of the house again.

Brian was always throwing legendary parties when his father was out of town, but was incredibly bad at covering his tracks, and so was always getting grounded. Proving that some people just don't learn, he had celebrated the end of his last grounding by throwing a blowout "ungrounded" party. He was grounded again, of course, and the length was extended to "indefinite" when his father had seen his grades. Brian had been my lab partner in Marine Biology, which turned out to be a very bad pairing, as we'd spent most of the semester talking, and very little time dissecting starfish. I had realized my grade was in jeopardy after the prom, and had buckled down with an intense cramming schedule. I had received a good enough grade on the final that I passed the class with a B–. Brian, however, had not been so lucky, and was now taking summer classes to make up for his F.

Ruth and her boyfriend, Andy, were sitting on the edge of the pool near the deep end, feet splashing in the water, holding hands. Ruth caught my eye and waved, and I smiled and lifted the hand that wasn't holding Nate's to wave back to her.

"I'm going to say hi to Ruth," I said to Nate, who was looking in Dave's direction.

"And I think I'm going to make the acquaintance of some pizza," Nate said, gesturing to the table near Dave, where boxes from Putnam Pizza were stacked high. "I'll save you some pineapple if they have it."

I set down our stuff on one of the lounge chairs and headed over toward Ruth and her once and current BF. Ruth and Andy had dated last summer at Science Camp, but had lost touch when camp ended. But Andy had come back into Ruth's life as a result of Promgate. I had asked Andy to be my impromptu prom date in order to get into Hartfield's prom. And when Ruth and Andy had seen each other again, they had immediately reconnected and had been together since.

Andy glanced up as I approached, and gave me a small nod before blushing red and looking away quickly. Ruth knew why I'd bamboozled Andy into taking me to his prom, but Andy had never gotten the full story, and seemed to believe that I had wanted our date to be real and still harbored a crush on him. He was slightly jumpy around me, avoiding being alone with me at all costs, as though worried I was just lying in wait for an opportunity to make my move. And he was even jumpier around Nate, rarely speaking to him or even making eye contact. I had told Nate all the details of Promgate, so he knew about Andy's role. But Andy's nervousness was probably the reason that the four of us still hadn't ever managed to have a double date.

"Hi," I said, approaching the two of them. I kicked off my flip-flops and sat next to Ruth on the edge of the pool, easing my feet into the just-heated-enough water.

"Hey," Ruth said, smiling at me. "Glad you made it."

"Good evening, Madison," Andy said stiffly, looking at me for only a second before looking away again.

"So I see Tricia's here," I said as I looked across the pool where she was laughing with Schuyler and Lisa. She caught my eye and gave me a wave, and I smiled back before turning to Ruth.

"Sure," Ruth said. "I mean, she's on the Constellation feed, so she saw Dave's invite." She paused and looked at me closely. "You like her, don't you, Mad?"

"Of course," I said quickly. "She's really nice." Ruth was still looking at me closely, like she was about to say something else, so I turned to Andy. "Did you know her at Hartfield?" I asked.

Andy jumped, as though surprised to be spoken to directly. "Not really," he said, mostly to the pool water. "I mean, she looks familiar, but I'm not sure. I was only there a few months before school ended, you know." He looked up, and when he saw I was still looking at him, blushed again, then cleared his throat and looked away. "Wow, is that pizza?" he asked a little too loudly, getting to his feet and hustling toward Dave. When he spotted Nate next to Dave, however, he veered sharply away in the opposite direction, and as a result, ended up standing by himself at the end of the pool. With an air of studied nonchalance, he stuck his hands in the pockets of his khaki shorts and looked up intensely at the night sky, as though a little stargazing had been his goal in getting up all along.

Ruth, watching him, shook her head. "Poor guy," she said.

"We could tell him," I suggested with a shrug. "Probably help lower his blood pressure a few points."

"Yeah," Ruth said, a little doubtfully.

"I know," I said quietly, and we both looked at the water in silence for a moment. I had a feeling we were both thinking the same thing. Even though we had pulled off Promgate, any number of us could still get in a lot of trouble if the truth came to light. And the eleven of us involved had all decided that it would be best to keep what had happened between us, as we figured the more people that knew about it, the more chance there was about someone spilling the beans. Nate didn't count. If anyone understood the importance of keeping secrets like this, it was him.

Though Nate had never admitted it outright to me, he had been instrumental in organizing his school's senior prank — one that had been epic enough to shut Stanwich High down for three days. I had heard lots of stuff about it, and while it was hard to separate rumor from truth, it had been confirmed that it had involved both a streaker and a cow, and I just hoped the two hadn't overlapped.

It had also involved stealing the mascot costume of Hartfield High, which, as far as I knew, had still never been returned.

Nate's headmaster had gone on the rampage, threatening to expel anyone involved, and even cancelling the prom in a futile attempt to get the names of those guilty. Nate hadn't been caught, and once he'd been able to graduate without a problem, I could tell that he'd relaxed a little. But the fact remained that he wasn't entirely out of the woods yet. He didn't want to raise any suspicion by actually asking what the protocol was, but he'd told me he was worried that if Yale found out what had happened, his acceptance might still be revoked. So I didn't have to tell Nate how important it was that nobody find out what had actually gone on at my prom.

As I looked around the party, I realized that most of those in attendance had played some role in Promgate. And it seemed like everyone would have something to lose if the truth came out. From Ginger, who was determined to get a scholarship to RISD and needed an impeccable record to do so; to Brian, whose father was always a heartbeat away from sending him to military school, and really didn't need any extra excuses.

"There's still lots of pizza here, people!" Dave yelled, causing a stampede in his general direction.

I turned to Ruth. "Za?" I asked her, and she groaned, shaking her head.

"*Pizza* needs to be abbreviated?" she asked. "Really?"

"Oh, totes," I said, pushing myself to standing.

Ruth laughed and stood as well, and Lisa and

Schuyler approached, accompanied by Tricia. As they got closer, I saw that there was something different about her makeup. I frowned and squinted, trying to get a better look.

"Hi, Madditude!" Tricia said with a smile.

"Hi," I said automatically. She was close enough now that she was doing the exact same Swiftian cat-eye thing I'd started doing lately—but her eyes were done with a lot more skill. "Your eye makeup . . ." I began, not even sure where I was going with this, just that I was surprised to see it.

Tricia's smile grew. "Do you like it?" she asked. "It's just something I'm trying."

I blinked at her, wondering why this sounded so familiar. "I do," I said. "It's . . ."

"Kind of like what you're doing, *non*?" Lisa asked, shaking her head. "*Très* not French, you guys."

"French women don't wear eyeliner?" Schuyler asked, frowning. "Like, at all?"

"Well, historically," Lisa started, and Ruth jumped in, perhaps sensing a long cultural lecture in the offing.

"I'm going to get some *za*," Ruth said, heading toward the pizza table, and I saw Andy leave his stargazing position and walk over to join her.

"Me too," I said as I headed for the pizza, crossing my fingers that Nate had, in fact, been able to secure me a slice of pineapple.

****

Three hours later, the party had more or less moved inside to the house. I'd had a slightly awkward moment

71

with Turtell when he'd started complaining that Kittson hadn't been in touch at all lately, and had asked me if I'd talked to her recently. I didn't want to tell him that his girlfriend had iChatted with me, but luckily, he—and everyone else—had been distracted by the sight of Mark's attempt at a swan dive that had gone horribly wrong and turned into a belly flop. It had rendered Mark immobile for the rest of the evening, and he'd spent the remainder of the party lying faceup on one of the pool rafts and moaning softly.

The pool was mostly empty now, except for Nate and me—and Mark, whose stomach was still bright red and clashed with his plaid bathing suit.

"You ready for this?" Nate called to me from where he was bouncing on the edge of the diving board.

"Ready," I called back from where I was treading water in the middle of the pool.

Mark lifted his head from the raft and whimpered when he saw Nate. "Don't do it, man," he said faintly. "You'll regret it."

But Nate just smiled and gave the diving board one more bounce before jumping off it, gaining an impressive amount of air, tucking into a cannonball, and landing in the pool with a splash that drenched me and set Mark's raft rocking from side to side. I ducked under the water and smoothed my hair back. When I surfaced, Nate was swimming toward me.

"Nicely done," I said as he reached me. He was tall enough that he could stand, and I swam closer to him and brushed his wet hair back from his forehead.

"Thanks," he murmured as he ran his hand over my own hair, then down my mostly bare back. I rested my hand on his chest for a moment, and Nate leaned down and kissed me, his hands encircling my waist, sending my heart racing. Whenever we were swimming together—which didn't actually happen that often, as neither of our houses had pools—I was always reminded by how much more *naked* you were in a bathing suit. There was just so much of Nate's skin on display, and I couldn't seem to stop myself from running my hands over his chest as we kissed.

We swam-kissed over to the side of the pool, my back resting on the cool tiles that lined the edges. I wrapped my legs around Nate's waist, and he started kissing down my neck. I shivered, even though the night was warm and so was the water. I looked up and saw the stars, bright and clear above us, with the underwater lights of the pool all around us, and just reveled in the moment, and how perfect everything felt.

"You know," Nate said, his voice low, a small smile taking over his face, "it's a lovely night for stargazing."

"I actually think Andy discovered that earlier," I said, linking my hands behind his neck.

"And I bet that the stars are lovely at the Bluff," Nate continued. He raised one eyebrow at me, and I couldn't help smiling back at him.

"Well, it *is* a lovely night," I agreed.

"It sure is!" Mark chimed in as he floated by. I looked over at him, startled—I'd totally forgotten Nate and I weren't alone in the pool.

"Think we should go?" I asked, and Nate nodded immediately. I unhooked my legs and stretched a toe down to touch the bottom of the pool.

"I'll get our stuff," he said, hoisting himself out of the pool and heading, dripping, toward the lounge chairs.

I swam over to the ladder and started to climb up it when Mark floated past again. "Hey, Mad?" he called.

"Yeah?" I asked, turning back to him and hoping he'd make it quick. When there was a Nate makeout session on tap, suddenly everyone and everything else just seemed like an intrusive, unnecessary interruption.

"That new girl who was here," he said, gesturing vaguely in the direction of the house.

"Tricia," I supplied.

"Right," he said. Mark started to sit up, then groaned and dropped back down again. "Do I know her from somewhere?"

"I doubt it," I said. "I mean, she goes to Hartfield."

"It's weird," Mark said. "Because she looks familiar." His raft started turning away from me, and he stretched out his hands to paddle the water, trying to turn himself around, but actually managing to propel himself farther away.

I glanced back toward the house. Through the glass doors that led to Dave's TV room, I could see the group playing Big Bass Champion—the game that combined Guitar Hero with Xtreme Sport Fishing. Most everyone was intently watching Brian trying to keep his balance on the rocking footpad—meant to simulate the movement of a boat—while simultaneously playing a

74

guitar solo. But Schuyler and Tricia were sitting apart, backs to the screen, talking and laughing. Schuyler had claimed that she couldn't watch the game, as it violated her recent moratorium on anything boat related.

"She was probably at the Hartfield prom," I said as I pulled Mark, who was drifting toward the shallow end, closer in. "And you and I spent more time there than anyone else."

"Except Sarah," Mark pointed out.

"Except Sarah," I conceded. While Mark and I had been ducking in and out of the Hartfield prom, Sarah had spent her night in the thick of it, falling for her prom date. Sarah and Zach had been an item since then, and were going strong, despite the fact that she was in the Catskills working at a theater camp, where she was terrorizing children and forcing them to read Strindberg. I hadn't heard much from her, except for occasional texts she sent me when she saw on Constellation that I was in the same area as Zach, and was worried I might bump into him without getting prepped.

Sarah and Zach had met as part of Promgate, when Sarah had delivered an unordered pizza to him. Zach had originally been Isabel's prom date, and we had needed for him not to be Isabel's prom date so that she could take Mark, who was pretending to be an earl. But to everyone's shock, Sarah and Zach had fallen for each other for real. And now Sarah was worried that someone might reveal to her boyfriend the less-than-legit circumstances under which they had actually met.

I saw that Nate had gathered up our stuff and pulled

(darn it) his shirt on. He was talking to Dave near the edge of the pool, and he caught my eye and tipped his head slightly to the driveway. "See you, Mark," I said, climbing the ladder the rest of the way.

"At the *Second* Concession Stand!" Mark called as he began to drift toward the shallow end again. "Don't forget, okay, Mad?"

"I won't," I called to him. I toweled off quickly, pulled on my jean shorts and a tank top, and stepped into my flip-flops. Then I walked over to Nate and Dave, squeezing some excess water from my hair.

"I think you're leaving because you can't handle my mad skillz," Dave said to Nate, arms folded across his newest ironic T-shirt. This one featured a long row of blond-haired people, and read *Finnish Line.* "You know you would lose in the Bass-Line showdown."

"Probably true," Nate said, giving me a smile and taking my hand as I reached him. "But we should get going. Madison has a curfew."

"Yes," I piped up. "I do. And I don't want to miss it."

Dave glanced down at his watch. "It's ten fifteen, Mad."

"Yes, well . . ." I said, squeezing Nate's hand once. "There might be, um . . . traffic."

Dave adjusted his thick black-framed glasses and rolled his eyes. "Sure," he said. "And you certainly wouldn't want to get caught in that. Have fun making out. You know that you two are getting almost as bad as Jimmy and Liz?"

I stared at Dave, feeling my jaw drop. "Hey," I said, stung. That was a serious accusation to level. And it also seemed that Dave had entirely forgotten his first few months of dating Lisa, when they would barely stop kissing long enough to carry on a coherent conversation.

Dave seemed to realize the gravity of this, and held up his palms. "I take it back," he said. "Thanks for coming out."

"Thanks for throwing this fiesta," Nate said, dropping my hand so that he and Dave could do their complicated guy-handshake that seemed to get longer and more intricate every time I saw them do it.

As Dave walked back to the house, I realized I hadn't said goodbye to anyone inside. I paused, wondering if I should just dash in. But I had a feeling it would take twice as long as it should . . . and I just really, really wanted to be alone with Nate. The Jimmy and Liz comparison had bothered me a little, but truthfully, for the first time, I could see where they were coming from. Making out with Nate was starting to seem preferable to—well, almost anything else. And especially saying goodbye to my friends and having to explain why I was leaving early and probably getting more of the kind of grief Dave had just given us.

"Hey, Dave," I called, and he turned around in the doorway. "Tell everyone goodbye, okay?"

Dave looked at me for a moment, surprised, but then nodded. "Will do," he called. "See you, Mad."

I tried to push down the feelings of guilt that were threatening to rise. But I was sure that my friends would be fine. Then I turned and hurried down the driveway with Nate.

CHAPTER 6

Song: Paradise By The Dashboard Light/Meat Loaf
Quote: "Oh, Earth, you're too wonderful for anybody
to realize you. Do any human beings ever realize life
while they live it—every, every minute?"—Thornton
Wilder, *Our Town*

We hadn't made it to the Bluff.

We actually hadn't made it very far at all. When we'd reached Nate's truck, I'd kissed him once, just to tide us over. But that peck had quickly turned into a real kiss, and Nate had pressed me against the driver's side of the truck. I kissed him back, and when his hands slid underneath my tank top, we had both realized that it might be a good idea to move inside the truck and avoid getting arrested for violating any kind of indecent exposure laws.

And then once we were in the truck, it had just seemed easier to keep making out there, rather than drive twenty minutes to make out somewhere else—and, thankfully, the truck was parked the farthest distance away from the party, so it wasn't like anyone was going to be passing by and interrupting us.

Nate had pulled off my top and I had taken off his shirt, and we stretched out together across the bench seat. We'd been making out for a while when Nate paused and pulled away, looking into my eyes.

"My Mad," he murmured, and I reached up and ran my hands through his still-damp hair. He moved his hands across my bare stomach and over my ribs, stopping as he reached the tie of my bikini. "Is this okay?" he murmured. I nodded—it was *more* than okay. My heart was hammering as Nate pulled the first string—at the very same moment that his phone rang.

Nate groaned. He seemed to be having some sort of internal battle with himself, but finally sat up. "I have to get that," he said, and I could hear how unhappy he was. "It's the ringtone for Maxwell's house." I propped myself on an elbow, trying to untangle my legs from his so that he could reach his bag on the truck floor. He pulled his phone out and flipped it open. "Hello," he said, and there was silence while he listened to what was being said on the other end. "Yes, but . . ." he said as he glanced over at me. "Tomorrow?" He frowned, and I could see that he was not liking what he was hearing. "I know, but the thing is . . . all right," he finally said. "I'll see you then." He pressed the button to end the call, then turned to me and sighed.

Pretty sure that the mood had been broken, I sat up and retied my bikini top. "What is it?" I asked.

Nate shook his head. "It's what you get for agreeing

to tutor on call. Maxwell and his parents are going to their house on Martha's Vineyard for two days, and they want me to come along and tutor him."

"Really?" I asked, hearing the disappointment in my voice. Two days? Nate was going to be gone for two whole *days*?

"Yes," Nate said. He dropped his phone back in his bag. "Apparently, they want him to learn to study in a distraction-heavy atmosphere, and not just in a library. Even though he hasn't yet learned to study in a library. But I thought it best I not point that out."

"Probably a good idea," I said. Nate ran his hand through his hair, looking preoccupied. "Should we call it a night?" I suggested. I had a feeling that even if we continued making out, Nate would be distracted.

"I think so," Nate said, checking his watch. "They want to leave really early in the morning, and I should get home and pack. But," he said, arching an eyebrow. He leaned over and kissed me quickly, running his hand down my back. "To be continued?"

"Oh, definitely," I said immediately. I pulled on my tank top and helped Nate put on his shirt. As I did, I straightened it over his shoulders and felt myself smile.

It was a shirt I'd given him just after we started dating, even though Lisa had been horrified, saying that she hadn't given Dave any presents until they'd been dating for three months. But when I'd seen it, I'd had to buy it for him. It was a polo that brought out the color in his eyes perfectly. But where there was normally an alligator, or a horse, on polo shirts, this one had a tiny camera. He'd told me that he liked it, but even better, he wore it a *lot*, which proved it to me. I ran my fingers across the camera, and Nate kissed the top of my head.

The drive home seemed ridiculously short, and we got there all too soon. I couldn't believe I wouldn't see Nate for two days. But I tried to spin it in a positive light—spending a few days apart might be good practice for being in an LDR come fall.

When we pulled up my long, winding driveway, I could see that the house was still dark—clearly, this crisis at the paper was taking a long time to resolve—which, at the moment, was completely fine with me.

Nate parked in the turnaround next to Judy, and we both got out of the truck. He met me around on the passenger side and kissed me goodbye. "I'll talk to you tomorrow," he said when we broke apart after a medium-length kiss. "I'm not sure what the reception sitch is going to be like out there, but I'll definitely give you a call."

"Oh em gee," I said, smiling up at him, "did you just use the word *sitch*?"

"Technically, I don't think it's a word," Nate said, giving me one of his half smiles. "And I just wanted to see if you were paying attention."

"A likely story," I said, raising my eyebrows at him. "I'm having an effect on you. You can admit it."

"Well," he said, his voice more serious now. He tucked that one lock of hair behind my ear. "I know that's true." I looked up at him, feeling that something in his tone had just definitely shifted. I had almost never seen Nate look so serious before.

"You okay?" I asked.

"I am," he said, but still in the same serious tone. "I'm more than okay. And there's actually something I've been wanting to say for a while now." Nate took a step closer and touched my cheek, letting his hand linger there as my heart started beating double-time. "Madison MacDonald," he said, looking right into my eyes, "I love you."

I closed my eyes and felt a smile take over my face. I didn't understand why I felt like I might cry, since I was positive I'd never been quite this happy. I opened my eyes and looked at my boyfriend, and realized my heart wasn't pounding nervously anymore. Rather, it was beating slow and steady, just for him. And suddenly, what I had been so scared to tell him wasn't frightening at all. It was the simplest thing in the world to say—just naming a truth about how I felt, one of the universe's understood facts. The earth was round. The sky was blue. I loved Nate Ellis, with all my heart.

I opened my mouth and took a breath, thrilled that I could finally say these words to him. "Nate," I said, smiling at him so wide that my cheeks were beginning to ache. "I—"

"Don't say it," he said quickly. He leaned down and kissed me, then pulled me into a hug.

I hugged back, but then leaned away to look at him, smoothing his hair back from his forehead. "What do you mean?" I asked. "Just listen to me for a second. I lo—"

Nate leaned in and kissed me again, stopping me from speaking. When we broke the kiss, he was smiling at me. "What's going on?" I asked.

"I just wanted to tell you how I've been feeling," he said. "But I don't want you to say it to me just because I said it to you. If you want to say it, I want it to be some other time, and because you want to. Not just because you're responding to something that I said."

"But—" I managed to get out before he kissed me again. "Wait," I started, but he stopped me again with a kiss, this time a *serious* kiss, lifting me off my feet, his arms tight around me. I gave up and just enjoyed kissing my boyfriend—who loved me. Even the thought sent a thrill through me. Nate *loved* me.

We broke apart sometime later—twenty minutes? Three hours? I was entirely unable to judge—and I looked at him, resting my hands on either side of his face. It felt like we had crossed over to some new level. We weren't just dating. We weren't just making out. We loved each other—even if Nate hadn't let me say it back to him.

"So," Nate said, still smiling at me.

"So," I echoed, matching his smile with my own.

"I should get going," he said. "Packing, and all that."

"Right," I said. I was grinning at him, probably looking like a total dork, but I didn't care. I wondered if Nate felt as giddy as I did. "Packing."

He kissed me again, clearly trying to make it a quick goodbye kiss, but I had other ideas, and kept the kiss going, turning it into a *kiss*. Nate broke away, breathing hard, shaking his head. "Okay, I really have to leave now," he said. "Or I'm not going to have the will-power to leave at all."

"All right," I said. I could feel that I was still smiling. I had a sneaking suspicion that I might never stop.

He gave me a very quick kiss, squeezed my hand, then turned and walked to his truck. "I'll call you tomorrow," he said across the truck bed.

"Have fun," I said. "If possible."

"Will do," he said. He opened the door and climbed behind the wheel, then backed out. I walked over to the driver's side door and leaned in through the open window.

"I'll miss you," I said softly. Nate, lit softly by the dashboard lights, smiled at me and touched my cheek.

"Me too," he murmured. He leaned in and we kissed quickly. "Good night," he said.

"Night," I said. I stood back and Nate headed down the driveway, lifting one hand out of the window to wave at me. I watched the truck's taillights until they faded from view, and then listened as the rumble of his engine got fainter and fainter and finally, all I could hear were the cicadas chirping, or squawking, or whatever it is cicadas do, all around me.

When I was very sure that I was alone, I spun around once in a circle, feeling like I now understood why people were always breaking into songs and dances in musicals. Because there were some moments in life that were just too big to be expressed in words alone. Had some invisible orchestra given me a downbeat, I would have burst into song right there. *Nate loved me.* I felt like I was a heartbeat away from floating off the ground.

I took out my phone and was about to text my friends, but stopped. I now got why Lisa and Dave might use a code to exchange "I love you." There was a piece of me that wanted to hold on to this moment between me and Nate, and keep it private for the time being. Of course, I would tell my friends soon. Probably tomorrow. But I just wanted to keep this knowledge close to my heart for a while, turning it over and replaying the moment in my head.

Still feeling my smile firmly in place, I turned to head inside, quite certain I was the happiest I'd ever been.

CHAPTER 7

Song: One Time/Justin Bieber
Quote: "Secrets are things we give to others to keep
for us."—Elbert Hubbard

At three A.M., my phone beeped with a text. I had been
having a really lovely dream—the details were fading as
I sat up and looked around, but I seemed to remember
that it had something to do with Nate, and he was most
definitely not wearing a shirt. I grabbed my phone off
the nightstand and squinted against the brightness
of the screen in the darkness of my bedroom.

INBOX 1 of 31
From: Kittson
Date: 6/22, 3:01 A.M.

MADISON!!! Are you awake?

I groaned. I was tempted just to put my phone aside
and go back to sleep, but there was a piece of me that was

worried. If Kittson was texting me at three o'clock in the morning, there was probably a real reason for it—and not just a wardrobe consult. Willing my brain to wake up a little bit, I texted her back.

OUTBOX 1 of 36
To: Kittson
Date: 6/22, 3:02 A.M.

I am NOW. You okay?

The response came almost immediately.

INBOX 1 of 32
From: Kittson
Date: 6/22, 3:03 A.M.

Go on iChat. Need to talk to you.

I turned on my bedside light and leaned over to the floor, hoisting my laptop onto my bed and booting it up. I hoped that everything was okay with Kittson, but my brain was still in my Nate-loves-me happiness haze, and it seemed like everything that wasn't concerning Nate was just a little bit fuzzy.

My iChat had loaded—still moving a little more jerkily than usual, thanks to my brother—and I accepted Kittson's invitation. A moment later, she was looking back at me, wearing an oversize Metallica T-shirt that I recognized as Turtell's.

"Hi, Madison," Kittson said in a voice that sounded slightly more hoarse than usual. She was looking down at the keyboard, and not at me. "Sorry if I woke you up."

"It's okay," I said, leaning forward and peering at my screen closely. There was something about her that seemed — off, somehow. "Are you okay?"

Kittson tossed her head, as though she was going to tell me she was fine, but then her shoulders slumped, and she lifted her eyes.

I clapped my hand over my mouth. I had never seen Kittson look so bad before. In fact, I had never seen her look bad at *all*. Kittson was always pulled together to a slightly absurd degree. But now her eyes were red and puffy, and she looked both exhausted and miserable, an unfortunate combination. I was not able to stop myself from gasping audibly.

"Thanks, Madison," Kittson said, glaring at me. "That's real nice."

"Sorry," I said quickly, trying to get my expression of horror under control. "I just . . . what happened?"

Kittson's bottom lip was trembling, and I realized to my shock that she was on the verge of tears. I had never seen Kittson even come close to crying before.

"Is it Glen?" I asked, remembering what he'd said earlier that night about Kittson not being in touch with him. Kittson's face crumpled, and she choked back a sob.

"I can't believe I'm telling you this," she said, looking up at the screen, then maybe seeing her own tiny reflection in the left-hand corner, and looking away quickly.

"But I don't know who else I can tell." She narrowed her puffy eyes at me. "I can trust you, Madison, right?" she asked.

"Of course," I said quickly. Admittedly, before the hacking debacle of the spring, I'd had a little bit of a problem with gossiping. But I had more than learned my lesson as far as that was concerned, and now really didn't gossip at all—something that Kittson herself had complained about only last week.

"You can't tell anyone this," Kittson said, her eyes still fixed on mine.

"I promise," I said, and I crossed my heart for good measure.

"Okay," she said. She took a big breath, like she was steeling herself. "It is about Glen," she said. "He called me out of the blue earlier tonight and wanted to talk about our relationship, and how he thinks that I haven't been in touch enough this summer."

"Okay," I said slowly, hoping that being surrounded by couples at Dave's tonight hadn't somehow caused this.

"And it turned into this big fight," Kittson said in a small voice. "About how he thinks that he's making all these sacrifices for me, planning on going to college when what he really wants to do is weld . . ."

"Weld?" I asked, baffled.

Kittson waved a hand dismissively. "Like a welder," she said impatiently. "With metal. Don't get me started. Anyway, it ended on this really bad note, and I was really pissed off. I needed to get out of the house, and I ended up going to this party."

"Uh-oh," I murmured. I suddenly had a feeling that I knew where this was going—nowhere good.

"Yeah," she muttered. "It was just this stupid guy," she said, her words spilling out in a torrent. "Just this lame preppy guy my parents have been trying to set me up with all summer. They're not exactly Glen's biggest fans, as you can probably imagine." She brushed some tears away quickly. "All we did was kiss," she said in a small voice. "And as soon as it happened, I knew it was a mistake, and I left." She let out a long, shuddery breath.

"Oh my God," I murmured.

"Yeah," she said, giving a short, humorless laugh. "And I just don't know what to do now. It was a total, idiotic mistake. But I don't know if I should tell Glen or not."

I looked at Kittson's unhappy face and thought back to all the times I'd seen Turtell looking at her when he didn't know anyone was watching—with an expression of utter trust and love and devotion. And then I thought about how, around prom time, he had threatened to beat up anyone who was going to win prom king because they were going to so much as *dance* with Kittson. I feared for every lame preppy guy on the Eastern Seaboard if he found out that she had made out with one of them. "I don't think you should tell him," I said after a moment.

Kittson looked up at me sharply, blinking in surprise. "Really?" she asked.

"Yeah," I said slowly, "really." I had given the same advice to Jimmy and Liz when they had both (unbeknownst to the other) found themselves in this situation. And since they'd both realized the error of their mistakes, things had worked out fine. Well, until the hacking had revealed these secrets to both of them, and they'd broken up acrimoniously for a week. But now they were fine again, and that's what mattered.

It wasn't that I thought secrets were a good idea or the way to go. But it just seemed easier to keep them sometimes, rather than telling the truth and hurting people who didn't need to be hurt.

Kittson frowned. "I thought your whole thing these days was all about *communication*," she said. "Or is that over now?"

I was glad to hear that she was being sarcastic again; it seemed like an indication that she was beginning to feel a little better. "No, that's not over," I said. I tried to suppress a yawn I felt threatening. The lateness of the hour was beginning to hit me. "I just think that telling him would do more damage than good. I mean, would you want to know if Glen had made a total mistake and hooked up with Shauna?" I asked, pulling out the name of one of Turtell's exes.

"Shauna?" Kittson asked, sitting up straight, her voice totally clear now. And dangerous. "Who's *Shauna*?"

"No, that was just an example," I said quickly, not at all liking Kittson's expression. "I guess sometimes, you need to keep secrets for the sake of the relationship. I mean, do you think Glen would be able to get past this?" Kittson met my eyes for a long moment, then shook her head. "Me neither," I said.

Kittson let out a long sigh. "Okay," she said. "I think

you're right." I noticed a more familiar expression—that is, one of slightly distracted impatience—coming back on her face. "Anyway. Is everything good with you?"

"Yes," I said. I felt a huge smile overtake my face. "Everything's *great*."

Kittson sighed, a little wistfully, and her image froze for a moment before coming back to life. I yawned again, and a second later, she yawned as well. "Sorry for keeping you up, Mad," she said. "Thanks for this." Then she signed off.

I looked at my screen, wondering if I'd done the right thing by telling Kittson not to tell Turtell. But a moment later, I pushed the thought away. I was still far too happy about what had happened with Nate to let it bother me. I shut down my computer, switched off my bedside light, and pulled the covers over me, resolving not to worry about it—and hoping very much to return to my shirtless Nate dream.

CHAPTER 8

Song: Exes and Øs/Stockholm Syndrome
Quote: "There is love, of course. And then there's life, its enemy." —Jean Anouilh

 M² ☺
Location: On A Blender Smoothie Shop. Putnam, CT.

 M² ♥
Location: On A Blender Smoothie Shop. Putnam, CT.

 M² ☺
Location: On A Blender Smoothie Shop. Putnam, CT.

The next day at work passed in a haze. I was pretty sure that people ordered smoothies and I made them, but mostly I existed in a happy world in my own head. My friends would text me and I would respond, but I was only half aware of what I was doing. My thoughts were on Nate, and counting down the minutes until he would be back and I could tell him that I loved him, too.

Luckily, it was a gray, overcast day, threatening rain, so there were far fewer customers than usual. But my nonparticipation at work meant that Kavya actually had to make a smoothie or two, which she claimed stressed her out so much that she needed to leave early to get a pedicure. And Daryl and John left midafternoon to head to their valet job—and to try and score some sweet Jack Johnson tickets—so I was closing up alone. Which was fine with me, as this gave me uninterrupted time to sit on the counter and stare into space, reliving the events of the night before.

Five minutes before I was due to close up, I was startled out of my reverie when my phone beeped with a text.

INBOX 1 of 32
From: Justin
Date: 6/22, 5:55 P.M.

Hey, Mad—I see on Constellation that you're at work. Can I swing by and get my wallet from you?—Justin

I let out a breath. It had been bothering me that I still had Justin's wallet, and even though it meant that I would have to stay at work a little later, I was happy to get it off my hands. And plus, it wasn't like Nate was around and I had anything important to do that night, anyway. I texted back right away.

To: Justin
Date: 6/22, 5:57 P.M.

Sure! Come on by. I'm just closing up.

A response from him came almost immediately.

INBOX 1 of 33
From: Justin
Date: 6/22, 5:58 P.M.

Great! Are you by yourself?—Justin

I frowned down at my phone, thinking that was a bizarre question, when it beeped again.

INBOX 1 of 34
From: Justin
Date: 6/22, 5:58 P.M.

I mean, is your coworker there too?—Justin

I *knew* Justin had been interested in Kavya, and this proved it. I felt myself smiling as I responded, adding my name as a joke I was pretty sure he wouldn't get.

OUTBOX 1 of 38
To: Justin
Date: 6/22, 6:00 P.M.

Sorry—just me. See you soon!—Madison

By the time I'd locked the freezer, rinsed out the blenders, and cleaned the wheatgrass machine, the bell over the door chimed. I looked up and saw Justin standing in the doorway.

"Hey," I said, smiling at him. Justin walked over to the counter, and I pulled his wallet out from my back pocket.

"Is that it?" he asked as he reached me. I nodded and he smiled. "I can't believe I forgot it. Thanks for coming through for me, Mad."

"Sure," I said. I held out the wallet to him, but he made no movement to take it from me.

"So here we are again," he said. I looked around, not exactly sure what he was talking about. The last time he'd come in? When he'd forgotten his wallet? Maybe seeing my blank expression, he prompted, "Remember, we came here on one of our first dates?"

I did, in fact. Lisa hadn't approved at all, saying that early dates should not involve Styrofoam or straws. Or drinks with names like Mango-Go. "Yes," I said, wondering where he was going with this. "Of course I do." I smiled and extended my wallet-holding arm farther out, trying to ignore the fact that it was actually beginning to ache a little.

"I really liked you back then, you know," Justin said. He had a small, half-fixed smile on his face that didn't seem to have any connection to the words that he was saying. "I thought it was so cute that you came

96

to my rugby games. I could tell you liked me, too."

I blinked at him and finally lowered my arm, which had begun to shake, making me realize it might be time to start doing dips, or push-ups, or something. "Yeah," I said slowly, gathering my thoughts, "I liked you, too. You know, back then. That's why we went out." I nodded with what I hoped was finality and held out his wallet to him once again. But Justin didn't even glance down at it and continued to look straight at me.

"You know, I don't think I ever told you how embarrassing it was for me when you dumped me over Friendverse during spring break."

I stared at him. This was ancient history. This had all happened *months* ago, and we had all moved on. Hadn't we? I had absolutely no clue why it was resurfacing now. "Wait," I said, giving my arm another rest, "you know I wasn't the one who did that. You know that my Friendverse got hacked."

"But I still got dumped, didn't I? Publicly?" he asked.

"Well," I said, feeling my forehead crease, "yes. But . . ." I tried to gauge from his expression what this was about. His face looked blank, which wasn't out of the ordinary for Justin. But there was something about it—maybe the fixed expression—that made me think that it was carefully blank, and masking something else. But I had no idea what. "Why are we talking about this now?" I finally asked, getting exasperated.

"We should have talked about it then," he said.

"I did try," I pointed out, even though the last thing I wanted to do was to belabor this conversation I wasn't even sure why we were having in the first place. "But you were going out with Kittson then, and didn't seem to really want to discuss it."

"Kittson," he said slowly. He took his hands out of his pockets, which gave me hope that we were getting closer to the moment when he'd actually take his wallet back. I was a few minutes away from just dropping it on the counter. He gave a short, bitter laugh, a kind I'd never heard from him before. "Yeah. What a disaster that was. After you dump me, *she* dumps me and starts dating that total burnout. And then when I say I want to get back together with you, you totally shoot me down."

"Justin," I said slowly, wondering why he was steering us forcibly down memory lane. "Where is this coming from?"

He shrugged and looked over at the happy smoothie couple pictures before glancing back at me. "I just think you treated me like crap last semester," he said bluntly, surprising me. "And then you totally used me at the prom."

"I didn't," I said quickly, feeling that this, at least, could be cleared up. "I'm sorry I couldn't explain it better at the time, but I really didn't mean it like that—"

"Whatever," Justin said, interrupting me. "I just wanted to make sure you knew where I was coming from with this."

"Okay," I said. "But listen, Justin. I really wasn't using you, I swear. I had thought that you were doing me a favor. As a friend. That's all." Justin stared at me, his small smile gone, and it seemed like he was hearing me for the first time in this bizarre—and for him, quite extended and multisyllabic—conversation. I held up his wallet for him, hoping that he could finally take it off my hands and I could go home. "Just like this is me doing you a favor," I said. I held it out once again, and Justin looked down at it, then shook his head.

"Actually," he said, and his voice was quieter now, and colder. "This wasn't you doing a favor for me. This was me doing a favor for someone else." He reached into his pocket, pulled out his phone, and started typing a quick text.

I stared at him, totally confused. "And who's that?" I asked.

"Oh," Justin said, giving me another small smile as he pocketed his phone, "I think you've met." As he said this, the bell above the front door jangled again. I looked up to the entrance and felt my heart stop for just a moment.

The figure there was wearing a gauzy tank top, fitted skirt, stacked pumps, blunt, dark brown bangs, and a satisfied smile.

I stared for just a moment, trying to make sense of what I was seeing.

Isabel Ryan was standing in the doorway.

CHAPTER 9

I stared at Isabel as she walked toward the counter, not entirely able to believe what I was seeing. Isabel wasn't supposed to be in On A Blender. Isabel wasn't supposed to be in Connecticut at all—she was supposed to be on Nantucket. Although, I realized with a sinking feeling in my stomach, I hadn't checked her location on Constellation in a few days. She easily could have come back, and I wouldn't have been aware of it. I had no idea why she was here now, but I didn't think it was to get a Pomegranate Paradise Pow or have a fun catch-up with me over all the great times we'd shared.

As she got closer, I could see that she looked extremely happy. And it was an expression that I didn't like to see.

It was like when I'd been in detention and the arson kid had looked gleeful. You knew that no good would come of it.

I looked over at Justin and realized that it wasn't a coincidence that she was here now. Justin had set this up. I had a sudden impulse to hurl his stupid wallet at his head.

"Justin," I said, not quite able to keep the hurt from my voice.

He didn't look at me, but focused on Isabel, his expression still blank, as though it was totally normal for him to lie to me. "Sorry, Maddie," he said, using the nickname that I'd always hated and that nobody but Ruth was allowed to use.

"Why are you doing this?" I asked, trying to make sense of what was happening. Justin and Isabel were here together? And that meant that they were . . . what? Friends? Dating?

Justin turned to me as the first rumble of thunder sounded from outside. And in that moment, it was like the mask he'd been wearing slipped off, and I could see what was underneath it, what he was really feeling. Justin was *angry*. Angry and embarrassed and . . . hurt? I squinted, trying to make it out, but the expression was only there for a moment before the blankness returned. Justin turned back to face Isabel, who had arrived at the counter, looking very pleased with herself.

I could see now that she was a little more tan, and her bangs had grown out a bit. But aside from that, she looked the same as she had the last time I'd seen her, when she'd been staring daggers at me across the Rosebud Ballroom.

"Well," she said. She stood right next to Justin, very close, and I noticed that he took a tiny step away from her. If she was aware of this, however, she didn't let on. Her smiled widened. "Madison MacDonald," she practically purred. "We meet again."

I couldn't help but roll my eyes at that. "Yeah," I said. "It seems we do. What are you doing here, Isabel?"

From the added height her four-inch heels gave her, Isabel looked down at me, and I struggled to stand up taller in my flip-flops, suddenly wishing I wasn't wearing a smoothie-stained shirt that read *Blend Me A Tenor*. "Seriously?" she asked, her tone contemptuous that I would even ask such a stupid question. "I would have thought it would be obvious, Madison."

I looked from her to Justin and back again. "Um, no," I said. "I just stayed open late to give Justin his wallet back."

She shook her head and gave a high, giggling laugh that made me wince. "God, I can't believe you bought that," she said. "I didn't think you would. I thought that even *you* had to be too sharp to fall for it. But Justin here"—as she said his name, she touched his arm, brushing her fingers over it for a few seconds longer than normal—"told me that you're always willing to help out your friends."

I was probably a little slow on the uptake, but it hadn't occurred to me until then that Justin had left his wallet behind on purpose. The thought gave me the shivers—that this, whatever it was, had been planned days in advance. "I'm sorry," I said, still trying to wrap my head around the two of them in cahoots. It was just bizarre to see them standing next to each other, like two chapters of my past had suddenly, without my consent, decided to join forces. "Are you two . . . together?" I asked.

Justin, who had been watching me this whole time with his expression unchanging, suddenly frowned and looked down at the checkered linoleum floor. Isabel stiffened slightly and glanced over at Justin, her grin faltering.

And just like that, I understood what was going on. I hadn't been a girl for seventeen years for nothing. As clearly as if they'd told me that this was the situation, I could see that Isabel liked Justin and wanted to go out with him. And there *was* something between them—maybe they'd made out, which, ew—but it was clear Justin didn't want to turn it into anything more.

"Not exactly," Isabel said, turning back to me with a slightly forced smile. "But that's not why we're here."

"Then please tell me why you *are* here," I said. "The shop is now closed, I've been working all day, and I'm not feeling particularly fond of either of you at the moment." Justin glanced up at me when I said this, and I frowned at him. I had no idea why he had thrown his lot in with Isabel, but I was going to make sure that he knew I wasn't happy about it. But rather than looking away, or ashamed, Justin just stared back at me coolly, his expression hard.

"Well, I had to talk to you somehow," Isabel said. She wasn't smiling now. Her tone had turned serious and businesslike. "And Justin was kind enough to assist with that. Really, we would have done this sooner, but I needed to make sure the conditions were right. I've been preparing this for a month, you know."

I swallowed and felt myself shiver again. But I worked very hard to make my voice sound even and steady as I asked, "Preparing what?"

Isabel began to smile again. "My revenge," she said, as though this was the most obvious thing in the world.

"Your revenge," I repeated. I said the word slowly, but my thoughts were racing, trying to figure out what she could possibly be using against me, trying to determine if she was bluffing. When I'd had a remarkably similar conversation with Dell at the tail end of our prom, it was obvious the things he'd tried to do to me—because he'd already *done* them. But aside from a coworker who refused to work, which I highly doubted was Isabel's doing, there was nothing in my life that had gone wrong. I looked at her closely, but Isabel just nodded, her expression unchanging. "Okay," I said. "Well . . . I'm sorry to tell you that whatever your revenge was, it actually wasn't that effective. Because everything in my life is really great right now. So nice try, but no banana." Immediately after saying this, I sighed. Clearly, staying in the shop after-hours was taking a toll, and making me speak in fruit colloquialisms.

But Isabel didn't seem bothered by this. Instead, her smile widened, like I'd just given her the answer she'd been looking for. "Your life really *is* good right now, isn't it, Madison?" she asked. "Your boyfriend . . . your three best friends . . . and don't think I haven't noticed how *popular* you are. Even after my cousin hacked you, you're still superclose with all your buddies, aren't you? Hanging out at the beach, going to pool parties . . ." Her smile was now gone. "My life, on the other hand, hasn't been going as well since you trashed it." She took a step closer to the counter.

Every impulse I had told me to take a step back—or find and wield some garlic at her—but I forced myself to stay absolutely still, looking right back at her.

"You should know," she continued, her voice growing ever colder, "what happened to me after what you did to my prom. I was officially reprimanded by our headmistress. I almost got suspended, because she thought I had pocketed the money allotted to pay the DJ— the DJ you stole. Not to mention the fact that you tricked my date into dumping me the night before. I was a laughingstock at school. Totally ostracized. I had absolutely no friends after that."

That seemed more about how Isabel's friends were lame than anything to do with me. "Really?" I asked, a little incredulously. I tried to remember back to Isabel's Friendverse profile when we'd looked at it during the Promgate planning session. I could have sworn I'd seen something about a BFF on there. "What about your best friend, um . . ." I paused, trying to recall it, but the name wasn't coming. Something with a *B*, but that was as far as I was getting.

Isabel blinked at me, surprised. "She doesn't matter," she said quickly. "Because my social life at Hartfield was *ruined*." She looked at me levelly. "Did you think I was just going to let that slide?"

"The only reason I did what I did," I said, matching her icy tone, "was because you had been trying to sabotage *our* prom from the outset. You stole our crown and wrecked my prom dress—"

"And it sure seems like you're really suffering, doesn't it, Madison?" Isabel interrupted me, voice dripping with sarcasm. "Not to mention what you did to Justin," she continued, touching his arm again. "*Using* him like you did. Unfortunately, all that little ploy managed to accomplish was introducing two people who had something in common—namely, a score to settle with you."

I looked at Justin, not quite able to believe that he was this upset about the prom thing. He met my eyes for a moment before dropping them again. But I realized his resentment might have been building for a while—and it explained some of his slightly odd behavior before the prom. But this—whatever *this* was—seemed to be taking things way too far.

"Justin," I started, trying to reason with the only rational person in front of me.

But Isabel shook her head and continued as though I hadn't spoken. "Really, I'm just doing what I have to, Madison," she said. "I mean, you got to wreck my life and walk away scot-free, and I'm afraid we just can't have that." She put her hands on her hips, and I felt a little bit like we were in a showdown, like the one I'd seen in an old Western with Nate, at our drive-in.

I realized suddenly that this whole thing had a feeling of déjà vu about it. I'd been in a similar situation—twice—and there had always been a certain dark-haircd, black-souled person present. I looked outside, searching for a lurking figure in a black hoodie. "Where is he?" I asked.

"Who?" Justin asked, sounding genuinely confused.

"Dell," I said, answering him but looking at Isabel. "Your charming cousin. I assume he's behind this?"

Isabel's lip curled in a sneer. "Frank," she said contemptuously. She shook her head. "I'm afraid my cousin is officially worthless. He's sticking to the little bargain you struck with him. I haven't even seen him except at a family reunion three weeks ago."

"Oh," I said, surprised. This all might have made more sense if Dell, as usual, had been the mastermind, trying to settle his old grudge with me. The fact that I was only dealing with Isabel—and Justin, although he just appeared to be along for the ride after letting himself be used as bait—made me relax a little. Dell was a skilled hacker who had managed to commit all kinds of internet fraud and, most likely, a number of unprosecuted felonies. If he'd been involved, I might have actually been concerned about what his intentions were. After all, he had managed to successfully derail my life once. But what was Isabel going to do to me? "What do you want, Isabel?" I said, crossing my arms. I was suddenly finished with being insulted in my place of work.

I wanted to get some dinner, go home, log on to iChat, and talk to my boyfriend.

"What I want is simple," Isabel said, smoothing down her bangs. "Oh, I'd had some larger thoughts—bigger, more complicated plans—but then it came down to an eye for an eye. Nothing more, nothing less." She raised an eyebrow at me again, and I got the distinct feeling that she'd been practicing this in front of the mirror.

I glanced at Justin, but he was still looking down at the floor. He seemed—for the first time that night—a little discomfited. He swallowed hard and stuck his hands back in his pockets.

"An eye for an eye," I repeated.

"Exactly," Isabel said. "I only want to do to you what you did to me. And that's to leave you totally friendless—no boyfriend, no best friends, no big social circle of everyone who, for some reason, thinks you're so great. No friends at all, in fact."

I had to bite my lip to keep from laughing out loud. The whole idea was just so preposterous. "Okay," I said, not quite able to keep myself from smiling. "So let me get this straight. You're going to break up me and my boyfriend and then turn all my friends against me?"

"Oh, no," Isabel said, shaking her head. "Of course I'm not going to do that." She looked at me and started to smile again. "You are."

CHAPTER 10

Song: Earthquakes And Sharks/Brandtson
Quote: "If you think things can't get worse, it's probably because you lack sufficient imagination." —Anon

I looked at her, trying to tell if she was joking. She didn't appear to be, which just made this whole thing all that much more ridiculous. I shook my head, beginning to get really annoyed that she was wasting my time. "Actually," I said, feeling my voice slide into sarcasm, "I don't think I feel like doing that. But thanks so much for the offer, Iz. Now if you wouldn't mind leaving, we actually closed at six."

I started to turn away when I realized I was still holding Justin's stupid wallet. I turned back, holding it out, fully prepared to just throw it at him if he didn't take it this final time. "Here," I said. "Take it or I'm going to drop it."

Justin continued to look down at the floor, so I just let it fall to the counter and headed to the back to get my bag, hoping that Justin and Isabel would take the hint and leave.

"One thing, Mad," Isabel said, stopping me. "There's something that I wanted to give you." I turned back to her and saw that she was removing a silver flash drive from a crowded-looking key ring. She held up the drive, then placed it on the counter and slid it across toward me.

I saw, to my surprise, that it was a flash drive I recognized. *Making Sure You'll Never Forget* . . . was written in tiny, curling script on one side, and . . . *Your Night To Remember!* was printed on the other. It was one of the flash drives that had gone in our prom gift bags, but I had no idea what it had to do with anything. I held it in my hand, now thoroughly baffled.

"You'll want to take a look at that when you get a moment," Isabel said, adopting a light, conversational tone. "I think that it should prove . . . illuminating."

"What is on here, Isabel?" I asked, staring down at the flash drive resting on my palm.

"Now, I'm not going to spoil the surprise by going into particulars," she said. I looked up and saw that she was smiling. Justin picked up and pocketed his wallet, but was still looking down. "But I think it should help . . . clarify your decision."

"My decision?" I echoed. She nodded, and I raised my eyebrows. "You're serious. You really think that I'm going to dump my boyfriend and ditch all my friends?"

"I think you just might," she said, her voice still light and pleasant, like we were discussing the weather or how cute her bangs were. "If you don't, I'm going to make public everything that's on that drive. And what's more, all the information will appear to have come from you."

I felt my jaw drop but closed it immediately, not wanting to let Isabel see me unnerved. But I was. At the moment, I was feeling very, very far from nerved.

"After all," she continued cheerfully, "you've done it once. I don't think it would be that hard for people to believe that you were capable of doing this again."

"But I didn't do it in the first place," I said, finding my voice, still staring at her. "I was hacked—"

"Mmm," she said. She smiled at me. "But I don't think people are going to believe that happened *twice*. Do you?"

I stared at her for just a moment longer before shaking my head and putting the flash drive back on the counter. "No," I said, pushing it back toward her. "You do whatever you want to with this. I don't want to see what's on it. I'm going to tell my friends that She Who Shall Not Be Named has returned, and that something is going to happen, so we can all deal with it together. But I'm not about to play your little game, Isabel."

I realized I had nothing more to say, really. How stupid was she, to think she could blackmail me into ending my friendships? Into breaking up with Nate? I shook my head and looked at Justin. "I really didn't expect this from you," I said, a little shocked at the quaver that came out on the last word. But it was hitting me, somewhere deep inside, that Justin had betrayed me. After what had happened with Ruth, I would have thought the second betrayal would have been easier. But it wasn't. Instead, it was like pressing hard on a cut that had just begun to heal.

Justin looked up at me, and I saw a flash of something—regret?—in his eyes. I couldn't be sure, as a moment later it was gone.

"All right, Mad," Isabel said conversationally. "It's your call." She shrugged and started to turn toward the door, Justin following behind her. "I was just curious," she said as she paused and looked back at me. "What do you think Nate is going to do when his acceptance to Yale is reversed?"

That stopped me cold, and I could feel my heart hammering. "What are you talking about?" I asked, trying my best to keep my voice steady, folding my arms across my chest.

"He was accepted early decision, right?" Isabel asked. I just stared at her, wondering how she even knew this. *I* wasn't even entirely sure of that. "Because," she continued, "if he didn't apply anywhere else—if he has no backups—then he's really going to be in trouble when Yale kicks him out, now isn't he?"

"Why would Yale kick him out, Isabel?" I was trying my best to sound calm. The very fact that Isabel was tossing around Nate's name was unsettling me. As far as I knew, she still thought my boyfriend was named Nathan. The fact that she'd not only found out his name but had clearly done research into his life sent a shiver down my neck that had nothing to do with the air-conditioning level in the store.

"Because," she said, drawing out the word, and I realized, all at once, how much she was enjoying this. This moment, right now, was what she'd been waiting for. It must have been like Christmas morning and a Lilly Pulitzer sample sale all rolled into one. I gritted my teeth. Isabel smiled. "I know that he was one of the engineers of the Stanwich Senior Prank. And I can prove it. And I also have proof that he was the one who stole the Hartfield mascot costume."

My breath caught and I gulped, forcing myself to keep my expression neutral and not betray any of what I was feeling. Which, at the moment, was a growing sense of dread. How — *how* — did Isabel know about Nate and the prank? I barely knew the particulars of the prank. But I did know that he had been involved. Could he still get in trouble, now that the school year was over? I had no idea. But the fact that Isabel had connected Nate and the prank was bad. It was *really* bad.

I glanced down at the flash drive on the counter, instinctively, and Isabel followed my gaze. "Not there," she said. "I'm keeping the irrefutable evidence of what your precious boyfriend did somewhere much safer than that."

I cleared my throat, and found that it took me a few tries before I was able to get out sounds that sounded like words. "How do I know you're not bluffing?" I asked. "About Nate?"

She gave me the kind of smile that I would imagine

lions give gazelles as they size them up for an entrée. "I guess you'll just have to trust me on that one," she said. "And decide if it's worth the risk."

I looked away, at the pictures of the far too happy, smoothie-clutching couples who were so thrilled about blended fruit and rollerblading. Their lives seemed much simpler than mine was at this moment. I turned back to Isabel, drawing on all my acting skills—even if they had been recently described by the local theater critic as "acceptably adequate"—to fake a bravado that I certainly wasn't feeling. "I don't believe you," I said.

Isabel shrugged, looking totally unconcerned by this. "Believe whatever you want," she said. "But I have information on all of you. Your friends. Everyone who was part of your little crew during the prom. You. And, believe me, it's stuff that none of you will want getting out."

"And how did you come by this information?" I asked, grasping desperately at straws.

Isabel smiled again. "I guess I should rephrase what I said earlier. It seems my cousin isn't totally worthless, after all. But he should really learn not to leave his laptop lying around at family reunions."

Outside, another low rumble of thunder sounded, letting me know that the storm that had been threatening all day was finally thinking about heading toward us.

Isabel glanced outside, and it seemed to break her out of the supervillain monologue she had been so clearly enjoying. "Anyway," she said, a briskness coming back into her voice. She nodded down at the flash drive.

"I'd recommend looking at that. And then make your decision. I'll give you until tomorrow morning—should we say ten?" she asked, as though we were making plans for brunch.

Justin was looking intently out the window, doing a very convincing imitation of someone who wasn't actually hearing or experiencing anything that was going on around him. She touched his arm again. Justin looked at her, and she nodded. "I think we're done for now," she said. She turned and yanked open the door, setting the bell jangling. Justin met my eyes for only a moment before ducking his head and hurrying out the door.

"Oh, and Madison," she said, turning around in the doorway, just as thunder sounded again, louder this time.

"What," I said, not even really phrasing it as a question. I saw that her smile was gone. She looked deadly serious.

"If you tell any of your friends about this conversation, or that something is going to be happening, I'll know. And then all bets will be off. Understand?"

I didn't nod, but just stared back at her. She held my gaze for a moment before turning and leaving, stalking off toward a red sports car parked outside the store.

The door swung shut behind her, the bell dinging faintly and then falling silent. And as thunder rumbled again, closer than ever, I felt my knees wobble and my legs threaten to give out. I let myself lean hard against the counter, feeling my heart pound, wondering what the hell had just happened.

CHAPTER 11

Song: Grin & Bear It/The Grizzly Situation
Quote: "But aside from that, Mrs. Lincoln, how did you like the play?"—Anon

I sat on my bed, my laptop on and open before me, heart hammering. The flash drive rested next to me on my comforter.

After Isabel and Justin had left, I had remained in the store for a few more minutes, trying to order my thoughts and thinking that now would be a really excellent time for Einstein's theorems of time travel to suddenly be proved, and transport me back to a moment before I'd ever even heard of Isabel Ryan. When that didn't happen, I had closed up the store, gotten into Judy, and driven home, thoughts still swirling.

When I turned up my driveway, I had been surprised to see that all the lights were off. It looked like my father was still dealing with the situation at the paper. I figured it must have been pretty serious, to take him away from his sabbatical. But the fact that he was gone actually suited my purposes fine, as I didn't think that I would have been capable of any kind of coherent conversation.

I had gone straight up to my room and had turned on my computer, but somehow was having trouble taking the plunge and putting the flash drive into my laptop. I had just been sitting and staring at it, and for long enough that my computer had gone into power save mode and my screensaver had kicked in. A montage of pictures from my photo library was now filling the screen—Nate and I, arms around each other, shots of all my friends in various configurations, one of Travis looking distinctly green on the deck of our Galápagos boat, and an old one of Ruth and me in fourth grade, dressed up as prom queens for Halloween. The screensaver scrolled on, filling over and over again with images of all my favorite people, and Travis.

I reached for the flash drive, picking it up and turning it over in my hands. It seemed much too small and innocuous to have the power possibly to damage me and everyone I loved. I touched my keypad and woke my computer back up. A picture of Nate and me, slow dancing at the prom, was the last image on the screen, and it froze there for a moment before fading out. Both of us looked so happy. In that moment, I had thought we'd gotten away with everything. I had no idea how wrong I'd been.

My hand hovered over the keypad, and I wanted nothing more than to message my friends, to iChat them and see their faces, and tell them everything that had happened. I wanted to talk to Nate. I wanted not to be the only one holding on to this information. And even though

I couldn't imagine how Isabel would know if I told any of them, she had seemed so absolutely serious when she told me that I didn't want to chance it. I swallowed hard and gathered my courage. And before I could talk myself out of it, I inserted the flash drive into my computer.

The flash drive icon appeared on my screen a few seconds later, taking a bit longer than normal to show up. It was labeled FOR MADISON. I clicked on it. There was just one folder inside, labeled DOSSIERS. When I clicked on that, there was another strange multi-second pause before the folder opened. And when it did, I could feel my heart start to beat faster. There were four-teen folders inside this one, a list of names stretching alphabetically down my screen.

- Zach Baylor
- Ginger Davis
- Sarah Donner
- Nate (Jonathan) Ellis
- Lisa Feldman
- Dave (David) Gold
- Andy (Anderson) Lee
- Madison MacDonald
- Brian McMahon
- Ruth Miller
- Kittson Pearson
- Mark Rothmann
- Glen Turtell
- Schuyler Watson

I scanned the list, not liking at all that Andy's and Zach's names were on it. I was getting a distinctly bad feeling as I looked at it, a sense that this was maybe going to be worse than I'd expected it to be. It was just so *organized*.

Realizing I couldn't put this off any longer, I took a breath and clicked open the first folder.

ZACH BAYLOR
Location: Hartfield (following)
- Has no idea date with Sarah D. was a setup. Dating Sarah D. since after prom. Still believes she works/worked for Putnam Pizza.
- Not involved with prom incident—seems to have no knowledge of it (possibly useful).

GINGER DAVIS
Location: Putnam (following)
- Dating Josh Burch (not following).
- Working at Putnam Historical Society for summer—receiving credit for this (NOT widely known) because she nearly failed English last semester.
- Pictures from BMM parties 4–35—GD in states of apparent intoxication (could be useful).
- Wants to go to RISD. Needs scholarship & impeccable disciplinary record to do this.
- Involved with prom incident, <u>suspect</u> directly (uncorroborated).

SARAH DONNER

Location: Reach4theStars! Theatre Camp, Catskills (following)

- Determined to be President of Thespians sr. year.
- Still might have ax to grind with Madison. (Useful? Possible ally? Investigate.)
- Deeply invested in relationship with Zach B./ fearful of him finding out truth about how they met.
- Directly involved with prom incident, but not easily proved. In Hartfield ballroom for duration of prom.

NATE (JONATHAN) ELLIS

FILE MOVED TO SECURE LOCATION

LISA FELDMAN

Location: Putnam (following)

- Dating Dave G., 1 year +.
- Working at Putnam Hyatt (internship).
- DIRECTLY involved with prom incident.
- Employers seem to have no knowledge of role in prom incident.
- Potential target.

DAVE (DAVID) GOLD

Location: Putnam (following)

- Dating Lisa F.
- Works at Putnam Pizza (ongoing).

- DIRECTLY involved with prom incident. Used job to create diversions, etc. Boss (Tony Carlucci) unaware of this.
- Hosted prom afterparty—parents seemingly unaware.

ANDY (ANDERSON) LEE
Location: Hartfield (following)
- Dating Ruth M., 1 month.
- Not directly involved with prom incident. Used as Madison's ticket into Hartfield prom.
- New to Hartfield. Relatively friendless/ vulnerable.
- Unaware of his role in prom incident/why Madison chose him for her date. Thinks it was genuine interest (possibly useful).

BRIAN MCMAHON
Location: Putnam (following)
- Attending summer school—failed Marine Biology.
- Directly involved with prom incident.
- Engineered the Young Investors Club investment in Save The Last Dance results, profiting $10k.
- Constantly in trouble with father for throwing parties w/out permission—serially grounded.
- Father has threatened to send him to military school should he step out of line again (update from 6/2).
- His house = location of meeting on 5/22.

MADISON MACDONALD
FILE MOVED TO SECURE LOCATION

RUTH MILLER
Location: Putnam (following)
- Dating Andy L., 1 month.
- Suspended (2 weeks) due to actions in spring hacking—it would take only one more incident for her to be expelled.
- Friendship with Madison et al. seemingly repaired.
- Indirectly involved in prom incident. Unclear when she switched sides.
- LOYALTY TO MADISON NOT ENTIRELY ASSURED. COULD POSSIBLY BE USEFUL AGAIN.

KITTSON PEARSON
Location: Hamptons (following)
- Dating Glen T., three months.
- Well liked by Dr. Trent/administration.
- Directly involved with prom incident.
- Skilled with computers—possible that she rigged prom results (unproven).
- CHEATED on Glen T. in the Hamptons. Glen unaware (for now).

MARK ROTHMANN
Location: Putnam (following)
- Directly involved with prom incident. Pretended

to be "Marcus James Selwidge Rothschild" to gain access to Hartfield prom.
- Working at Second Concession Stand during summer—constantly updates status re: loneliness. Potentially useful.
- Single.

GLEN TURTELL
Location: Putnam (following)
- Dating Kittson P., three months—jealous, protective of her.
- Directly involved with prom incident.
- Constantly in trouble w/administration, Dr. Trent.
- ONE incident away from expulsion.
- Unaware of Kittson's cheating. USEFUL.

SCHUYLER WATSON
Location: Putnam (following)
- Ex of Connor Atkins—they broke up after prom, have not reunited.
- Has NOT revealed to anyone but Madison the facts with the Choate scandal, or why she left school. Cause of Connor breakup?
- Directly involved with prom incident.
- Easily manipulated, scared of others finding out about her past—weakness that can be used.

"Oh my God," I murmured. I took a steadying breath and closed my eyes for a long moment, then opened them again. But the facts were still there, staring at me from the screen in black-and-white. This was like when I'd come back from the Galápagos and found my Friendverse hacked—but was somehow much worse. The Friendverse hacking was mostly concerned with hurting me. But looking at the information that had been collected, it was clear that I was no longer the target.

It was my friends.

I leaned back against the throw pillows that were propped against my headboard, my heart beating hard. Isabel hadn't been kidding, or exaggerating. There were literally files on me and my friends, and in them were all our secrets. And some secrets I hadn't even been aware of, like Ginger's failing English, and that all it would take would be one more infraction for both Ruth and Glen to be expelled. And it was really troubling that this much information could so easily be found on us. I realized that Isabel had been actively looking for it, and that we were dealing with someone who had an unbalanced mind and an evil streak a mile wide. But it was clear that a lot of this information had been gleaned from Friendverse profiles and status updates. And though I had tried to encourage all my friends to make their updates private, it appeared that nobody had listened to me.

But *how* had Isabel found out about Kittson hooking up with the lame preppy guy? I was fairly sure that Kittson wouldn't have told anyone except me. And she would *never* have told Isabel. But I suddenly remembered my defense when Liz was accusing me of spilling the beans about her ill-advised hookup this spring—that there was the lame preppy guy to consider. For all I knew, he knew Isabel. Or other people at the party might have seen Kittson kissing the LPG. Which was the problem with secrets, I realized as I looked at the long list of them that Isabel had compiled. They didn't just belong to you.

I scrolled to the top of the page, looking at my absent folder, and then Nate's. It was really troubling me that they weren't there. That Isabel would bait me with the fact that she had information on us, but wasn't going to let me see what it was.

And it wasn't just the facts she'd gathered, I saw as I read through the profiles again, feeling my stomach drop. It wasn't just the information itself. It was that the information had been analyzed, dispassionately, to see how it could best achieve the most destructive results. It had been examined with a view to hurting, and potentially seriously damaging, all my friends.

I stared at the screen until my eyes watered, and then closed them for a long moment, thinking. What was I going to do about this?

My iChat dinged, and I opened my eyes and saw an invitation from Kittson. Glad for a distraction—any distraction—I accepted, and a moment later, there she was. She was back in the wicker room, but now looked much, much happier.

"Hi," she said, smiling wide.

"Hi," I said, trying to keep my face from betraying any of what I had experienced that night. I quickly minimized the dossiers, as though Kittson could somehow see through her computer what I was looking at on mine.

"I was just, um, doing some reading. Nothing interesting. At all. Just, you know, Wikipedia."

"Wow," she said, rolling her eyes. "Way to have a rocking Sunday night, Mad. I just wanted to thank you for your advice. I called Glen, and we made up and things are really great now!"

I felt my face relax into a smile for the first time since Isabel had dropped her bombshell. "That's great, Kittson," I said. "I'm so happy for you guys."

"Me too," she said, pulling her hair up and examining her reflection in the tiny image of herself, then dropping it again. "What do you think?" she asked, smoothing down her hair. "Should I get layers?"

"Well," I started, not even thrown. It was totally normal for Kittson to switch the subject to her hair within a conversation. The fact that she was doing it was actually a good sign, as it showed me that she was feeling better.

"No," she said decisively, not waiting for me to finish. "I think they'd do weird things to my texture. Anyway." She focused back on me. "I think you were absolutely right. I would have just upset things by telling him about my hookup with that guy. I mean, it didn't mean anything. So why wreck what we have for something that didn't even matter?"

"Right," I said slowly. A tiny piece of me was still wondering if this was the right advice to have given her. But things were good with the two of them. Kittson looked happy. And if she had told Turtell the truth, I was 100 percent positive that neither of those things would be true. And also, that lame preppy guys might find them-selves in mortal peril.

"So what's happening with you?" she asked, raising her eyebrows expectantly.

I glanced down at the minimized folder and then made myself look back up at her, forcing a smile. "Nothing," I said brightly. "Same old."

Kittson frowned and leaned toward the screen, scrutinizing me. "Something's wrong," she said after a moment. "What is it, Madison? Tell me."

It really was getting to be discouraging that my friends—not to mention Nate—could always seem to tell when I was lying. This was not a great testament to my acting skills, acceptably adequate or no. I was about to say something when I heard the sound of the garage door opening, which meant my father was home. "I have to go," I said to Kittson, glad to be able to tell her the truth. "My dad's home."

She looked at me, narrowing her eyes. Then her expression relaxed and she smiled again. She was still clearly riding the happiness of the Turtell wave, and wasn't going to let any suspected weirdness on my part bring her down. "All right," she said. "But call me *soon*, okay? I don't think I'm coming back to Putnam until August and I'm feeling totally out of the loop."

"Sure," I said quickly. "Bye, Kittson." I closed out my iChat and then, after a moment's deliberation, logged myself out so that none of my other friends would be able to see that I was online. I pulled up the dossiers and looked at them for another moment before putting my computer to sleep.

Then I headed downstairs to say hi to my father. At this point, I would have even talked to Travis, if he'd been there. Anything to distract me from my own thoughts.

****

"Is there any more vanilla?" my father asked, leaning over to look into my carton. I held it out to him, but didn't relinquish it until he handed over his rum raisin, which he had been hogging. "Thanks," he said, dipping his spoon into the *Gofer To Go . . . fer!* container with a deep sigh.

When I'd arrived downstairs, I'd seen my father beelining for the freezer and removing all the ice cream. While this was not a good sign in terms of the night my father had had, it did help me realize that ice cream was precisely what I required at that moment. We had settled around the kitchen table, eating directly out of the cartons, something that my mother never would have allowed if she'd been there. But my mother was in London, so we were free to eat ice cream as it was meant to be consumed.

I'd started to ask my father about what was happening at the paper, but he'd just shaken his head and pointed to his carton. I had understood what he meant—and what's more, appreciated a moment to try and get my own thoughts in order—so we ate in silence, the only sounds in the kitchen the ticking of the clock and the scrape of the metal spoons against the plastic containers.

When he had polished off the vanilla, my father sighed and pushed the container away from him. I did the same with the rum raisin, feeling the beginnings of an ice cream headache setting in. My father took off his ancient Cubs hat, the one he always wore when he was on deadline, and tossed it onto the counter. "It's a mess, kid," he told me, shaking his head.

This was very true, but I had a feeling that he was talking about his problem, not mine. "What's going on?" I asked.

My father sighed again. "It's this thing at the paper," he said. "One of my favorite young baseball players—nothing but future ahead of this kid—is about to be implicated in a steroid scandal. The story's going to break tomorrow."

"Did he do it?" I asked, leaning forward.

My father shrugged. "I don't know. We don't have the facts yet. Which is why I've been in the newsroom, arguing with the editor. I don't think we should go to print until it's been proved, and isn't just speculation."

"But," I said, trying to come up with some positive aspect to this, "if he didn't do it, then his name will be cleared, and everything will be okay. Right?"

My father gave me a sad smile. "I wish the world worked that way, kiddo," he said. "But rumor can ruin people. You don't realize how much is built on a reputation until you see one about to crumble before you."

I could have told him I knew that all too well. "But people can come back from that stuff," I said, thinking about how, with the exception of the occasional sidelong glance I still received, most people seemed to have forgotten about the hacking incident. "Right? If it's disproved, he'll be fine."

My father just shook his head again. "I'm afraid that goes against who we are as people. Everyone latches on to the scandal. It's *interesting*. It's what people want to believe. You'll find there's a much smaller audience for people who want to hear the truth. And once impressions are made, it's almost impossible to reset them. This is going to follow this kid his whole career. He'll be the 'suspected' steroid user in every piece that ever gets written about him from now on. And it's just so hard to see it and know you can't do anything. . . ." His voice trailed off. He stared into space for a moment, then glanced up at the clock. I looked up as well, and was shocked to see that it was close to midnight. I could feel the tiredness seeping into my bones. It had been a very long night.

"I should get to bed," my father said, standing and stretching his back. He picked up his Cubs cap and whapped me lightly on the head with it. "You too, kid."

"Right," I said. "Sure." He cleared the spoons from the table and loaded them into the dishwasher while I put the ice cream that was left back in the freezer. My father started to head out of the kitchen, then turned back to me.

"You doing okay, Mad?" he asked. "Did you have a good day at work?"

I made myself smile at my father. "It was great," I said, mentally crossing my fingers that my acting ability would be strong enough and that he would be tired enough to just accept this explanation.

My father gave me a weary smile and nodded. "Oh, to be a carefree teenager," he said wistfully as he headed out of the kitchen. "Night, sweetie."

"Night, Daddy," I called after him. I stood in the kitchen for a moment, not quite able to stop myself from letting out a short, humor-free laugh. Carefree teenager. *Right.*

****

It was three A.M., and I was lying in bed, staring at the glow-in-the-dark stars on my ceiling, the ones that Ruth and I had put up back in middle school. Even though I was exhausted, my mind was swirling, and it felt like sleep was many miles off. I had looked at every angle of the situation, but always came back, over and over, to the same inevitable conclusion.

I had no choice.

I had to do what Isabel wanted, or all my friends' lives were going to be damaged—some severely and irreparably. I couldn't stop thinking about how, at the end of the prom, my assistant headmaster, Dr. Trent, had tried to get me in trouble for wandering around the hotel—on a tip that came from Isabel. He had listened to her then. Why should I assume he wouldn't listen to her now? Especially when he had been so eager to see me in trouble for Dell's expulsion? And he was always happy to see Turtell in trouble. It meant I couldn't just dismiss what Isabel had told me. I knew her well enough to know that if she threatened to act, she would.

I closed my eyes and saw the possible carnage playing out in front of me. Zach dumping Sarah when he found out that she had lied to him. Andy and Ruth breaking up when he found out the inadvertent role he'd played in Promgate. Ruth not getting valedictorian, but instead getting expelled. Brian potentially going to *military school*. Ginger, so incredibly talented, losing her chance at a scholarship to RISD. Glen getting expelled. Me, potentially suspended. Or worse. Senior class secretary undoubtedly taken away, and I would possibly not be able to get into the schools I wanted to, with a serious disciplinary infraction on my record. And Nate . . . my stomach lurched when I thought about Nate, and my eyes opened again.

Nate might not be able to go to college. Nate going to Yale had been an inseparable part of him from the moment we met, and the thought that he might not be able to—the thought that his future might be destroyed because of *me*—was almost too much to handle. I felt like I now understood why Victorian ladies were always turning faint and going into swoons. I would have liked to go into one myself, if I knew how. Just something to shut out the oppressive reality of the world.

Was I really going to let all these terrible things happen, when they could all easily be prevented? Was I really going to be that selfish?

I closed my eyes again and rolled over on my side. I didn't understand how, only a day ago, I'd felt the happiest I'd ever been. I hugged my pillow tighter, wanting nothing more than to drift off and forget all this for a few hours. But even though I lay there in the quiet darkness, perfectly still, sleep didn't come. And outside my window, closer than ever, I heard thunder rumble one more time before it finally started to rain.

CHAPTER 12

FROM: Madison
TO: Ruth, Schuyler, Lisa
Date: 6/23, 8:34 A.M.

GUYS. There's something really weird going on
with Isabel. I'm not going to be able to explain it
properly—and you're not going to believe me—but
The Evil One is back. And she's planning on doing a
lot of damage to us. We're going to have to pretend
not to be friends for a little while, just . . .

Sitting at the kitchen table, I paused and looked at the
half-composed e-mail on my laptop screen. When I'd
woken up early that morning, thinking a little more
clearly, I realized that just because Isabel was making

threats didn't mean I had to capitulate to them. After all, how would she know if I told my friends—and Nate, of course—what was really going on? We could keep up a facade that everything had fallen apart until we figured things out, but we could figure it out *together*.

I took a bite of my breakfast (two frosted strawberry Pop-Tarts) and a sip of my morning Diet Dr Pepper (with my mother gone, my father and I had both reverted to terrible nutrition) as I read over my words. The more I typed, the better I was feeling about this. And it was just past eight thirty—so I had plenty of time to talk to my friends before Isabel's deadline.

My cell rang, and I saw that the number was blocked. I hesitated before answering, but then remembered Nate had said his service might be wonky—so maybe he was calling from Maxwell's house line.

"Hello?" I asked.

"Madison."

I drew in a breath as I recognized the voice. It was Isabel.

"What?" I snapped, looking at the time on my computer screen. "It's not ten yet."

"I am doing this even though I don't have to," Isabel snapped back at me. "I'm giving you a chance not to make a mistake."

I felt myself frown. "What do you mean?" I asked.

"I mean, I told you not to tell anyone what I'd said or that I'd contacted you," she explained crisply. "And I told you what the consequences would be if you did."

I stared at the unsent e-mail in front of me, and looked around quickly. It wasn't like Isabel could see what was on my computer screen. "I haven't," I said, glad that I could be entirely truthful on this point.

"No," Isabel conceded. "But you're thinking about it, aren't you?"

I suddenly felt very creeped out. How had she known? "Isabel," I said slowly, "how . . ."

"I told you I would know," she said. "I know. And I'm giving you a chance not to be stupid, Madison. You play by my rules, or your friends, and your precious Nate, are going to get hurt."

"How did you get all that information on my friends?" I asked, trying to keep my voice from betraying the fact that my thoughts were spinning. "It came from Dell?"

"Mostly," she said. "I added some of my own, of course. But he was undeniably helpful. Frank's very smart about certain things, you know. And one thing he's always advocated is having information on your enemies."

I closed my eyes. There had been a time in my life, I was almost sure of it, when things were fairly normal and I wasn't being blackmailed and people didn't keep dossiers on me and my friends.

"I hope you've come to a decision," she continued, her voice growing more serious. I glanced at the clock, but this didn't seem like the moment to mention I still had an hour and a half. I was feeling more and more like I was being painted into a corner, and my options were being taken away from me. But I still had to know for sure before I made a not-entirely-metaphorical deal with the devil.

"I need to know something first," I said.

"And what's that?" Isabel asked, beginning to sound annoyed.

"I need some proof," I said. "About Nate." It was all very well for Isabel to tell me that she knew he was involved with the prank, but that might just be speculation. Isabel could have just heard this rumor from somewhere. After all, Nate had been one of the main suspects of the prank—he'd been called before his headmaster over and over again. But since they'd never been able to prove anything, he'd never gotten in trouble. Nate's involvement in the prank was the biggest thing she could threaten me with revealing, and I had a feeling she knew that.

"Proof," Isabel said. There was a small pause, and then she said, "That's fair." Then there was a longer pause, then a rustling and the faint sound of metal hitting metal. I pressed the phone to my ear and could hear the sound of keys clacking on a computer. "Well," she said, "right now, I'm looking at a picture of your boyfriend breaking into Hartfield. And he seems to be wearing a polo. But instead of an alligator, it looks like . . ." There was a pause, and I heard more clacking of keys. "A camera, maybe?"

I swallowed. That was indisputable evidence. The one time Nate and Isabel had met, Nate had been wearing a tux. She wasn't his friend on Friendverse, so she didn't have access to any of his pictures. The only way she could know about that shirt would be because she was looking at a picture of it. A picture that had the power to potentially wreck my boyfriend's life.

"Okay," I said after a moment. The word caught in my throat and came out scratchy and a little tremulous. My heart rate was speeding up, and I felt on the verge of panicking. Clearly, my body knew that I was wandering headlong into something that was a bad idea, and was trying to tell me to get out of it—flight or fight. But instead, I was choosing to do neither. "Okay," I repeated, my voice steadier this time. "All right."

"All right what?" Isabel asked.

I made myself take another breath, this one mostly so I wouldn't throw my phone across the kitchen. "All right," I said. "I'll do it. I'll say goodbye to my friends. Okay?"

"And Nate," Isabel added, causing my stomach to drop.

"And . . . that," I said, when I started to say his name and found that I couldn't, not without betraying the storm of emotions I was currently trying to weather.

"Good," Isabel said. I heard the smugness come back into her voice. "I really do think you're making the right decision, Madison. And it is only fair. You have to admit that."

I wasn't about to admit anything, and certainly not that, to her. "Are we done now?" I asked. I was feeling, with every minute passing, that I needed to end the call and give the whole Victorian swooning thing another shot. Either that or go to bed for about five years. But mostly, I needed to not be talking to Isabel any longer.

"Almost," she said, and her tone became clipped and businesslike. "Here's how this is going to work. After you bid your friends farewell, you're going to unfriend them all on Friendverse, Status Q, and Constellation. And you're going to do this today."

I felt my heart begin to race even faster, which was not a good thing, since I was already feeling like I'd just run a marathon. "No," I said faintly. I had hoped to take some time to get used to the idea, and figure out how I was going to do this, and then break the news to my friends. I was not going to be at all ready to do this in a few *hours*. "Today? Not possible."

"I think you'll find it will be possible," she said, her voice frosty. "Unless you want me to let all this out. Or send the e-mail I've composed to Nate's headmaster . . ."

"How do you *know* all this?" I asked again, my voice breaking midsentence.

"I thought you would have understood by now," Isabel said, sighing loudly, "there's not a lot I don't know about you and your soon-to-be-ex-friends. So unless you want everything getting out, you'll do it today. Everyone on the list."

"Fine," I said, forcing the word out, trying to concentrate on how much I hated Isabel right now, so I wouldn't have to think about what I was going to have to do.

"And Nate," she added. *"Today."*

"Nate's out of town," I said. I heard her draw in a breath, and I jumped in before she could speak. "He's working," I said shortly. "And I'm not going to do it over the phone, Isabel. You can forget that."

"No," Isabel said. "A big conversation like that? You'll want to do that in person."

I let out a breath, glad that Isabel had conceded this. I couldn't even think about what it would mean to do this yet—my heart gave a sharp little pain every time I thought about it. But I knew without a shadow of a doubt that I wasn't going to be able to do it over the phone. Nate deserved more than that. "Yes," I agreed hoarsely.

"And you'll have to come up with a reason," Isabel continued. "One that he'll believe, since you were so disgustingly *smitten* with him only a few days before. But," she added, her voice turning sly, "when he sees on Constellation that you were hanging out after-hours with your ex-boyfriend, it should give him some idea of why it's suddenly over."

My stomach plummeted like I was on a roller coaster that had just gone around its first loop. I hadn't thought about that. I had never even *considered* what that might look like, since that had been the furthest thing from my mind. I suddenly realized how hurt Nate might get as a result of all this, and the thought made me feel physically ill.

I needed to get off the phone with her. This whole conversation was terrible. It was like being bitten to death by fire ants—somehow, hundreds of little tiny stings that were so much worse than just getting punched once, or something. "Okay," I said shortly. "So—"

"And as for you," she continued, as though I hadn't

spoken. "You're going to make your Constellation feed public, same with Status Q and Friendverse. I'm going to keep tabs and make sure that you haven't gone back on our agreement. If you do—or if you tell any of your friends or Nate that I am the reason this is happening, I'll know and I go public with everything. Understood?"

"How?" I blurted. I could hear the edge of hysteria in my voice. She was just a high-school almost-senior, like me. She wasn't the CIA, or the IRS. How was she doing this? "How are you going to *know*, Isabel?"

"Because I will," she replied calmly. "You tell a group that large something that big, and someone's going to say something. In their statuses, in their quotes, in messages they send to other people or write on their friends' walls. Your life is public, in case you hadn't noticed, Madison, and it exists on the internet. If you say something, I will know. And then the very next thing I'll do is release this information. Understood?"

"Yes," I muttered. I wouldn't have admitted it for almost anything, but she had a point. Getting *everyone* to not say anything about this—or pretend we weren't friends when we still were, which was what I'd been hoping to pull off—had no chance of lasting. It would be as impossible as convincing everyone to leave Constellation, Friendverse, and Status Q. I might as well ask them to cut off a major appendage.

"Good," Isabel said. She sounded content now, and relaxed, and I could hear that she was smiling again. "I really didn't want to have to do this," she added, almost conversationally. "But you brought this on yourself, Madison. You don't mess with me. And now you know it. Have a *great* rest of your summer, Mad."

She hung up, and I was left staring at the phone in my hand. I was gripping it so hard that my hand was shaking. I unclenched my fingers and put it down in front of me on the table. My thoughts weren't racing anymore—they were just centered on what I had to do today. I had to hurt everyone that I loved.

I looked at the half-written e-mail on the screen in front of me. Then I deleted it entirely. I took a breath, and logged on to Constellation. It was time to get this over with.

CHAPTER 13

Song: Why Can't We Be Friends?/War
Quote: "True friendship is a plant of slow growth, and must undergo and withstand the shocks of adversity before it is entitled to the appellation."—George Washington

 Queen Kittson ➔ **M²** Thanks so much for the talk yesterday, Mad! Come out here and hang if you get some time off from your fruit stand, or whatever it is that you're doing.
Location: Blue & Cream. East Hampton, NY.

 Nate Stuck inside an isolated beach house while it pours rain outside, and I try to teach geometry. Suddenly, The Shining is beginning to make a lot more sense to me.
Location: 65 Vineyard Drive. Martha's Vineyard, MA.

 Young MacDonald ➔ **M²** Mad, tell me if you go and see Kittson! I made a lanyard for Olivia that I want you to give to her.
Location: Camp Arrowhead. Pocono Pines, PA.

 Young MacDonald ➔ **M²** Girls like lanyards, right?
Location: Camp Arrowhead. Pocono Pines, PA.

Schuyler Just because it is raining doesn't mean you should skip the sunblock! You can still get burned!
Location: Central Pool, Stanwich Yacht Club. Stanwich, CT.

 Schuyler And I know this because I just did. ☹
Location: Central Pool, Stanwich Yacht Club. Stanwich, CT.

 Rue I have the WHOLE DAY OFF. I am going to celebrate by doing anything except watching Dora the Explorer.
Location: 28 Waverly Terrace. Putnam, CT.

 Lord Rothschild → Rue Come down to the beach and hang out with me!
Location: Second Concession Stand, Putnam Beach. Putnam, CT.

 Lord Rothschild And that invite is open to EVERYONE! The beach is great today!
Location: Second Concession Stand, Putnam Beach. Putnam, CT.

 Lord Rothschild Well, except for the rain. But there's lots of parking!
Location: Second Concession Stand, Putnam Beach. Putnam, CT.

 be tricia Rain, rain, go away! Come again sometime in October! ☺
Location: Hartfield Day Spa. Hartfield, CT.

 Dave Gold I am the reigning Big Bass CHAMPION. Please show me appropriate respect the next time that we meet.
Location: Hott Wheelz (KING). Putnam, CT.

 Nate → Dave Gold I really think that what we should be talking about is the fact that you're now the King of a toy car store. Not good, dude.
Location: 65 Vineyard Drive. Martha's Vineyard, MA.

La Lisa → Nate, Dave Gold THANK YOU.
Location: Putnam Hyatt. Putnam, CT.

Dave Gold → La Lisa, Nate They are not TOY CARS.
They are miniature automotive models built to scale.
Location: Hott Wheelz (KING). Putnam, CT.

Nate → Dave Gold Just keep telling yourself that.
Location: 65 Vineyard Drive. Martha's Vineyard, MA.

Rue → M² Mad, are you working today? Want to hang
out? I'm up for anything other than finger painting or
watching anything Wubbzy related.
Location: 28 Waverly Terrace. Putnam, CT.

Schuyler → M² Mad, is everything okay? Didn't hear from
you last night.
Location: Central Pool, Stanwich Yacht Club.
Stanwich, CT.

La Lisa → M² Oui, Mad—what's up with the silence
mysterieuse?
Location: Putnam Hyatt. Putnam, CT.

M² → Rue, Schuyler, La Lisa So sorry, guys. Stuff's been
happening this morning. Can we all meet at Stubbs when
Shy and Lisa are done with work?
Location: 76 Winthrop Road. Putnam, CT.

Schuyler → M², Rue, La Lisa Sure! 5:30?
Location: Central Pool, Stanwich Yacht Club.
Stanwich, CT.

La Lisa → M², Rue, Schuyler Tres bien! C'est un
rendezvous!
Location: Putnam Hyatt. Putnam, CT.

Rue → M², La Lisa, Schuyler Sounds great!
Location: 28 Waverly Terrace. Putnam, CT.

Rue → M² Mad, I've got nothing else going on today. Totes free. ☺ Want to hang out?
Location: 28 Waverly Terrace. Putnam, CT.

M² → Rue I can't. Sorry.
Location: 76 Winthrop Road. Putnam, CT.

Rue → M² Oh. Um, okay.
Location: 28 Waverly Terrace. Putnam, CT.

Nate → M² Mad, is everything okay? Haven't heard from you. Miss you & hope you're good.
Location: 65 Vineyard Drive. Martha's Vineyard, MA.

Nate → M² Mad?
Location: 65 Vineyard Drive. Martha's Vineyard, MA.

For once, I was the first to arrive at Stubbs. I got my latte, along with everyone else's current usuals, from Vince the barista and made my way slowly over to the area we had long ago staked out as ours. I sat in the armchair that was always saved for me. I looked across at the couch that Lisa and Schuyler shared and then next to me, at the wooden chair that was Ruth's. It had been left empty for her even during the two months when she hadn't been hanging out with us. I wondered, a little numbly, if my friends would leave this chair open for me when I stopped hanging out with them, or if someone else—like Tricia—would start sitting there. Trying to push away the visual of Tricia literally taking my place, I set everyone's drinks in front of their normal spots. If I was going to confuse and alienate all my best friends, I'd figured that the least I could do was buy them coffee first.

I took a sip of my iced latte and checked the time on my phone. My friends weren't due to arrive for a few more minutes yet, and I wanted to just stay in this moment for a little bit longer. Everything was going to change all too soon, but for right now, as far as everyone else knew, everything was status quo.

I took another sip, grateful for the caffeine that helped me feel a little more awake, and let out a long breath slowly, like I did before I went onstage. I tried not to think about what was about to happen, instead concentrating only on the grizzled sailor on the Stubbs sign, the rain that was lashing the plate glass window, and the fact that, for a few minutes more, I could pretend that nothing in my life had changed.

The bell on the door jangled, and Ruth came in, looking half drenched, squeezing water from her ponytail. She smiled when she saw me and headed over to our spot. I smiled back automatically, then felt something very cold grip my insides when I realized the enormity of what I was going to have to do. My smile faltered, and I looked down at my Stubbs cup to try and regain my composure.

"Hey," Ruth said, settling into her wooden chair and pulling it a little closer into the circle. "Can you believe this weather? My umbrella died halfway across the parking lot."

I swallowed hard. "That sucks," I said, but I could hear how not-normal my voice sounded, how strained and shaky. Ruth looked at me sharply, concerned, and I knew she'd heard it as well. "I got you your *ush*," I said, gesturing toward her small soy latte with one pump of vanilla. The vanilla was a new addition, and I had been thrilled to see it, as it said to me that Ruth was willing to let go of her routines and try new things. I thought it was no coincidence that she'd changed her drink around the time she'd started officially dating Andy.

"Thank you," Ruth said, digging in her purse for her wallet.

I shook my head. "On me," I said firmly. "Really."

Ruth glanced up at me, maybe again hearing something in my voice I hadn't intended for her to. "Okay," she said, dropping her wallet back in her bag. "Thanks, Mad. You didn't have to."

"I did," I said quietly. Ruth had lifted her Stubbs cup halfway to her lips, but now she stopped and set the cup back on the small table in front of her.

"Maddie," she said, using the nickname in one of its few permitted circumstances. She leaned forward, looking concerned. "What is it? Something's wrong."

I looked at my former BFF, and current FF. Despite everything that had happened with us, she was still the person who knew me best, and I didn't think I was a good enough actress to deny this and have her believe me. I just looked at her in silence for a second, all too aware that these were the last moments of our friendship.

"Maddie?" Ruth asked. "Come on, you're scaring me."

"Just promise me something," I said, the words rushing out. I looked down at my Stubbs cup, knowing that if I kept seeing Ruth's worried expression, I was going to break down and tell her everything. And she would undoubtedly make a pro and con list and would assure me that we could figure it out together.

"What?" Ruth asked, still looking concerned and now looking confused, as well.

"I just . . ." I took a shaky breath and made myself keep going. "I hope that you and Andy stay together. I hope you guys are really happy. And I hope that you can be there for Schuyler and Lisa."

"Why are you talking like this?" Ruth asked, looking more and more confused, and no less worried. "What's going on?"

Before I could deflect that question, the bell jangled again, and I looked up to see Schuyler and Lisa rushing in, both looking fairly waterlogged.

"Mon Dieu," Lisa grumbled, shaking the water from her curls, which had expanded to about three times their normal size, "did I suddenly move to Seattle? *C'est ridicule.*" She flopped down dramatically on the couch, then leaned forward when she saw her drink. *"Pour moi?"* she asked, and I nodded. *"Merci!"* she said, smiling at me and picking up her cup.

Schuyler looked around the coffee shop anxiously, twice, before sitting down next to Lisa and picking up her drink.

"What?" Lisa asked, turning and looking around as well. Ruth and I followed suit, and the only other person currently in Stubbs—he looked like one of the laptop-tethered college students who had recently descended on the coffee shop—clearly thought we were staring at him (which, technically, we were). He blushed bright red and accidentally knocked over his coffee, then gave a little yelp as the coffee headed toward his laptop. He hoisted it valiantly out of the path of the coffee, which then, unimpeded, ended up soaking the front of his pants.

I turned away from the spectacle—I had a feeling it was going nowhere good—and back to Schuyler, who was doing a terrible job of appearing nonchalant. "Shy?" I asked.

"It's nothing," she said, fiddling with her coffee cup lid. "I was just checking to see if Connor—or *Roberta Briggs*—was here." She said Roberta's name in the same way that people normally said *anthrax*, or Lisa said *Euro Disney*.

"Why would you need to wonder about that?" Lisa asked. "*Pourquoi?* Check your Constellation to see where he is."

"I can't," Schuyler said. "He's not on it anymore."

This was surprising enough to cause silence to fall at our table, and for me to nearly forget that, soon, I would have to steer the conversation in a very unhappy direction. "Wait, what?" I asked, baffled.

"I don't understand," Ruth said, brow furrowed. "He's not on Constellation?"

"No," Schuyler said miserably. "He's not on Friendverse, or Status Q, either. It's like he's just *vanished*. And I have no idea where he is, or what he's doing, or who he's doing it with." As soon as she said this, Shy turned the same color as her hair. "Not like that," she said quickly. "I didn't mean it like that." Then she paused, and her complexion suddenly changed direction and started heading back to pale again. "But *OMG*," she said, looking stricken, "do you think—"

"Un moment," Lisa interrupted. "I still don't understand why Connor would do that." She turned to Ruth and me, eyebrows raised. "Do you think it's possible that he joined a cult?"

I took a sip of my latte, thoughts racing. Connor had *left*. Connor had just cut himself off from what constituted a social life at Putnam High. It had never even really occurred to me that you could do this—or that you would want to. Even after the hacking incident, I had never even considered leaving Friendverse. It just wasn't an option.

Right?

"I don't know why he did it," Schuyler said. "But I hate not knowing where he is. It's like . . ." She looked up at us, and took a breath before continuing. "It's like he's disappeared. And my last connection with him is now gone. And I just . . . really miss him." She said this last part softly, and very fast.

Lisa opened her mouth to say something, but then paused and looked at me. "Mad?" she asked. *"Votre opinion?"*

Ruth turned to me as well, and I could see from her worried expression that she hadn't let my earlier strangeness slip her mind in the midst of the Schuyler drama.

I looked around at the faces of my friends one last time, fixing them in my memory. Then I took a deep breath and shook my head. "No," I said, trying with all my might to keep my voice steady. "I can't help."

Schuyler blinked at me, Lisa frowned, and Ruth leaned forward. "Maddie," she said, urgency in her voice. "What's going on?"

"I'm so sorry," I said, and despite my best efforts, my voice broke on the last word. "But I have to go now. And I won't be coming back. I can't—I can't be friends with you anymore."

Lisa was staring at me, utterly confused, like I was the one speaking in a foreign language. Schuyler had turned even paler than she normally was, and Ruth was biting her bottom lip, looking like she was about to cry.

Lisa was the first to recover the power of speech. "I'm sorry," she said. She shook her head. "Madison, is this some sort of joke? Because it is not funny."

Somewhere in the back of my head, I registered that she must have realized how serious the situation was, since she had spoken entirely in English. "It's not a joke," I said, feeling my heart hammering, forcing the words out. "And I wish that I could tell you why I'm doing it. But I can't."

"Maddie," Ruth said, and I saw that her brown eyes were filling with tears. "Don't do this."

"She's not serious," Lisa said, tossing her curls, but without enough bravado to pull the gesture off. "Madison wouldn't decide to end our friendship out of the blue with no reason. She *wouldn't do* something like that." Though she was using the third person, she was directing this right to me, her eyes locked onto mine.

I felt my bottom lip start to tremble, and I knew that I wasn't going to be able to keep things together for much longer. And I knew that the longer I stayed there, with all my best friends, the closer I was going to come to breaking down and confessing everything. "Sorry," I choked out. "But I have to go—"

"Something isn't right," Schuyler said quietly, surprising me. She was leaning forward on the couch, looking at me closely. She shook her head slowly. "Last spring, you helped me when you didn't have to. At all. You risked a *lot* to help me then. And I don't believe that the Madison who would do something like that would walk away from us now."

I swallowed hard, blinking back the tears that were threatening to spill. There was a piece of me that still couldn't believe this was happening—and that I was the one who was bringing it about. I forced myself to stand on legs that were shaking, and shouldered my bag. "I'm sorry," I whispered. I took a breath to try and compose myself. "I just need you guys to trust me that I have to do this, okay? And just . . . don't try and contact me. I can't . . ." My voice broke, and I looked away, forcing myself to focus on the Stubbs sailor and his pipe, until I got myself under control enough to finish. "I want you all to know," I said very fast, looking around at them, "that you've been the best friends I could have ever imagined. And I didn't realize, really, how lucky I was until now. And I'll never forget you. But . . ." My voice trembled, and I felt the first hot tear hit my cheek. "But I have to go," I choked out. Through my tears, which made everything fuzzy, I looked at my friends looking back at me—stricken, hurt, confused. Then I rushed toward the door, yanking it open and setting the bell jangling.

I stepped outside into the pouring rain, only remembering as I did so that I'd left my umbrella by my chair in the coffee shop. I hunched my shoulders against the rain and turned toward my car when I heard the Stubbs bell jangle again. Ruth rushed out and stood facing me, rain running down her face, quickly getting drenched.

"Maddie," she said.

I just shook my head quickly and took a step back, away from her. "I'm sorry," I said. "I can't—"

"I'll be here," she said, interrupting me for the first time in nine years. Her voice was clear and steady, and she was emphasizing her words. "If you need me. Okay?" She looked at me searchingly, like she was trying to figure out why I'd suddenly turned everything upside down. "I'll talk to you later."

The phrase hung between us until I shook my head. "No," I said finally, making myself say it. "You won't."

I turned away from the hurt that was spreading over Ruth's face and ran across the parking lot to my car, not even trying to stop myself from crying now, tears just flowing freely, and mixing with the rain that was running down my face.

CHAPTER 14

Song: Breakable/Ingrid Michaelson
Quote: "Doing what's right is no guarantee against
misfortune."—William McFee

My phone had started ringing, and then beeping with
texts, and chiming with Constellation messages as soon
as I reached my car. I had no doubt that it was my friends,
calling to try and find out what had happened—if this
was all some elaborate joke, or if I had hit my head on
something hard. Once inside my dry car, I took my phone
out of my bag, preparing to check my Constellation messages, as was my ingrained habit. But at the last moment
I stopped myself. The phone in my hand started to ring
again, and I saw the call was from Ruth—though I had a
feeling Lisa and Schuyler were currently clustered
around her, and would be waiting to talk to me
as well.

I looked down at the picture that came up when Ruth
called, one of the two of us that Lisa had taken at my sev-
enteenth birthday party last month. Ruth was looking

at the camera, smiling, but there was something in her expression that indicated that she was about five seconds away from cracking up. I was next to her, already laughing hysterically, pointing at something off-camera. I wished I could remember what it was we'd thought was so funny. Especially since right now, I had a feeling that I might never laugh, ever again.

I wiped my eyes, trying to pull myself together a bit. The phone was still ringing, and before I lost my nerve, I pressed the button to ignore the call. Then I turned my phone off, watching the screen until it powered down and then faded to black. I started Judy and drove home in silence, even turning my iCar off, so the only sound in the car was that of my ragged breathing and the windshield wipers turned up to their highest speed, *whap*ping back and forth.

I reached home and stepped inside the quiet, dark house, remembering that my father was working at the library. I stood in the doorway, dripping, and felt myself missing my mother for the first time since she'd left. If she hadn't been in England, she would have been home now, and the lights would have been on, the stock report playing on her financial channel while she worked in the kitchen. She would have lectured me about forgetting an umbrella and told me to take a hot bath. But instead, there was only dark and quiet and the sound of the kitchen clock ticking. For just a moment, it was all just so lonely that I almost cried again. But I still—unfortunately—had a lot more to do today. I kicked off my wet shoes, took the stairs to my room two at a time, and sat down at my desk with my laptop. Then I logged on to Friendverse and started typing.

Friendverse Message
 From: Madison MacDonald
To: Ginger Davis, Sarah Donner, Dave Gold, Brian McMahon, Kittson Pearson, Mark Rothmann, Glen Turtell, Tricia Evans
Date: 6/23, 6:15 P.M.

Hi guys,
I'm so sorry to have to do this, and without any explanation. But as of today, I can't be friends with you any longer. I wish I could tell you why, but you'll just have to trust me that it has to be like this. I promise it's nothing personal. You guys are the best, and I'm going to miss you all more than I can say. Don't ask why or message me on Constellation about this. Please just trust that I'm doing what I have to.

Mad

I pressed SEND and watched the message disappear, knowing that it was heading to my friends' inboxes, to no doubt confuse and hurt them. I had included Tricia on the list even though Isabel hadn't included her on the dossier. But I knew that it would hurt my friends even more if I stopped being friends with all of them but kept in contact with Tricia. It seemed better, perversely, to just cut myself off from everyone.

I logged out of Friendverse immediately, and out of Constellation as well. I had no doubt that perplexed and worried messages and posts were piling up, but I didn't feel up to reading any of them at the moment. Right now, I was feeling utterly overwhelmed by what I still had to do.

I had to break up with Nate.

The thought was so terrible that I actually had to close my eyes, as though that would make it go away. But it wasn't going away. It was just sitting there, a cold, hard fact, refusing to be ignored.

Was I really going to be able to dump Nate without an explanation? Was I going to be able to leave him as confused and hurt as all my friends? I could feel myself on the verge of tears once again as I thought about what I was going to have to do to my boyfriend—and soon.

Feeling like I could go to sleep for about twelve years, I pushed myself away from my desk, climbed up on my bed, and curled into a ball. Next to me, on my bedside table, I could see the carved tortoise, standing atop a stack of Nate's unread spy books. I turned to face the other wall; they were too painful to see right now.

But a second later, I sat up straight, heart pounding. I looked at both the books and the tortoise. I had just realized that there might be something I could do after all.

****

Around eight, my father came home bearing Chinese takeout, and he seemed too preoccupied by the steroid scandal (which had broken that morning) to notice that I was not exactly my normal self. But he did comment that he hadn't seen me go this long without my phone since our trip to the Galápagos.

I had left my phone turned off, and hadn't logged back on to Constellation to see what the damage was. As a result, I was feeling incredibly disconnected from what was going on. Once I'd finished this whole terrible thing, and had had the conversation with Nate, I'd log back on and see just how bad things were. But until then, I was determined to remain in a state of Constellation blackout.

My father headed to bed early, and I realized I had no idea what to do with my time. Since I couldn't go on to Constellation, iChat, talk, or text with any of my friends, I was a little bit stuck. While I racked my brain for what I could do, it hit me for the first time just how lonely my life was probably going to be now. Perhaps this was the moment to finally learn to knit.

I ended up downstairs in the family room, watching *Point Break*, from Travis's stack of DVDs. Since it was about surfing bank robbers, and featured Keanu Reeves as an undercover FBI agent, it wouldn't have been my first choice of an evening's entertainment. But all of my first choices seemed to remind me of Nate or my friends, and this one had no associations with either. Things seemed grim when Patrick Swayze realized that Keanu had pretended to be his friend to spy on him but at the end, Swayze surfed into the sunset, and the credits rolled.

I was considering trying to go to sleep when the house phone next to me rang. I saw that the caller ID read ELLIS, and I snatched it off the cradle. "Hello?" I asked, speaking more softly than usual, even though I had no doubt my father was fast asleep and dead to the world.

"Hi," I heard an achingly familiar, gravelly voice say on the other line. "This is Nate Ellis calling. Apologies for the late hour, but I was trying to reach my girlfriend."

I felt myself smile involuntarily, but the smile disappeared only a moment later when I realized that there was a ticking clock on that title, and I was about to say goodbye to it forever. "You've got her," I said.

"Sorry to call so late," he said, and I could hear him muffling a yawn. "But I just got back. I tried calling your cell, but it was going right to voice mail. And my phone's charging, since I didn't bring a charger with me and kept it on for two days. I'm actually not sure it's ever going to turn on again. So to make a long story short—"

"Too late," we chimed in together, my heart giving a sad little thump as we did.

"Right," Nate said, and I could hear a laugh in his voice. "Seriously. Anyway, I couldn't text you or anything, and I just wanted to say hi."

"No, this is great," I said. "My phone's off, so . . ." I paused, turning over what he'd just told me, and hoping that maybe a tiny piece of luck was on my side. "So have you checked Constellation or anything tonight?" I asked, trying as hard as I could to keep my voice light and untroubled. Though it had gotten harder, lately, to remember exactly what light and untroubled felt like.

"Not yet," Nate said, and I could hear him speaking around another yawn. "I wanted to call you first."

My heart gave another slow, sad thump at that. At how sweet my boyfriend was, and how he so didn't deserve what I was about to do to him. "Oh, great," I said. It actually was, for the purposes of what still hadn't happened. If Nate logged on to Constellation and saw the messages that were no doubt piling up among our mutual friends, he'd know something was wrong. And if Nate was concerned, and asking me questions, and wanting to help, I knew there was no way I'd have the strength to lie to him and keep up the ruse. And I had to. I had to do it for him, even if he didn't realize it now—even if he never realized why. "So I know you're tired," I said, crossing my fingers that he wasn't too exhausted, "but I was wondering if maybe you wanted to meet up tonight? Just for a little bit?"

"Now?" Nate sounded surprised, but I could hear that there was a bit of a smile in his voice as well. "Really? Can you get permission to go?"

This was a bit of a sticking point, but I'd passed the point of worrying about getting in trouble with my father. And if he ended up grounding me, what was he going to be keeping me from? He'd probably just help me put my knitting plan into effect a little earlier. "Absolutely," I said as confidently as possible.

"Well . . . great," Nate said, and I could hear that he was really smiling now. "How about I pick you up, and—"

"No!" I said, more emphatically than I meant to.

"I'll meet you," I said quickly, trying to cover. "It's faster that way."

"Okay," Nate said. He sounded a little skeptical, but clearly wasn't going to argue. "Should we meet at the diner?"

"How about the Bluff?" I asked. It had stopped raining a few hours ago, and I was just hoping that the ground wouldn't be too muddy to make this a real option. It was where, if this had to happen, I wanted it to happen — in the place that had always been ours alone, and where we could be utterly private, our location unknown to anyone else.

"Sure," Nate said after a moment, maybe doing the same muddy ground calculation that I had. "But are you sure I can't come get you, my Mad?"

I had to press my lips together hard after hearing that, to pull myself together before I felt that I could speak again without Nate hearing that something was wrong. "No, I'll meet you," I said quickly. "I wouldn't want you to go out of your way."

"I don't mind, for you," he said. I closed my eyes, thinking that if there had ever been a moment for Nate to have been uncharacteristically grumpy and mean, this would have been it. The more nice things he said, the harder this was going to get.

"So, the Bluff," I forced out. "I'll leave now. See you there in twenty?"

"Totes," Nate said, and I heard one of his low, slow laughs on the other end. "Can't wait. SYS!"

"SYS," I repeated, forcing my voice to stay upbeat,

and then pressed the button to hang up the phone. I hadn't realized how hard it was going to be to lie to Nate—and we hadn't even been face-to-face. But I was just going to have to get through this. I wasn't quite sure how yet, but maybe I'd figure it out on the drive to the Bluff.

I hurried into the kitchen and scrawled a note for my father, something about needing to pick up some emergency "feminine products." I knew that if he happened to wake up and find me—and the car—gone after midnight, this would be the one excuse he would accept without question, and not want to talk about in the morning.

Then I headed up to my room and took the carved tortoise from my bedside table. I turned it over in my hands once before dropping it into my purse. I picked up the note I'd worked on that afternoon. I read it over once more, then folded it and dropped it into my bag as well.

I turned to go, resting my hand on my bedroom light switch. When I came back to my room, I knew it would look exactly the same, even though my life would be utterly destroyed. I shut off the light and walked downstairs slowly, heading toward Nate, and what still had to be done.

CHAPTER 15

Song: It Ends Tonight/All-American Rejects
Quote: "Those things which are precious are saved only by sacrifice."—David Kenyon Webster

When I got to the Bluff, Nate's truck was already parked, right at the edge of the driveway where the gravel ended and turned into grass. I pulled behind him, put Judy into park, and killed the engine. I unbuckled my seat belt, but didn't get out of the car right away. I took just a moment, trying to prepare myself.

The driver's side door of the truck opened, Nate emerged, and I knew that my moment was over, and this next part—this terrible task—had now begun. Nate was smiling at me, and I smiled back, automatically, the way I had always done, like his smile was somehow tied to mine. As I saw him walking toward my car, I opened my door and got out. I realized, seeing him, how much I had missed him after only two days. I didn't let myself think about how much I was going to miss him when two days turned into forever. I slammed my door and turned to face my boyfriend.

"Hi," he said, closing the remaining distance between us. He slipped his arms around my waist and there was a part of me that knew I should push him away, give him the cold shoulder, begin this process. But I didn't quite have the fortitude to do it, and instead, I wrapped my arms around his neck, pulling him close to me. It seemed only fair that I get to kiss him one last time. And though our kiss was as knee-weakening as ever, it was spoiled for me by the knowledge that it was our last one.

I broke away from the kiss and wrapped my arms around Nate in a tight hug. "Hey," he murmured, stroking the back of my head, which I had buried in his shoulder. "You okay?"

I nodded against the soft cotton of his T-shirt. "Fine," I murmured, glad that he couldn't see my expression. "I just missed you, that's all."

"I missed you, too," Nate said, leaning back a little. I looked at his face, which was pretty much my favorite thing in the world. I rested my hands on either side of it, and felt that his cheeks were warm.

"Did you get sunburned?" I asked, tracing my thumb gently over the edge of his jaw.

"Amazingly, yes," Nate said, with one of his half smiles. "Apparently, Schuyler was right, and you *can* get sunburned even when it's raining."

"Never doubt Schuyler when it comes to matters of SPF," I said, feeling myself smile. I was on the verge of launching into the story of Schuyler's epic sunburn the summer before, but stopped myself. The longer I stood there, just talking to Nate like nothing was wrong, the harder this was going to be. I probably shouldn't have kissed him in the first place, but that ship had sailed. "So, um," I said, taking a deep breath and a tiny step away from him. I looked down at my flip-flops on the gravel, trying to get up my courage. "The reason that I wanted to see you tonight was . . . there's something that I wanted to say to you."

I looked back up at Nate and saw that, improbably, a huge smile was slowly spreading over his face. "Yes?" he asked. He sounded nervous, but also really happy and hopeful.

The reason why came crashing down on me like a ton of bricks. Nate was excited by what he thought I was going to tell him. The last conversation we'd had involved him telling me he loved me, but wanting me to wait and say it back to him in my own way. Nate thought I was about to tell him that I loved him, too.

This made what was about to happen so, *so* much worse that my breath caught in my throat and I had to fight for a moment to get it back. The timing was bad enough, but what I was fighting hard against, since it made me want to yell and break things, was the *unfairness* of it all. I loved him, too. And I wanted to be able to tell him, and for us to share in what in normal circumstances would surely have been a really wonderful, special moment. But instead, I wasn't going to say it back to him. Instead, I had to break his heart and mine, in one fell swoop.

"The thing is," I started, tearing my eyes away from his face. I knew I wasn't going to be able to do this to him if I had to look at his open, hopeful expression. My voice turned trembly, and I swallowed hard and forced myself to continue. "I wanted to say . . ."

"It's okay," Nate murmured. He tilted my chin up and smiled at me, looking right into my eyes. "You can say it."

He tucked that one lock of hair behind my ear, and rested his hand on my cheek. I leaned my head against his hand for just a moment and closed my eyes, knowing it would be the last time that he would touch me. Then I opened my eyes and moved my head away, breaking our contact and looking back at him. "I'm sorry," I forced out. My voice was shaking, and felt totally out of my control, like even my vocal cords knew this was a bad idea and were trying to prevent me from saying these words.

Nate's smile faltered a little. "About what?" he asked.

"That I have to do this," I said. I took another step back, farther away from him, even though the distance between us felt like it was physically hurting me.

"Do what?" Nate asked, and his smile was almost totally gone now. A crease had appeared between his eyebrows. He reached out to me, but I took another step back. I had a feeling that if he touched me, I wouldn't have the strength to push him away again.

"This," I choked out in what was little more than a whisper. I could feel tears in the back of my eyes, but I clenched my fists, fighting against it, trying not to let myself cry until I'd gotten through this. Which pretty much made it the world's worst reward.

"Mad," Nate started, taking a step toward me, looking worried.

"Don't," I said sharply, taking another step away. I was practically backed up next to Judy at this point. I saw confusion take over Nate's face, as well as a flash of hurt in his eyes that I'd never seen before. Hurt that I had caused. And I wasn't done yet. "I'm sorry," I said again. "I just . . . need to say this." Nate nodded, still looking baffled. He let the hand that had been reaching out to me drop, and the space between us seemed to expand into a chasm. "I think," I started. I took a breath and then let it out. I knew the words that I had to say. But it didn't seem conceivable to me that I could say them, since they were so contrary to everything that was true.

Then, in a series of images, I saw Nate getting called before his headmaster, Nate's acceptance from Yale rejected, Nate's dazzling future dimmed forever. And it gave me the resolve I needed to continue.

"I think we should break up," I forced out. As soon as I said these words, the tears started to fall, one sliding out from each eye. But my vision was clear enough to see Nate's reaction. It was as though I'd just struck him with a physical blow. He recoiled and took a step backward. Hurt and confusion were plain to see on his face, which, only moments ago, had been so filled with happiness. I swallowed hard, though my throat felt tight, and it was getting hard to breathe normally.

Nate looked away from me and out to the Bluff, to

the open, empty space that we'd filled with laughter and feverish kisses and long discussions about what might have been. He turned back to me, and I could see just how shocked he was. "I don't understand," he said, his voice lower than usual, and a little choked.

"I'm sorry," I said again, hating these words and how useless they were in the face of everything that was happening. "I wish I could . . . tell you why. But I can't." More tears were falling now. I wasn't sobbing—I had a feeling that would come later tonight—but I also knew I wasn't going to be able to stop myself from crying. I brushed some tears away, and my hand came back black. Clearly, this new eyeliner thing was not compatible with my current emotional state.

"Is it because of . . . what I said?" Nate asked, his eyes searching mine.

"No!" I said. I hadn't meant to be so emphatic, but it was as though the word was yanked out of me. "No, not at all. I just . . ." I wiped my eyes, though that was a futile gesture, and took a breath to continue, but stopped when I realized there was nothing, really, that I could tell him. No reason that would make all of this make sense. And I hated that I not only had to hurt him deeply but had to leave him in a state of confusion, with no answers. "It just has to be this way," I whispered, looking back at him.

Nate was staring down at his shoes, his shoulders hunched forward slightly, as though to protect himself from any other bombshells I might decide to hurl at him. I could see that his brow was furrowed, and his chin was trembling ever so slightly. Finally, he nodded, and then looked back at me, and what I saw in his expression made me want to start crying harder. There was a distance in his eyes now that I'd never seen before. One that hadn't been there just moments ago, and the sight of it brought home how real all of this was. There was truly no going back now.

"And there's nothing I can say," Nate said. "Right?" He looked at me closely, as though trying to see if he could get any kind of explanation for why I had chosen to make both of us so unhappy.

I shook my head slowly, and the chasm between us seemed to open even further, until it felt like we were standing on opposite sides of the Grand Canyon. Like the space between us was so vast, it was absurd to think that we'd ever touched each other.

"If this is what you want," Nate said, his voice sounding a little jagged.

"It is," I made myself lie. I wiped my eyes again, even though my tears were showing no signs of abating. Possibly ever. I was seized by a sudden, strong desire to get out of there, and fast, which was so strange to me, since before that moment, I never wanted to leave where Nate was. It had always been an internal battle to force myself away from him. But I couldn't be here any longer—next to him, not kissing or touching or laughing, but instead, causing him great unhappiness. Being in his presence, in these new, awful circumstances, felt like it was physically hurting me.

"This is for you," I said, my voice shakier than ever.

I reached into my bag, pulled out the tortoise, and held it out to him.

Nate's eyes darkened as he looked at it and he shook his head. "I don't want it," he said, his voice more choked than ever.

"Please," I said, still holding it out to him. "I want you to have the set." Implied in this was something that made me feel like someone was squeezing my heart—that Nate would, at some point, give the other one to *someone else*. But I needed Nate to know that I was serious about this, and to get him not to ask me why, or try and get back together with me. I had to let him know that this was a real breakup, and this was the only way that I could think to do it.

Nate stared down at it for a long moment, then reached out and took it, grabbing the tortoise's head, our hands not touching. He turned it over in his hands, and when he looked back at me, his eyes were more distant than ever.

"And this," I said hurriedly, reaching into my bag and holding out the note to him. "Just . . . read it later, okay?" I asked. "When you're at home, with all your things." Nate reached out and took the end of the piece of paper, but I held on, the letter taut between us.

Nate glanced up at me, surprised, and I looked right into his eyes and spoke with urgency, knowing that this was my only chance to get this message across. "I just want you to remember that I gave this to you here," I said. "At the *Bluff*." I looked at him closely. "I wish I could give you the key," I said as I let go of the piece of paper, knowing he would probably think I meant our song, but hoping he would know that I meant something else.

Nate stared at me, and I had no idea if the hints I had given him had gotten through. I looked back at him and realized that there was nothing more to say.

"Bye," I whispered, the words scratching at my throat. I turned away from the sight of him by his truck—confused, unhappy, hurt, and holding a wooden tortoise.

I yanked open my door and started the engine. I buckled my seat belt and looked over at Nate one last time. His eyes met mine, and after a second, I forced myself to look away. I put Judy in reverse and backed out of the driveway. Then I put the car in drive, leaving my boyfriend—my love—behind, not once letting myself look back.

CHAPTER 16

I had made it home and gotten back inside seemingly undetected. If the quiet stillness of the house was anything to go by, my father was still sleeping. I headed into the kitchen and retrieved the note I'd left for him, crumpling it up and throwing it away. Then I headed up to my room, taking the steps slowly, leaning on the railing.

I had stopped crying on the way home, mostly because I had concentrated hard on the mechanics of driving, putting on the poppiest, happiest songs I had on my iCar, cranking the volume, and letting the lyrics wash over me, trying to lose myself in their upbeat choruses about finding summer love. A curious sense of numbness had settled over me, but I had a feeling that it was just temporary. It was like I could see a whirl-pool swirling just under the surface of a placid lake. Everything might seem okay on the outside, but I knew that, before long, I would be pulled down into it. It was just a matter of time.

I didn't even turn on the lights when I reached my bedroom. I kicked off my flip-flops, dropped my bag in the doorway, and walked across my dark room. I headed directly to my desk, where my laptop was. I opened it and it whirred to life, making me wince a little as the brightness of the screen lit up the dark room. I logged on to Constellation and immediately clicked past the home page, but not fast enough to avoid seeing that I had forty-eight new messages. I went to the settings page and pulled up my profile.

I looked at it for a long moment, especially at the very last line—my relationship status. I couldn't stop myself from remembering when I had changed it from single. Nate and I had done it together, back in April, sitting in the back of his truck with our laptops. He'd logged into his Friendverse and changed his status, which sent a notification to me, asking me to confirm that I was, in fact, taken by Nate Ellis.

"Taken *with*, is more like it," I'd said to him then, and he had smiled suddenly, happily, like I'd surprised him, in the best way. And I'd confirmed that I *was* dating Nate, and had watched the screen as my status changed from single to taken, and I'd immediately gotten a bar-rage of congratulatory messages from my friends.

I looked at the line on my profile that I hadn't

thought I'd ever change. I gave myself just a moment longer to read the proof of who I'd once been—Nate Ellis's girlfriend—and now would no longer be. Then, trying to do it fast, like ripping off a Band-Aid, I brought up the CHANGE SETTINGS menu. I made my changes, pressed SAVE, and waited for the small moment it would take for everything to become official. You didn't need to get a confirmation e-mail when you ended something with someone, so Nate, at least, wouldn't have to confirm that we were no longer in a relationship. There would just be a notification waiting for him the next time he logged in, just in case it might have slipped his mind or something.

The changes had gone through, and I stared at my profile, trying to process that this was who I was now.

**M²/
Madison MacDonald**

Song: No song
Quote: No quote

Age: 17
Permanent Location: Putnam, Connecticut
Current Location: 76 Winthrop Road, Putnam, Connecticut

Followers: 54
Following: 0

About Me: Nothing to say.

Single

I stared at the screen until my eyes burned. I could feel myself on the verge of tears, real tears, the kind Schuyler had cried over Connor that had nearly dehydrated her. Somehow, seeing my profile had been the remaining proof I needed that this was real. I was no longer friends with my friends. Nate and I were over. And there was no undoing this.

My computer dinged, telling me I'd just received a new private Constellation message.

 From: Isabel
Location: Undisclosed
To: M²

Well done. Hope it wasn't TOO painful. Don't worry—I'll keep up my end of this. But know that I'll be watching. Have a great summer!

I was relieved that I'd prevented disaster but furious that she'd been able to do this to me at all. Not wanting to see her message—or face—any longer, I logged out of Constellation and shut my computer down. But before it turned off, a message popped up, asking me if I wanted to first save my changes to the last document I'd written. The note I'd drafted to Nate filled the screen, and I found myself reading through it once more.

Nate,

Does one not tell?
When a new thought

Takes hold it sticks.
Better let a change kommence, meaning an initial loss
ends doubts.

It's
Letting one version end
You once understood
Tragically, once's over.

Madison

I swallowed hard against the lump in my throat.
I had no idea if Nate would understand what I'd meant.
Reading it over now, it seemed impossible that he would.
Everything suddenly seemed totally hopeless.

I could tell that I was about to cry, but I also
knew—which made me want to cry even more—that it
wouldn't accomplish anything. I had lost my friends. I
had lost Nate. It was as though the solid ground I had
always taken for granted had suddenly been jerked out
from under me, and I had no idea now how to stand or
walk. I closed my eyes and felt one tear, then another,
trickle down my cheek. I didn't even bother to wipe them
away, but just let them fall.

I stood up on legs that felt shaky and walked slowly
over to my bed. The thought of getting changed into my
pajamas, or even brushing my teeth, was much too challenging to even contemplate. I climbed up on my bed and
pulled the covers over me, still fully dressed.

I turned on my side and closed my eyes. There was

a piece of me that was still trying to fight against this, cursing Isabel and the unfairness of it all. But that piece grew fainter and fainter, until I could barely hear it any longer. There was no point in fighting against what had happened—it had happened, it was over, and there was nothing to do but accept it. The tears flowed faster as the new reality of my life stretched out before me. The calm surface broke, and there was the whirlpool, waiting for me, ready to pull me down into its depths.

I gave up the fight and let myself be pulled under.

TUESDAY

WEDNESDAY

THURSDAY

FRIDAY

CHAPTER 17

Song: Sink To The Bottom/Fountains of Wayne
Quote: "In the real dark night of the soul it is always
three o'clock in the morning, day after day."—F. Scott
Fitzgerald

 La Lisa → M² Madison. WHAT IS GOING ON? Call me
back. I'm worried.
Location: Stubbs Coffee Shop. Putnam, CT.

 Schuyler → M² Seriously, Mad, none of us understand
what's happening. Is there a cult involved? Do you need to
be deprogrammed or something?
Location: Stubbs Coffee Shop. Putnam, CT.

 Rue → M² I hope everything is okay. I'm here if/when you
need to talk about this, Maddie.
Location: Stubbs Coffee Shop. Putnam, CT.

I was aware, on some level, that time was passing.

My father had knocked on my door on Tuesday morning, surprised to find me still in bed, and I'd murmured
something about having the flu. My mother, if she'd been

at home, would have insisted on taking my temperature to check my story. She had been disinclined to believe me when it came to matters of illness ever since she'd figured out, sophomore year, that the days I'd had the flu had matched up precisely with the days I had Chemistry tests. But my father, always more trusting, just took me at my word. He had been headed to the library, and offered to stay home to take care of me. But I'd muttered something about just sleeping anyway, and he'd finally left, telling me he'd call in and check on me throughout the day.

I was glad that he was going. All I wanted was to go back to sleep. I changed into actual pajamas, got back into bed, and pulled the covers over my head once again.

 Queen Kittson → M² What do you MEAN you can't be friends with me anymore? What is THAT? I am NOT happy about this, Madison. Is this one of your "jokes"? If so, it is not funny. AT ALL. I want an explanation. And an apology. CALL ME.
Location: Amagansett Beach. East Hampton, NY.

 King Glen → M² WTF, Mad? You know I've always had your back. What's with the e-mail brush-off? Not cool.
Location: Putnam Motors. Putnam, CT.

 Gingerly → M² Mad, I don't understand what's happening. Is everything all right? Worried about you. ☹
Location: Putnam Historical Museum. Putnam, CT.

Days went by. My father knocked on the door occasionally, and though I could hear him and murmured responses back, it was as though he was miles away and I could only dimly make out what he was saying. Every time he was standing in my doorway, talking to me, it seemed to be a massive imposition on what I really wanted to be doing, which was going back to sleep. Underneath my covers, it was quiet and still and there was no outside world that I would have to think about for too long, if I could just drift off again.

When my father had asked me about work on Wednesday morning, I had remembered, as though from a different lifetime, that there had been a smoothie shop I had once worked at. I sent texts to Kavya, Daryl, and John, and elusive manager Gary, telling them that I was sick and should stay home until I felt better, for public health reasons. Then I put my phone down—but not before I saw that I had twenty-three new voice mails. I scrolled through the numbers, but didn't listen to any of them. None of them had been from Nate. And I really didn't think I could bring myself to listen to what anyone else had to say.

Dave Gold ➔ M² Mad, what's going on? Everyone's worried. Tell me and I'll make you all the pineapple pizza you want. Promise.
Location: Putnam Pizza. Putnam, CT.

Lord Rothschild ➔ M² Mad, what did I do? Are you still mad about the Selwidge thing? It was totally my bad! Just tell me what's happening, okay?
Location: Second Concession Stand, Putnam Beach. Putnam, CT.

Brian M ➔ M² Okay, what? I don't understand what's happening here. And what did you do to Ellis? He looks like someone stole his dog.
Location: Putnam High School Science Wing. Putnam, CT.

It got dark outside, and it got light again. I stayed where I was, curled in a ball underneath the covers. Thankfully, I didn't dream. Or if I did—because Ruth had told me once that we were always dreaming, whether we recalled the dream or not—I didn't remember. Which was what I wanted. I wanted to forget—about the past, both recent and distant, and about the future I was going to have to face at some point, and about the fact that I knew I wasn't going to be able to stay in bed forever.

 johnmakesthesmoothies ➜ **M²** Hiya Mad. So I'm sorry you're sick and whatnot, but are you coming back into work ever? Because Kavya can't touch anything or she gets boils, or something, and Daryl thinks the blueberries are looking at him again. And we can't figure out how to open the register, so we've just been keeping the money in an envelope under the counter.
Location: On A Blender Smoothie Shop. Putnam, CT.

 johnmakesthesmoothies ➜ **M²** Okay, um, maybe I shouldn't have said that on the internets.
Location: On A Blender Smoothie Shop. Putnam, CT.

 johnmakesthesmoothies ➜ **M²** I was JUST KIDDING before. Ha ha ha!!
Location: On A Blender Smoothie Shop. Putnam, CT.

 darylparksthecars ➜ **M²** hey.
Location: On A Blender Smoothie Shop. Putnam, CT.

 darylparksthecars ➜ **M²** yeah, what john said. when r u going 2 be around again?
Location: On A Blender Smoothie Shop. Putnam, CT.

darylparksthecars ➔ M² oh, and this is daryl.
Location: On A Blender Smoothie Shop. Putnam, CT.

From the quiet safety underneath my covers, I could hear life going on around me, a world I felt myself drifting further and further away from. I could hear cars driving by on the street outside. I could hear my father walking around downstairs, opening and closing the fridge, watching baseball. He'd knock on my door, and bring me peanut-butter-and-banana sandwiches that I left untouched. I could tell that he was getting worried, and I was sorry about that, but there wasn't anything I could do.

My world had shrunk down to the size of my bed, and I liked it that way. It was quiet, and peaceful, and nobody was out to hurt me, or was forcing me to hurt other people. At some point, before I drifted back to sleep once more, it occurred to me that if I'd just stayed there to begin with, I could have avoided a lot of this mess.

Sarah♥Zach ➔ M² Mads, what is happening? Is this some kind of performance art? Very confused up here in the Catskills . . .
Location: Reach4theStars! Theatre Camp. Catskill, NY.

be tricia ➔ M² Hi Madly! Is everything all right? We're all worried about you! Hope you're okay!!!
Location: Stanwich Yacht Club. Stanwich, CT.

Jimmy+Liz ➔ M² Mad! What is going on? Is it true you broke up with Nate? Why? We miss you & are worried. (both of us)
Location: Putnam Beach. Putnam, CT.

On Friday, my father stood in my doorway with the phone, talking to my mother in London. "I don't know," I could hear him saying in a low, worried voice. "She hasn't gotten out of bed in days. She says she has the flu. . . ." There was a pause, and I could hear my mother, faintly, talking on the other end, an ocean away.

I heard my father's footsteps coming closer, and sighed and pulled the covers away from my face. I winced at the brightness of the room, and the light that was hurting my eyes.

"Mad?" he asked from the foot of my bed.

"What," I muttered, turning my face into my pillow once more.

"It's your mom, kid," my father said, holding out the phone to me. "She wants to speak to you."

Even though it felt like my mind was working more slowly than usual, I knew that refusing to talk to her—while we were on an international phone call—was just going to make things worse. Feeling like I was moving through molasses, I sat up slowly, getting a head rush as I did so. When I was sitting up all the way—and exhausted by this—I reached out for the phone. My father handed it to me, and I lifted it to my ear with effort, as the phone seemed much heavier than it had a few days ago. "Hi, Mom," I rasped. I cleared my throat, but it felt like my vocal cords had rusted over in the days of not speaking.

"Madison, are you okay?" my mother asked me over a slightly crackling connection. She sounded equal parts concerned and skeptical. "Because your father is worried. I'm worried. If you're actually sick, you are going to the doctor. But if you're just moping, it's time to get out of bed and go back to work. Okay?"

I started to open my mouth and tell my mother why this wasn't exactly *moping*, but decided against it, as the very thought of trying to explain tired me out. I looked at my father, standing at the foot of my bed, and saw how anxious he seemed. I knew that this wasn't an idle threat. If I told her that I just wanted to go back to bed, I'd find myself en route to the doctor, who would no doubt tell me that there was nothing wrong with me. "Fine," I muttered into the phone. "I'll get up."

"Good," my mother said. She took a breath, and when she spoke again, I could hear that the concern hadn't entirely left her voice. "But what is this about, honey?" she asked. "Did something happen with your friends? With Nate?"

Just hearing Nate's name felt like a slap in the face. I cleared my throat again, trying to keep my voice neutral. "No," I lied through my teeth, hoping that the connection was bad enough that my mother wouldn't be able to hear this. "Everything's fine. I've just been . . . tired."

"All right," she said, but I could hear some disbelief lingering in her voice. "But I'm going to be calling and checking in. And I don't want to hear that you've gone back into hibernation, okay?"

"Sure," I said, trying my best to sound convincing. "Sounds great."

"Good," she said. "Now let me talk to your father again, okay, sweetie? Love you."

"Love you, too, Mom," I said. "Bye." I handed the phone back to my father, who smiled at me and headed out of my room, talking to my mother, closing the door behind him.

Sitting up in bed, I looked around my room, still squinting at the sunlight streaming in through my windows. I wanted nothing more than to lie back down again, pull the covers back over my head, and return to my quiet cocoon. But apparently, that was no longer an option. I tried to remember what day it was as I glanced over at my bedside clock. If it was Friday—which I wasn't entirely sure of—it was still early enough that I could make it to work on time.

I pushed myself out of bed on legs that felt weak and wobbly—which made sense, considering I hadn't been eating much over the last few days. I walked into my bathroom, hand resting on the wall for support, and cringed when I saw my reflection. I tried to remember the last time I'd washed my hair, but gave up when that became too challenging.

My reflection showed me just why my father had been worried. I looked exhausted. I was pale, my hair was tangled, and my eyes were puffy. But most of all, I looked . . . defeated. Like there was no life in me anymore. I didn't like it, and stared at myself for only a moment longer before turning on the water in the shower, preparing to join the world once again.

CHAPTER 18

Song: Wake Up/Arcade Fire
Quote: "The course of true anything never does run smooth." — Samuel Butler

"What happened to you?" Kavya asked as I pulled open the door to the smoothie shop. Sitting in her usual spot on the counter, she looked up from her phone and frowned at me. "You look like crap."

I glanced in the reflection of the window and felt a momentary wave of relief that she hadn't seen me earlier that morning, when I'd looked about fifty times worse. I had thought I'd managed to pull myself together a bit, but even so, I could see that she had a point. Mostly, I just looked — and felt — worn out. It might be enough to push me into finally trying a wheatgrass shot. "Hey," I murmured, with a voice that still felt scratchy. The molasses feeling had lingered. The lights of the shop were brighter than I remembered, and everything seemed louder after the quiet solitude of my bed.

I walked slowly over to the counter and ducked under it, walking past Kavya and into the back hallway to hang up my purse. Out of habit, I took my phone out of my purse, ready to put it in my jean shorts to have with me for the day. But after a second, reality hit me and I put the phone back in my purse. There was no point in having it with me during the workday—it wasn't like I had anyone that I could talk to. "Where are Daryl and John?" I asked, zipping my purse back up.

"In the freezer," Kavya called, her voice punctuated with the faint sounds of her texting.

I had a pretty good idea of what they were doing in the freezer, but I climbed the two steps up to it anyway and pulled open the heavy silver door. The first thing I noticed when I stepped inside was that it wasn't cold. Which struck me as a problem, since being cold was pretty much its main function. Daryl was sitting on the ground, flipping a coin in the air and catching it on the back of his hand, while John teetered on a ladder, peering at the contents of the top shelf.

"Hi," I said. John turned around quickly at the sound of my voice, and the ladder wobbled dangerously. After it had settled again, Daryl looked up at John, frowning.

"Dude," Daryl said, extremely after the fact, "your ladder's moving."

"Glad you made it back, Mad," John said, turning around and sitting on the rung above him. "Do you know how to open the register?"

"I'll give it a shot," I said. I looked around the freezer

once again for some explanation of why they were both in there, and why it was currently so balmy. "Is the freezer broken?" I finally asked.

"Nah," John said. "We just turned it off while we were in here. The switch is right outside the door. I can't find the mangoes, and it was getting really cold."

I was about to point out that it probably wasn't good for the fruit to keep defrosting and refreezing, but didn't feel like I had the energy to go into it, and just nodded. "Okay," I said. "I'll see you guys out there."

"Glad you're back," John said, standing up and setting the ladder swaying again. "We missed you."

I gave him my best attempt at a smile, but it felt like I hadn't used those muscles in a very long time, and I was no longer sure, exactly, how to go about it. I stepped out of the freezer and closed the door behind me, just in time to hear a loud crash and then, several seconds later, Daryl's voice saying, "Dude. Ladder."

Kavya didn't appear to have moved since I'd left. I pushed myself up to sit on the counter by the register side, feeling exhausted after even that small—and unchallenging—interaction.

"So?" Kavya asked, looking up at me during a break in her texting.

"They're getting mangoes," I said, nodding at the freezer. "In theory."

"Not them," Kavya said dismissively. She closed her phone and raised her eyebrows at me. "I mean, where were you? Were you really sick? I thought you were lying, but after seeing you now, I totally believe it."

"Kind of," I said, not wanting to get into it. I glanced out the door, thinking that now would be a great moment for a potential customer to wander by in search of iced, blended refreshment, but the shop remained empty. I turned back and saw that Kavya was still looking at me, waiting, going so far as to ignore her bleating phone. "It's a long story," I said with a sigh, wondering how to distill this to the Cliff Notes version. "Well—you're on Friendverse, right? So—"

"Ugh, no," Kavya said, shaking her head, her voice heavy with disdain. "Why, are *you*? Friendverse is *so* six months ago."

I stared at her, stunned by this. "Wait, what?" I asked.

Kavya gave me a patronizing smile, clearly happy to impart her California wisdom. "Friendverse is what everyone was on *last* year. But there was a mass exodus this spring. I mean, they add Status Q and Constellation in the space of a couple months? Just pick one thing and stick to it, am I right?"

"So," I said, trying to get my head around this. Like I had when I'd learned that Connor had defected from all the sites, I was still having trouble understanding how this was even possible. "Does that mean you're not on *anything*?"

"Um, *no*," Kavya said slowly, as though I wasn't too bright. "Everyone in L.A.—everyone cool, that is—is on Zyzzx." She sighed. "Have you even heard of it?" she asked.

"Zyzzx," I said, repeating the way she'd said it. I'd started hearing about this site a few months ago, but nothing specific, except that nobody knew how to pronounce it.

"Yeah," she said. "It's pretty much the only place to be. And it's all about actually *connecting* with your friends, not posting stupid quizzes for the world to see. I'll see if I can get you an invitation." She looked at me closely, as though appraising my social status, and frowned slightly. "Maybe."

"Wait, you need an invitation?" I asked.

"Um, yeah," Kavya said, picking up her phone and starting to type on it again. Clearly, she had been separated from it for as long as she was able. "Zyzzx is exclusive. You need an invite from a current member to join it. But I'll see what I can do for you."

"Thanks," I murmured. I wasn't sure what it meant yet, but I couldn't stop thinking about Kavya's dismissal of Friendverse, Status Q, and Constellation. The fact that there might be an alternative was something I'd never even considered before.

"Mangoes!" I glanced up to see John, looking a little worse for wear, hoist the cardboard box triumphantly over his head. Daryl shuffled along behind him, taking his usual spot on the counter by the blenders, and picking up the remote for the store's TV. He flipped channels until he found one of his *telenovelas* and cranked the volume. Kavya rolled her eyes and sighed loudly, and it occurred to me, not for the first time, that four employees were far too many for a very small smoothie shop.

When the bell above the door jangled, signaling a customer, I was thrilled to actually have something to do—until I turned and saw who the customer was.

Kittson Pearson, looking both very tan and very angry, was barreling across the store toward me.

I could feel myself start to panic. I had no idea how to handle this. If Isabel was watching me on Constellation, she would see that Kittson and I were aligned, and I would have no way of letting her know that I wasn't going against her rules. Somehow, I hadn't considered the possibility that one of my friends might come looking for me. And if this was going to happen, I never would have thought that Kittson would have been the one to show up.

"Madison," she fumed, taking her white sunglasses off and perching them on top of her head, like a headband. "I am *not* happy with you right now."

I glanced around at my fellow employees, all of whom were ignoring their phones, boxes of mangoes, and Spanish-language soap operas, respectively, in favor of the drama currently unfolding in front of them. "I know," I said, trying to keep my volume down, even though there was no real point to that, as everyone else was only a few feet from me and could hear every word I was saying. "But I can't talk to you."

Kittson stared at me for a long moment, and then shook her head. "No," she said firmly. "I just came back from the Hamptons," she said. "On a *bus*. You are going to talk to me."

"Can I get you a smoothie?" John asked, nudging me aside to give Kittson a lopsided smile. "Because we . . . you know . . . have them here."

"Yeah," Daryl echoed a moment later.

"I'm not here for a smoothie," Kittson said, rolling her eyes.

"Well, you *are* in a smoothie shop," Kavya said, getting up from the counter. I could see her giving Kittson the fellow-pretty-girl once-over, and I saw Kittson doing it right back to her.

Kittson looked at Kavya for a long moment, and I knew her well enough to tell that she was deciding between a comeback and asking Kavya what eye shadow she was wearing.

"Kittson's a friend from school," I said quickly, trying to prevent a potential showdown. "But she was just . . . um . . . leaving."

Kittson blinked at me, and I saw real hurt cross her face. "Madison," she said, her voice soft and a little surprised. "What is happening? Talk to me. I'm worried." She paused. "And angry," she added. "Let's not forget that."

"I know," I said. I could feel my heart beginning to race. I needed to get Kittson out of there, and fast. I hadn't gone through all of this only to have everything ruined because she refused to take a hint. "But . . ." I looked around helplessly, and my eyes fell on the freezer, the door propped open with the bottom of the ladder. It took a moment for my brain to kick into gear, but once it did, I realized there might be a way to talk to Kittson in private. "Okay," I said, nodding. "Let's talk. Follow me."

****

"What is this?" Kittson asked as she stepped inside and I pulled the metal door to the walk-in shut.

"It's a freezer," I said. I turned to her and pointed at her purse. "Your phone," I said, hearing the urgency in my voice. "Shut it off."

Kittson, maybe hearing something in my tone that told her I wasn't kidding, pulled out her phone and turned it off without comment. "If this is a freezer," she said, dropping her phone back in her bag, "why isn't it cold?"

"Never mind," I said impatiently. Even though I didn't think that there was a way for Isabel to see that Kittson was here with me, I didn't want to take the chance and prolong this interaction. "Look, I'm really sorry," I said quickly. As I said the words, I realized just how much I meant them. I *was* sorry—that all this had happened, and that I was putting my friends through this without giving them any kind of explanation. "I'm sorry," I repeated, less flippantly this time. "I wish I could tell you what's happening. But I can't. And you're just going to have to believe that I'm doing what I have to."

Kittson looked at me steadily. "Madison," she finally said, "this is getting weird. And why can't you tell me what's going on? It's not like anyone can hear us. We're inside a freezer."

"I know," I said. "But . . ." I looked at Kittson, who was standing with her arms crossed, a concerned expression on her face. And it was like an invisible hand squeezed my heart a little. I hadn't realized how hard it was going to be to face one of my friends and not be able to talk to them. And I felt a wave of affection for Kittson, this girl who I hadn't even been friends with at all a few months ago. I cleared my throat and looked down at the concrete floor. "I can't," I murmured. Silence fell between us in the freezer, and though there was a piece of me that really wanted her to stay, there was another piece of me that wanted her to leave, and as quickly as possible. Because having her there and not being able to talk to her was somehow worse than not talking at all. I looked up to see her staring at me, shaking her head.

"I don't know who you are and what you've done with Madison," she said, her voice clipped. "But the Madison MacDonald *I* knew wouldn't be giving up like this. The Madison I knew didn't walk away without a fight." She looked at me for another long moment, disappointment clearly written all over her face.

I felt my shoulders slump a little. Her words stung, but there was nothing I could do. "I need to get back to work," I said quietly.

Kittson looked at me searchingly for another moment. "You're really not going to tell me what this is about?" she asked.

I looked away, so I wouldn't have to see her expression when I shook my head. "I think there's a customer," I said, now just wanting this to be over as quickly as possible.

"How can you tell?" Kittson snapped.

"Because," I said, heading over to the door and starting to pull it open, "on the front door, there . . ." I stopped short, realizing what I was about to say, and how it might—*might*—be able to give Kittson a hint as to what

200

was really going on. "On the door," I said, turning to face her, "there is a bell." I put the most emphasis on the last three words.

Kittson frowned, but a second later, understanding passed over her face. "You mean . . ." she started.

I pulled open the door the rest of the way. "I should get back," I said, holding the door open for Kittson, who still looked lost in thought. "Just so you know," I said quickly, suddenly remembering that her secret was not, in fact, safe with me. "I didn't tell anyone about the thing that happened in the Hamptons. But I'm not the only one who knows." I looked at her steadily, hoping that she understood what I meant.

She wrinkled her nose for a second—as she always did when she was thinking hard—but then nodded. "Okay," she said. "Thanks for the heads-up." She stepped out of the walk-in and I shut the door behind her, then hit the switch on the wall to turn the freezer back on, hoping we hadn't done too much irreparable damage to the fruit. "But whatever this is," Kittson said in an urgent voice, causing me to turn back and look at her, "don't just give up like this. It's not like you, Madison."

She stared at me for a moment longer, like she wasn't quite sure who I was. Then she shook her head, put her sunglasses back on, and headed out of the smoothie shop.

CHAPTER 19

"So," my father said in what I'm sure he thought was an
offhand voice. He had brought home Putnam Pizza for
dinner, and I had been setting the table, getting out the
plates and his hot-pepper flakes, but paused when I
heard this.

"What?" I asked. There was something in his tone
that put me on the offensive. My father had seemed so
relieved when he'd come home and seen me upright
and mobile and not back in bed that I thought I was off
the hook.

The rest of the day at work had been fairly unevent-
ful, except for when Daryl had accidentally locked
himself in the freezer (since turned on). But rather than
trying to get out, or calling for help, he had decided
instead to pass the time until someone found him eating all the frozen raspberries. He'd gone home early with

a stomachache, and we'd had to explain to customers for the rest of the day that the Razzle-Dazzle Raspberry was no longer available. I had gone through the motions of my job, but I hadn't been able to stop my mind from circling around what Kittson had said. And the expression on her face when she had stared at me, like she was disappointed in me.

"When I was picking up the pizza tonight," my father said, taking the seat and opening the lid of the pizza box. He motioned to me to take the first slice, and I saw that there was, in fact, pineapple on half the pie. This was never a sure thing, as Putnam Pizza's owner, Big Tony, looked askance at pineapple on pizza. The other half appeared to contain every meat topping that Putnam Pizza offered. Clearly, my father was taking full advantage of my mother's absence. "Your friend David was working," my father continued, taking a slice of his own and raising his eyebrows at me. "He asked if you were all right and said to tell you hello."

"Oh," I murmured, looking down at my pizza. I took a breath and tried not to let any of the emotions that I was currently feeling show on my face. "That was nice," I said as brightly as possible, then took a bite, to buy myself some time in case he wanted to follow this up with questions I wouldn't be able to answer.

But my father just looked at me, concerned, before hot-peppering his slice and changing the subject to the research trip to Cooperstown that weekend. He thought that in light of my recent illness, he should cancel—or, better yet, I should come with him. Not thrilled with either of those prospects, I drew quickly on any acting ability I possessed to assure him that I was fine. I had a strong suspicion that unless I could get him to believe me, I would find myself spending a lot of time in a museum devoted to baseball. It took some convincing on my part, but my father finally agreed to go—alone—with the stipulation that he'd be calling frequently and checking in on me.

After dinner, my father headed into his study to work on the book, and I ended up in front of the television, primarily so that my father would see I hadn't immediately retreated back to bed, even though the idea was incredibly appealing. I was just flipping channels until I ended up on a marathon of *Man vs. Mountain*, a reality show where contestants are dropped in a hostile mountain environment and have to win competitions and occasionally eat rats to survive.

When the rat eating got to be too much for me, I started flipping channels again, and ended up on *Network*, an old movie that Nate and I had seen at the drive-in a few weeks ago, incongruously paired with *Legally Blonde*. Even though watching it reminded me all too much of Nate, I didn't flip past it. I was just in time to see the movie's famous scene, in which the newscaster has a meltdown on air, screaming into the camera that he was "as mad as hell, and not going to take it anymore." I watched the scene unfold, then paused the movie. The lines were still reverberating in my head, even though I didn't know exactly why.

I flipped back to the reality program, where the two contestants who had been at bitter odds all season were now huddled behind a yurt, forging a secret pact. "Nobody will suspect it," the more devious of the two (he was widely suspected of faking his vegetarian beliefs to get out of the rat eating) was saying. "But in order to survive, we're going to have to work together. An *alliance*. Are you going to eat that gruel?"

I flipped back to the movie and unpaused it. The newscaster, sweat running down his face, repeated his line over and over again, and I found that I was unable to look away from the screen. He was as mad as hell . . . and not going to take it anymore.

I turned off the television and sat in the quiet room, my mind whirling. I thought of Kittson's expression when she had asked me just who I had become. About Schuyler talking about what I'd done for her in the spring. About how my friends had looked when I'd told them goodbye. How satisfied Isabel had been when she'd played her trump card. And how, really, I'd just gone along with it. I had believed Isabel when she'd told me that I had to do what she wanted. I hadn't seen any other way out.

But what if that actually wasn't true? What if there was another way out, one I hadn't even considered? What if I didn't have to just accept that this was the way things had to be?

My thoughts were racing, and it felt like I was finally waking up after all those days asleep, like my head was just now breaking the surface of the water that had pulled me under. It had been peaceful down there, yes, but I couldn't stay there forever. Especially not when there were things to do.

I jumped up from the couch and yelled a good night to my father. Then I headed up to my room, my heart pounding. I closed the door and paced the length of my room, thinking. I didn't have a plan—I didn't have anything anywhere near the same vicinity as a plan—but I had an idea. And it was better than nothing. But mostly, I was angry. Angry at Isabel, and at Justin, but mostly at myself, for going along with their little scheme.

I grabbed my phone and scrolled through my contacts until I reached a certain number—a number I had never thought I'd end up calling. But I couldn't think of anyone else that I could turn to. Isabel had said I could no longer be friends with my friends. But she hadn't said anything about my enemies.

My phone still in my hand, I logged on to Constellation. Once there, I changed my screen name and my photo and I updated my status.

 Mad as hell . . . and not going to take it anymore.
Location: 76 Winthrop Road. Putnam, CT.

I smiled for the first time in days as I looked at my status. Then I took a breath and placed the call.

****

He was already waiting for me in Putnam Park when I arrived the next morning. I could see him as I approached the park's entrance, sitting on one of the benches, a lone figure all in black, contrasting with the bright pastel warm-up suits of the senior power-walkers doing laps around the lake.

He had sounded shocked to hear from me, which made sense, considering that I had been pretty surprised to find myself calling him. When I'd suggested Putnam Park—for old times' sake—as our meeting place, there had been a long pause. But he had agreed and we'd settled on a time.

I took a breath, gathered my thoughts, and walked over to his bench. He glanced up at me as I approached.

"Hello, Dell," I said, sitting down next to him. "Fancy meeting you here."

CHAPTER 20

Song: In The Never Ending Search For A Suitable Enemy/Joy Zipper
Quote: "I do not accept excuses. I'm just going to have to find myself a new giant, that's all." — *The Princess Bride*

 dudeyouregettingame — Not happy with the whole "nature" thing and suspicious of people who claim to enjoy it.
Location: Putnam Park, Putnam, CT.

 Mad — Just getting coffee. Alone.
Location: Stanwich Sandwich & Coffee. Stanwich, CT.

We had changed locations almost immediately, when Dell started getting some kind of allergy attack from the freshly cut grass. He'd suggested we adjourn to Stubbs, but I had a feeling that I would run into someone I knew — and wasn't allowed to hang out with — there, so I'd suggested the coffee shop in Stanwich. I did this only after I'd remembered that Nate would be tutoring at the library so I could be sure we wouldn't run into him. Nate was the one who had introduced me to Stanwich Sandwich & Coffee, and the last thing I wanted to do was bump into him post-breakup on his home turf.

Dell and I took separate cars, but arrived at almost exactly the same time. As I watched Dell climbing down from a big black SUV, it took me a moment to place why his car looked so familiar. Then I realized I had seen the car ferry Isabel away after she'd convinced Schuyler to hand over the Hayes crown. It was memories like this one — coupled with the realization that I'd seen Dell once before at SS&C, when he and Ruth had met to discuss strategy after my hacking — that made me wonder if coming to Dell for help was really the best idea. But it was the only idea I had at the moment. So, despite some misgivings, I'd joined him inside the coffee shop.

Sitting across from him in the back booth, I picked up my unfamiliar, non-Stubbs latte and took a careful sip. It wasn't bad. It just wasn't what I was used to. Over the rim of my ceramic mug — SS&C was funkier than Stubbs, and much less corporate, and if you were staying, they gave you real mugs — I glanced across the table at Frank "Hold the Frank" Dell.

He looked the same as he had when I'd seen him at the prom. His dreadlocks were still gone, and his dark hair was buzzed short. He was still pale and on the short side, but he seemed less tightly wound than I remembered. But this might have had something to do with the fact that the last two times I'd seen him, we'd been batting threats and ultimatums back and forth. I was sorting through the events of the past week and trying to decide where to begin, when Dell started speaking.

"I haven't done anything, Madison," he said, a little testily. He looked up at me from his quad-espresso, extra foam, and sighed. "I've been keeping to our agreement. So I don't know what this is all about."

"You don't?" I said, looking at him closely. It was the one thing I just wasn't sure of. Isabel had seemed very convincing when she told me Dell wasn't part of this, but I wasn't entirely sure I wasn't about to show my hand to the mastermind of this whole thing.

"No," he said, staring at me, looking baffled. "Should I?"

"I'm not sure," I said slowly, watching his reactions carefully. "It involves your cousin."

Dell blinked at me. "Isabel?" he asked, frowning. "That's weird. What did she do?"

It looked to me like Dell was telling the truth. Being in Thespians had given me access to seeing a *lot* of bad acting, and I didn't think that Dell would have been able to fake that kind of reaction if he was the one pulling the strings. And the truth was, I really had nobody else I could turn to for this. Unbelievably, Dell was my only hope. "Well," I said, taking a breath and preparing to launch into the story, "she—"

I stopped short when the door to the coffee shop flew open with a bang that rattled the panes in the windows. I looked over and saw a petite girl dressed all in black, wearing a motorcycle helmet. She took it off and shook out her long blond hair as she scanned the coffee shop.

I started to turn back to Dell, but there was something about the girl that seemed familiar. I glanced back at her, and saw to my surprise that she was looking directly at me. She was holding up a phone, and looking from it and back to me. Then she nodded, put the phone in her pocket, and to my shock, headed toward me.

Dell cleared his throat, and I looked across the table and realized he hadn't noticed the girl's arrival. "Well?" he asked impatiently.

I opened my mouth to say something at the same moment that the girl arrived at our table. She slammed her helmet down on the surface, making both Dell and me jump.

"So," she said, glaring at me through long, swingy blond bangs. "Madison MacDonald."

I stared at her, confused, until I suddenly remembered who she was. And I was not quite able to stop myself from letting out a small groan, since things had just gotten much worse.

Peyton Watson, Schuyler's stepsister and the scourge of Europe's best boarding schools, had decided to drop in.

"Hi," I said faintly, feeling a little like I had just walked into one of my nightmares. I had only met Peyton once before, but that had been enough for me. Her presence at the Watson house had been the reason that, earlier this summer, I had refused all of Schuyler's invitations to come and hang out, even though she had a really great pool. The last time I had seen Peyton, she'd been fully Gothed out. She'd since changed her look, I saw now as

I took in her ripped black jeans, black tank top, leather jacket, and black Converses—but I don't know if I could have said, exactly, what this look *was*—besides, that is, something to annoy Schuyler's father.

"What," Peyton said, glaring at me through her heavily mascaraed eyes, "do you think you're doing?"

Not having expected this question, I glanced across the table at Dell, then down at my mug. "Coffee?" I ventured after a moment.

Peyton turned to Dell and sized him up. "Who are *you*?" she snapped, sounding annoyed. But from what I knew of Peyton, this wasn't exactly abnormal, as annoyance seemed to be her default setting.

"Hhhegh," Dell choked out. He blushed bright red, then cleared his throat and tried again. "Hi," he said, more successfully this time. "I'm Frank Dell. But you can call me Dell. Or Frank. Or something else altogether, if you don't like those options . . ."

I stared at Dell, shocked, since generally the first thing he did upon meeting people was lecture them about never calling him by his first name. But then I saw the way that he was looking at Peyton. It was the way I'd only before seen him look at expensive electronic equipment—utterly besotted. Which was actually pretty surprising. It wasn't like Peyton wasn't pretty—she really was, underneath all the scowls and mascara—but she was not exactly giving out a flirty and interested vibe.

Peyton frowned at Dell for a moment longer, and he gave her what I'm sure he thought was a suave smile, but actually just made him look confused and slightly in pain. After a moment, Peyton turned her attention back to me, plunking herself down on my side of the booth, forcing me to slide over and make room for her. "I don't know who you are," she said, pointing across the table at Dell, "but—"

"Dell!" Dell jumped in helpfully, looking thrilled to be spoken to directly. "Or Frank. Or something else—"

"But I'm here to talk to Madison. So . . ." Peyton tipped her head toward the front door. "Scram." Dell jumped to his feet, but then paused and started to sit again. Hovering over the bench, Dell looked over at me, then back at Peyton, clearly in the grips of indecision.

"He's staying," I said, annoyed. Maybe Peyton's demeanor was rubbing off. "We have things to talk about." Dell smiled and sat down the rest of the way.

"So do we," she said, frowning at me.

"Since when?" I asked, still not able to wrap my mind around what she was doing here—and how she had tracked me down in the first place. But a moment later, the answer to the second quandary hit me. I had, per Isabel's orders, made my Constellation feed public. Anyone could see where I was. Including, it seemed, my former friend's slightly unhinged stepsister.

"Since you totally ditched Schuyler," Peyton said, narrowing her eyes at me, "she's been upset all week. You can't just dump your friends for no reason."

Dell leaned forward across the table. "You ditched Schuyler?" he asked, raising an eyebrow.

"Not just her," Peyton said, looking across at Dell.

"All her friends. And her boyfriend, apparently. No explanation given. So that's what I'm here to get." She turned back to me and crossed her arms over her chest.

"Is this the reason?" Dell asked, looking from Peyton to me. "Why you wanted to meet?"

"Yes," I said. "It is." I took a sip of my latte and looked from my former foe to Schuyler's stepsister. These were not the people I ever would have chosen to bare my soul to in normal circumstances. But normal circumstances had, it seemed, long since decided to depart. "Okay," I said, pushing my mug to the side and taking a deep breath. "Here's what happened."

****

I finished telling the story and took a restorative sip of what was left of my now very cold latte. Recounting the events of the past week had been more difficult than I'd anticipated, and it had forced me to relive some very painful moments. But I had gotten through it, and I suspected the next time I had to tell the story—if there was a next time—it would be easier.

Neither Peyton nor Dell spoke immediately. Dell was looking across the coffee shop, lost in thought, fingers tapping on his chin. Peyton shook her head and downed the last of the espresso shots that Dell had been fetching for her. "Here's what I don't get," she said. "Why did you agree?"

"Because," I said, a little testily, "I didn't think I had a choice. And she was threatening to get my boyfriend—" I stopped short, realizing that this word choice was no longer true. "My ex-boyfriend," I corrected, forcing the word out around the lump in my throat. "She was threatening to get him kicked out of school."

"So?" Peyton shrugged. "Do you have any idea how many schools I've been kicked out of? Believe me, it's not the end of the world."

"But this is *college*," I said, feeling that Peyton had missed the point. "And it would have been the end of the world, for Nate." It still hurt to say his name, but I made myself go on. "I couldn't let something like that happen to him, and have it be my fault." I looked across the table at Dell, who still had not spoken. "You swear you didn't know anything about this?" I asked.

"I had no idea," Dell said, looking back at me. He frowned and shook his head. "Believe me, if I'd known Isabel had been stealing information off my computer, I would have done something of my own."

"Right," I said, feeling that we shouldn't lose track of this piece of information. "You know, Dell, this whole thing is pretty much your fault."

"I told you, I didn't do anything," he said, raising his eyebrows at me.

"No," I said, "but if you hadn't had all that information there to begin with, Isabel couldn't have gotten it."

"Yeah," Dell scoffed. "Like that was an option."

"Compiling information on those who might wish to do you harm for counter-negotiation purposes," Peyton said, as though it was the most obvious thing in the world. "Totally standard."

215

"Yes," Dell said, looking across the table at her, smiling dreamily.

"So what now?" Peyton asked, turning to me. I blinked at her. I had thought that once I'd given her the explanation she'd demanded, she would be on her not-so-merry way. But it seemed that she was settling in, as she slipped off her leather jacket, revealing just her black tank top underneath. Dell, seeing this, turned even paler than usual, and missed his mouth the first few times he attempted to take a sip of his drink.

"I . . . don't know," I said slowly. I had no plan, other than to share this information with the most devious person I knew in the hopes that he might help me come up with one.

"Well, what do you want?" Dell asked. "What's your objective?"

What I really wanted was to go back in time, before any of this had happened, and my life had still made sense. But I had a feeling that wasn't going to happen. "Well," I said slowly, thinking, "I want to take away the hold that Isabel has over me," I said, "and I want to be able to tell my friends what happened, without her finding out." I also wanted to be friends with them again, but wasn't sure that was going to happen—not after the way I'd ditched them. "And I want to get the proof she has against Nate." I knew it was too much to hope for that Nate and I might be able to be together again. Not after how hurt he'd looked at the Bluff. I had a feeling there was no coming back from that.

"Okay," Peyton said, nodding. "Doable."

"Definitely," Dell agreed.

I looked between the two of them, shocked. "Wait," I said, "what do you mean, doable?"

"I mean that it's feasible," Peyton said. She looked across the table at Dell. "Don't you think?"

"Absolutely," he said. "It's not going to be easy, but it's certainly possible."

"And you both are just . . . volunteering to help me?" I asked, baffled. I had been anticipating that Dell would have been disinclined to help me, or would have at least insisted on charging me for his services. And I wasn't sure how Peyton had gone from scowling at me to joining Team Mad.

Proving she wasn't quite done with the scowling yet, Peyton glowered at me. "You do not," she said, "get to hurt my stepsister and get away with it. Plus, this Isabel chick sounds like she needs to be put in her place."

I glanced at Dell and studied his expression closely. I realized I wasn't sure where his loyalties were. After all, Isabel was his cousin, and they'd joined forces once before.

"I'm in," he said. He shook his head, his face darkening. "Nobody steals from me without consequences. And . . ." He met my eye, then looked down at the table again. "It is my fault," he muttered. "This wouldn't have happened if it wasn't for me. And I'm sorry about that, Madison."

I stared at him. Dell had never apologized, for anything—not for hacking me, not for helping mastermind the whole prom debacle. And what's more, it seemed genuine. It was really the proof that I needed. There was no turning back now. "All right," I said. "Well . . . thank you both."

"Now," said Peyton, clearly ready to get down to business. "If we're going to do this, we're going to need more than three people." She grabbed a napkin from the center of the table, extracted a pen from her bag, and pushed them both toward me. "People we can trust," she added.

I nodded and took the pen and napkin from her, realizing that of all the people to have come back into my life, she was probably the best equipped to help me pull this off. When least expected, fate had handed me a wartime consigliere. I paused for just a moment to be grateful for this. Then I took a deep breath and began to make the list.

CHAPTER 21

Song: Constellations Above Us/ The Jack Parsons Project
Quote: "Your fight is my fight."—Justin Bieber

 Mad Spending the night at home. Just hanging out chez MacDonald. Totally ordinary. The ush. Ho-hum. **Location: 76 Winthrop Road. Putnam, CT.**

I stood on the doorstep of Dave's house and tried to tell myself that there was no reason to be nervous. But my palms were sweating as I shifted from foot to foot. I was also without my phone, as I'd updated my status from my house and had left it there, so my location would be there and not changing. But I felt totally cut off without it. My hand kept reaching in my bag for it, before I would remember that it was no longer with me. And I couldn't remember the last time I'd rung someone's doorbell. If the door wasn't open, I would always just text. But I no longer had that capability. It was like I had traveled back in time to some terrible era before cell phones, like the 1500s, or the 80s. But I knew that it wasn't actually the ringing of the doorbell that was worrying me—it was what would happen after the door was opened and I went inside.

Earlier, at the coffee shop, I had made out a list of the people that I knew I could absolutely trust, while trying to keep the number of people involved as small as possible. As Isabel herself had pointed out, secrets get harder to contain the more people that know about them. And if the plan—such as it was—that Peyton, Dell, and I had started to talk about was going to be pull-off-able, it was imperative that Isabel not know that it was going to happen. After I'd given Peyton the list, she told me she'd organize people and tell me where and when. I'd gotten a text from her an hour before, telling me to meet at Dave's at eight, and that Dell would be joining us later. But I had no idea what I was walking into—who was going to be there, what she might have told them, how they were going to be feeling about me at the present moment. It felt incredibly strange to be worried about seeing my friends again. It just served as a reminder of how fully everything had changed.

I pressed the doorbell, hearing a muffled chime play inside the house. As I waited for someone to come and answer it, I suddenly realized that this was exactly what Ruth must have felt the first morning she rejoined our group again.

I couldn't hear the sound of approaching footsteps, and I adjusted the heavy canvas bag on my shoulder—it contained my laptop—and tucked my hair behind my ears. I wished for the umpteenth time that night that I had my phone with me. I was preparing to ring the bell a second time, crossing my fingers that Dave's parents wouldn't be home, and if they were, they wouldn't be in the middle of dinner or something, when a low, motorized whirring sound caused me to turn around. I couldn't see anything, but a second later, something collided hard with my ankle. I looked down and saw a miniature monster truck—painted black with red lightning bolts on it—rev back, turn itself in a circle, and start to head in the direction it had come from.

I just stared at it for a minute, not having expected this to be the result of ringing the doorbell. The truck stopped, turned around, and revved toward me again, before turning in the other direction. Unbelievably, it seemed like the truck wanted me to follow it. Dave was probably controlling the truck, and he was somewhere close, where he could see me. But as I looked around, I didn't see him anywhere. The truck spun itself in a small circle, and jolted forward once again before turning around and facing me, revving its engine, as though it was getting impatient.

Figuring that following the miniature truck seemed like the best—if most unexpected—course of action, I followed it away from Dave's front door and around the side of the house. It would zoom forward ahead of me, then pause and turn around to face me, as though checking I was still following, before turning back and jolting forward once again. As I followed it to the pool area and then around the side of the pool, I was looking all around me, checking over my shoulders, trying to find out where Dave—or whoever it was that was operating the truck—was operating it *from*. But I couldn't see anyone, which made this whole thing that much stranger. The truck led me to the door of the pool house, backed itself up, then gunned its tiny engine and zoomed through the plastic pet door in the bottom of it. Figuring this meant I'd reached our destination, I reached out and pulled open the door.

I stepped inside and had to blink a few times, since I wasn't sure exactly what I was seeing. Dave, Lisa, Schuyler, and Ruth were sitting on one of the pool house couches, while Kittson, Glen, and Mark were sitting on the other. Peyton was sitting apart from everyone, on the counter of the pool house's small kitchen. Everyone's attention was turned toward a huge TV screen, which was broadcasting . . . everyone sitting on the couches, and the pool house, back to them. It was a little bit like being in a carnival house of mirrors.

I realized that with everyone staring at the TV, my entrance had not yet been noted. I closed the door behind me a little harder than necessary, and one by one, my friends began looking over to me.

"Hi," I said, hearing the hesitancy in my voice.

"You made it," Dave said, giving me a smile. Today, he was wearing a shirt with arrows pointing to boulders arranged in a circle, with words underneath that read *Stonehenge Rocks*. He had a black controller in his hand, and I noticed that the truck was at his feet, and moving back and forth. "Wasn't sure if you were going to follow Greased Lightning there. It sure took you long enough."

"How—" I started to ask, but wasn't able to get my question out, as I found myself being hugged, suddenly and fiercely, by a petite curly-haired person.

"Mad!" Lisa said, trying to sound angry but not quite pulling it off. "*Qu'est-ce tu penses?* What were you thinking? You should have told us—"

"Well—" I started, before Schuyler hugged me from the other side.

"I hope it's okay that I told Peyton," she said, her words coming out in a tumble. "But I didn't know what to *do*, and I knew something was *wrong*, and—"

"Hi."

I looked in front of me and saw Ruth standing there, twisting her hands together, her bottom lip trembling slightly.

"Hi," I said back, hearing my own voice catch. Then, before I knew it, she was hugging me, too, and I hugged back, feeling for the first time since the spring that I had my best friend back. We had both made mistakes, but now, it felt like everything that had come before—the hacking, my recent behavior—no longer mattered.

I closed my eyes for a second, surrounded by my very best friends, who, it seemed, weren't holding grudges against me, and were just happy to see me again.

In that moment, I felt utterly ashamed that I had ever taken them for granted—truly becoming one of "those girls" as I pushed them aside for Nate, convinced they'd always be there. It had taken me actually losing them to realize how foolish and careless that had been of me. As I took in the room around me—filled with people who'd come through for me in the past, and were coming through for me again, even though I'd tried to push them away—I realized just how much everyone meant to me, and how close I'd come to losing the most important people in my life.

And even though I had cried more in that past week than I had ever cried in my life, I suddenly felt like I was going to start again. But not because something was wrong—but because something was back to being right.

****

"So here's what I don't understand," Kittson said a few minutes later.

My tearful reunion with my BFFs had been broken up when Dave had started circling the mini monster truck around our ankles, and we had rejoined the others on the couches. At first, I hadn't felt up to saying much, just looking around the room at my friends, and savoring the fact that I was there, among them, with nobody furious at me. After the last few terrible days, I hadn't thought that possible. But it was, and I was silently vowing to never, *ever* take them for granted again.

Dave had showed me how the truck had seemed to know where I'd been and why the TV (since turned off, as it was proving far too distracting) had been showing a live feed from the pool house. There was a small camera attached to the top of the truck, and Dave could watch what it showed either on his phone or stream the feed to the TV. Dave had just bought the camera a few days before, and was clearly having a little too much fun with his new toy, if Lisa's impatient sighs were anything to go by.

I looked across at Kittson, who was sitting on Turtell's lap. Turtell had seemed almost as happy to see me as my best friends had been, though I had a feeling that probably had more to do with the fact that my situation had brought his girlfriend back to town.

"What's that?" I asked Kittson from my place next to Ruth on the couch. I knew that Peyton had given people the broad outlines of what had happened with Isabel, but I wasn't sure how much detail she'd gone into.

"Why didn't you tell me yesterday?" Kittson asked. "I mean, we were in a *freezer*. Who was going to hear? But no, I have to hear the story from Schuyler's weird relative."

"*Shh,*" Schuyler hissed, glancing in Peyton's direction. I seconded that emotion. I certainly wouldn't dare call Peyton weird within hearing distance and expect to survive it. But she simply looked up from where she was drawing on her black Converses with Wite-Out, rolled her eyes, and focused back on her sneakers again.

"Because I didn't want Isabel to find out I was talking to any of you," I said. "She has information on all of you that she was threatening to let out if I did." I looked over at Peyton, who met my eye and nodded, capping her Wite-Out. "I thought you guys should see it," I said, reaching into my bag, and pulling out the sheets of paper I'd printed out that afternoon—all of Isabel's dossiers on my friends who were present. I handed them out—each person only getting the one with their information on it—and twisted my hands together, waiting, as everyone read in silence.

"This is messed up," Turtell said after a moment, shaking his head. "What is *wrong* with this girl?"

"Does anyone else find this kind of creepy?" Mark asked, looking up from his paper. "I mean, I don't want anyone keeping files on me."

"It's not all her," I said, feeling that credit—or blame—should be assigned where it was due. "She stole a lot of this information off Dell's computer."

"He did say," Dave said slowly, looking up from his paper, "that he had information on all of us. And that he was going to use it. At the prom. Remember?" Dave shook his head, balled up his paper, and tossed it on the ground. Then he picked up the controller and ran the mini truck over it, back and forth, until the paper was flattened and covered with small black tire tracks.

"But still," Schuyler said. She set her paper aside, looking slightly sick. "This seems to be taking things way too far."

"Isabel blackmailed you into taking the Hayes crown," Lisa pointed out. "We know this girl is crazy. *Comme une folle.*"

"The worst part isn't any of this, though," I said. This was the part of going against Isabel that really made me feel ill. My friends' secrets, though damaging, weren't fatal. And Isabel didn't have proof of most of them. But

226

Nate was another whole story. I swallowed hard and continued. "It's Nate."

Everyone in the room suddenly got very quiet, and out of the corner of my eye, I saw Kittson move even closer to Turtell, and Dave and Lisa join hands—as though just hearing about a breakup might be contagious, and they needed to guard themselves against it.

"Does this," Dave started slowly, "have something to do with why you guys broke up?"

I nodded, though it hurt my heart to hear someone else talk about the situation. It hit home for me that the breakup wasn't just something that had happened between Nate and me. Rationally, I knew that the news would have gotten out, where it had undoubtedly been talked about and speculated upon. But hearing Dave bring it up somehow made the whole thing seem that much more real. "Isabel has proof," I said, "that Nate was one of the engineers of the Stanwich Senior Prank. She has evidence that shows him stealing the mascot costume. If she gave it to Nate's headmaster, he might not be able to go to Yale."

Lisa let out a pretty impressive stream of French curses, and I gave her a small smile, to let her know I appreciated the support.

"That," Dave said, his voice low and angry, "is crossing a line."

"I couldn't let it happen," I said. "And she told me I had to break up with Nate and stop being friends with all of you, or she'd release all this information. And that's why . . . I did what I did."

"Does Nate know?" Ruth asked me quietly. I thought about the note I'd written him, but I'd pretty much given up hope that he'd understood it. I shook my head.

"But you're telling *us*," Schuyler said. I looked over at her and saw that, even in this high-stress situation, with her hair hanging loose, she wasn't chewing on it, and her voice was clear and steady. Taking this in, I felt a little surge of pride at just how far Schuyler had come.

"I know," I said. "Because I'm going to try and fix this, and I was hoping that I could get your help." I looked around at everyone, suddenly feeling panicky. "But none of you can update or post or blog about this or the fact that you saw me," I said. "Otherwise, Isabel might retaliate."

"Of course we're helping," Turtell said, crumpling up his own paper and tossing it in the path of the truck. Dave threw the controller across to Turtell, who caught it with one hand and began running the truck over his own paper. "No-brainer."

Mark looked around. "If we're pulling together another *crew*," he said, using air quotes around "crew," and a second too late, "should we call Sarah?"

"You mean just to keep her informed?" I asked, a little puzzled. Last I had heard, Sarah was forcing eight-year-olds to perform Eugene O'Neill. And if this all fell apart, I knew I'd have to get in touch with her—and with everyone else who Isabel had information on—but we weren't there yet. And if we could figure this out, we might be able to avoid being there altogether.

"No," Mark said. "She's back. I guess she had to

leave her camp because of her uncompromising creative vision."

I had a feeling I knew what that meant, and found myself suppressing a smile. But I was also realizing how out of the loop I was. "Why don't we just keep this between all of us for the moment?" I asked. Suddenly, I realized that Turtell was the only one who'd pledged his support. "If you guys are in, that is," I added, with a sinking feeling in my stomach. "I mean, I'm the one that Isabel has the biggest problem with. I'm the one she's blackmailing."

Dave shook his head. "Of course I'm in," he said. "This isn't just about you, Mad. She's trying to hurt all of us."

"C'est vrai," Lisa agreed. Then she turned to me and shook her head. "But you should have told us all from the beginning."

"Yeah," Kittson agreed. "Especially me."

I caught Ruth's eye and saw her trying to suppress a smile. "But what's done is done," she said quickly. "Mad did what she thought was the best thing at the time. And now we can figure out where to go from here."

"Right," Mark said emphatically. Then he paused and looked around. "So what happens now?" he asked. "Do we have a plan?"

I glanced at Peyton. I had something more along the lines of a vague idea that I hoped might shape itself into something, but *plan* was probably too strong a word to use at this particular moment. Before I could answer him, Peyton's phone beeped. She looked down at it, typed a response, then met my eye and nodded. I took a breath and prepared to explain what I had a feeling would be, for everyone else in the room, an unexpected turn of events. "So here's the thing," I started, just as the door to the pool house swung open and Dell stepped inside.

CHAPTER 22

Everyone in the room seemed to freeze, except for Turtell, who steered the mini truck right toward Dell, stopping it just before hitting his ankle, but keeping it close, its engine revving.

"Dell!" Mark yelled, jumping up and pointing at him, as though the rest of us might not have caught this. "Dell is here!"

"Alors," Lisa said, standing up and facing him, crossing her arms over her chest. "You have a lot of nerve, showing up here." And despite the seriousness of the situation, I had a feeling that she was thrilled to finally be able to say that phrase out loud.

Dell looked at me and sighed. "Really, Madison?" he asked.

"I was getting to it," I said defensively. "I invited him," I explained, looking around at my friends and taking in seven almost-simultaneous shocked reactions.

"Good evening, Peyton," Dell said in a voice that was much lower than the one he normally used, as he walked up to stand next to where she was sitting on the counter. Peyton narrowed her eyes at him and he took a large step away, but without losing what I'm sure he thought was an ingratiating smile. His attempts at suaveness were somewhat undercut by the fact that he was wearing a bulky black backpack.

"Wait, I'm sorry," Ruth said, looking from Dell to me. "But what's happening here?"

"I didn't know who else I could call," I explained. "I wasn't allowed to talk to any of you. And Dell's on our side. *Aren't you?*" I directed this last statement right to him, and Dell jumped, tearing his eyes away from Peyton.

"I am," he said. He looked around the room, took a small step forward, and cleared his throat. "I wanted to apologize," he muttered. "I understand Isabel got this information because it was on my computer. And I want to help make things right."

"Ha!" Mark said, in what was probably the least convincing fake laugh on record. "Like we're supposed to believe that?"

"Yeah," Turtell said. He glared at Dell and cracked his knuckles. "Not buying it."

"We don't have a choice," I said, knowing as I said it that it was, for better or worse, absolutely true. "We have to trust him."

"And let's look at the facts," Dell said, ticking them

off on his fingers. "I haven't gone back on the arrange-
ment we made in May, even though as you can see,
I had ample means. I haven't done anything retaliatory.
Also—"

"Yet," Kittson said, arching an eyebrow. "If your
little plan had succeeded, I would have lost my rightful
crown as prom queen." She looked around the room, letting the weight of this sentence sink in. "We should all
think about that."

"Seriously?" Peyton asked, looking at Kittson with
her eyebrows raised. "That's what bothers you here?"

"Also," Dell repeated, keeping his list going, "let us
not ignore the fact that I was just going about my business when Madison contacted *me*. I didn't approach her."

It looked like Dave and Lisa were both on the verge of
saying something, and I jumped in before this would turn
into a debate. There was no backing out now. "Guys,"
I said, "I told him the situation this afternoon. He's in.
And if he wasn't, he would have told Isabel already, and
we would have known he had, because all of our information would be out there."

"I don't know," Ruth said, shaking her head. She
looked over at Dell, who held her gaze for a moment
before looking down at the floor. "Are we forgetting that
he has a slight habit of double-crossing people?"

"Are you forgetting that you have the same habit?"
Dell shot back.

"Man," Peyton said, looking back and forth between
them, "Putnam's certainly gotten a lot more interesting
since the last time I was here."

"I do not believe," Ruth said, right to Dell, her voice low and angry, "that you are doing this out of the kindness of your heart. What's in it for you?"

I thought I saw something pass quickly over Dell's face, but then it was gone, and I couldn't be sure I'd seen anything at all.

"Well, I don't know what to tell you," he said. "But I'm doing it because it's something I need to do. Nothing more."

Dell's words hung in the air, but they didn't appear to have convinced anyone. Turtell revved the truck a few more times, prompting Dave to signal for him to give the controller back.

"Madison," Dave said, intercepting the controller flying through the air before it whacked Schuyler on the head, and looking at me gravely, "I just don't know."

"I hear what you're saying," I said. I looked around at the faces of my friends, all of whom looked much less pleased with me than they had a few minutes before. I was suddenly glad that we'd had our happy reunion before I'd dropped the Dell bombshell. "But the fact is, we need him."

"For what?" Schuyler asked. She didn't ask it contemptuously, but like she genuinely wanted to know.

"His computer skills, for one," I started. "And—"

"Not necessary," Kittson scoffed. "Anything he can do, I'm sure I can do just as well."

"Really." Dell raised an eyebrow at her. "Care to prove that?"

"No," I said quickly, before we got too far off track.

"The real reason he's invaluable is because he has access to Isabel. None of the rest of us can get in touch with her without raising her suspicions."

"Not to mention," Peyton added, hopping down from the counter and going to sit next to Schuyler on the sofa, crossing her legs underneath her, "from what I understand, he's the last person that this Isabel girl is going to expect any of you to be talking to, let alone working with. It's priceless misdirection."

Everyone was silent for a moment, and then Lisa shook her head. "We're working *with* Dell," she said, as though still trying to make herself believe it. *"Un coup de théâtre, non?"*

"Oui," I said quickly, even though I had no idea what she meant. I'd found, over time, that it was usually the fastest way to get Lisa to move on and not discuss etymology. I looked around the room. "Guys?"

After a moment, everyone nodded, Ruth just barely. I noticed that her brow was still furrowed. She looked anything but convinced, but I figured I would just talk to her about it later.

"All right, then," Dell said briskly, "first things first." He slid his backpack off his shoulders and sat down on the couch next to Mark, who moved away farther than was probably necessary, frowning at him.

"What's that for?" Kittson asked, watching as Dell pulled a laptop out of his backpack.

"This," Dell said, booting it up and looking at us over the screen, "is for finding out where she's keeping this information."

235

****

While Dell hunched over his laptop, typing furiously, I turned on my own computer, which was still acting weird, moving much more slowly than usual. I sighed as I waited for it to boot up, and glanced over at Lisa, who was focused on her phone, typing rapidly. I looked around: Peyton and Schuyler were deep in conversation, Kittson was examining her nails, Turtell and Dave were trying to get the truck to run up the wall, Mark was trying to peer over Dell's shoulder at what he was typing, and Ruth was getting a water out of the pool house fridge.

Lisa paused in her typing and looked up at me. "It's Tricia," she said, holding up her phone. Lisa's phone beeped, and she looked down at it and sighed. "She wants to know what's going on over here, since everyone seems to be gathering here, and who exactly is here, and can she come and hang out. . . ."

"Well . . . no," Peyton said bluntly. "She can't. Who is this girl again?"

"Our friend," Schuyler said. She looked at Lisa's phone and bit her lip. "I feel bad about not including her, but . . ." She shrugged and I nodded. While Tricia had probably seen that everyone else had aligned at Dave's without her, when I'd made out the list for Peyton, I'd limited it to people who'd been through Promgate, rather than bringing in new people who might get in trouble.

"I know she can't come over," Lisa said while typing, "but I'm trying to let her know that so she doesn't get suspicious."

236

"But she doesn't even know Isabel," Ruth said, leaning against the kitchen counter, bottle of Poland Spring in hand. "So who cares if she gets suspicious?"

"I'm just trying to be extra safe here," Lisa said. "I mean, they both go to Hartfield. Maybe they have friends of friends in common, and Isabel would be able to see if she posted something."

I shook my head, realizing how right Isabel had been—our lives were being lived in public. And it was very hard to know where, exactly, information would go. I just hoped we could pull this off, and soon, because I didn't think we'd be able to keep up this media blackout of certain information—like the fact that I was friends again with seven people that I wasn't supposed to be—for much longer. And plus, I was beginning to experience serious phone separation anxiety.

"Okay," Dell said, looking up from his computer. "I've been searching my files, and it's pretty obvious what she's taken from me. I mean, she didn't even try to cover her tracks."

"And you really didn't notice?" Ruth asked, coming to join us on the couch once again.

"I assumed that since my laptop hadn't left my *room* that it was safe," Dell said, a little irritably. "Clearly, I will revise such assumptions in the future."

"What did she take?" I asked.

"Well, the files that you saw," he said, typing rapidly. "And . . ." He typed in silence for another moment, then nodded. "She took the Hartfield security video," he said, frowning. "She took it from my hard drive."

"The proof that she has against Nate?" I asked, look-ing hard at Dell. "That came from you?"

"Yes," he said, still peering at his screen. "When I heard about the prank, I hacked into the Hartfield secu-rity system, just to see if I could. And there was the video, clearly showing who had done it. So I copied it and wiped it from the Hartfield system. I figured that it might be useful leverage, at some point."

"So it's a video file?" I asked, and Dell nodded. I tried to get my head around whether there was any salvaging this at all, or if this thing might have already gone viral. "How do we know that she hasn't made copies of it?"

"Because I encrypted it," Dell said, looking up from his screen to me. "Your leverage is lost if there are doz-ens of copies of something. It can't be copied. And if you try, you transfer a nasty little virus to your computer, as an added bonus."

"Not bad," Peyton said in an offhand voice, but she looked fairly impressed. Dell blushed bright red and started typing again, but so fast that I had a feeling it was probably gibberish.

"So if we get this file back from her," I said, feeling my heart hammering, "then we've got the proof back about Nate and the prank. The only copy. Right?"

Dell nodded. "Right. It's just a matter of getting it back."

"Yeah," I said. My own computer had finally booted up, and I opened a blank document, ready to write down some thoughts on how that was going to happen. Just as soon as they came to me.

"Well, the file's probably on her computer, right?" Dave asked. "So we just get to her computer, and you can take it off. Easy."

"Let's find out," Dell said, typing furiously again. I glanced at Ruth, who just shook her head, looking lost. Ruth was fairly hopeless with computers, which was maybe the universe's way of balancing things out, since she was fairly brilliant with everything else.

"What do you mean, 'let's find out'?" Kittson asked, looking interested in spite of herself, leaning forward along with Mark to look at Dell's screen.

"I mean," Dell said, "I have access to her laptop. Just give me a second to pull it up."

I blinked at Dell, certain I'd heard right, but figuring that I must have misunderstood. "How can you pull it up?" I asked.

A small smile crept over Dell's face—a genuine smile this time, not the ones that he was trying to impress Peyton with. "Well," he said, with a small shrug, "I have remote access to her laptop."

"Does she . . . know about that?" Mark asked, peering over Dell's shoulder for a closer look.

"Not as such," Dell said, his smile growing.

"So how did you do that?" I asked, a little stunned by this turn of events. I had known that Dell was a skilled hacker, but I hadn't known he was that good.

"There are a number of options," Dell said. "You can send someone a link, with the software embedded. They download it without realizing, and you get access to monitor their computer remotely in real time.

239

You can also insert a flash drive with a program on it that copies the contents of their computer. The only downside is if the person installs new spyware or password protections, your access is wiped out. And it can cause computers to run more slowly, so people tend to notice something is wrong."

I looked down at my own computer, which no longer felt like my familiar pink laptop, but instead, felt like a time bomb. I thought about how much more slowly it had been running lately, and about the flash drive Isabel had given me, and the folder I'd blithely opened.

"Dell," I said, looking up from my laptop. "I think we may have a problem."

****

"You were right," Dell said grimly, looking up from where he'd been going through my laptop. "Isabel's gained access to this machine."

"Oh my God," I murmured, leaning back against the couch. I felt a little bit sick at the sheer invasion of my privacy, and how far into my life Isabel's scheme had extended.

"She would have been able to see anything you did," Dell said. "Constellation, iChatting, even what you wrote on Word documents."

"iChatting?" Kittson asked, looking right at me.

I nodded, and I saw her turn a little pale and glance at Turtell quickly before looking away. But Isabel had given me the flash drive *after* Kittson had told me about her ill-advised hookup in the Hamptons. Strange. Still, at least I now knew how Isabel had seen that I'd started to send my friends the warning e-mail.

I racked my brain, trying to think of anything that I might have done on my computer that she would have been able to see. There was my message to my friends, which just showed that I was following her instructions, and my note to Nate, but on the surface, that was fine. And I couldn't think of anything else that might have implicated me at all. I felt a sudden relief that I hadn't actually started typing out our plan on my computer—since it would have meant that she would have seen all of it.

"I can get it off your laptop," Dell said, looking back down at it. "It's simple—a spyware update will take care of it."

"Great," I said. "Thanks." I wanted to get her off of my computer as fast as possible. The fact that she was peering in on my life like this was giving me the creeps.

"Wait," Peyton said sharply. She nodded at my laptop and smiled. "I think we might be able to use this to our advantage."

CHAPTER 23

Song: Okay I Believe You, But My Tommy Gun Don't/
Brand New
Quote: "When trying to rescue friends from a tree,
make sure the plan doesn't involve having everybody
stand on your back."—A. A. Milne

An hour later, we had what could almost be called a plan.
We had hooked Dell's computer up to the TV, so we could
all see what was being sketched out. We'd been passing
around the laptop as we took turns adding ideas—except
for Peyton, who said she wasn't able to touch a computer
until next year, for reasons she declined to go into—
making Dell wince a little every time it passed to someone new. Ruth was hitting the keys especially hard when
it had been her turn, but it seemed like Dell's presence
had been accepted, as nobody "accidentally" dropped his
computer or ran it over with a mini monster truck.

Dell hadn't been able to find the Nate file anywhere
on Isabel's computer, which had put a momentary hitch
in our plan, until Ruth, using her scientist's brain, had

made me talk through exactly what I'd heard when Isabel had described the Nate photo to me. I had thought back as hard as I could, and when I'd described how I'd heard the sound of metal hitting metal, her eyes had lit up, and soon, another piece of the plan was falling into place.

I looked up at the screen now, lifting my legs automatically as the monster truck, piloted somewhat erratically by Dell, swerved around the room. I was just hoping the plan would work. It *had* to.

~~ISABEL RYAN IS A LYING, SNEAKING LITTLE—~~
~~Madison's Nine~~
~~REVENGE!!~~

The Plan
Objectives:

Take AWAY Isabel's power re: secrets
Get back "Nate stealing mascot" evidence
Do this <u>without</u> her realizing it/before she can retaliate

Monday, July 1
4 P.M.
J working 1st concession stand
J distracted—invitation
Madison, Peyton, Schuyler, Mark—J loses phone

4:30 P.M.
Madison—J texts IR—makes plans to meet at SYC at 7

6:30 P.M.
J arrives OAB
Glen, Dave, Ruth—J chills out

7:00 P.M.
D&J—IR arrives SYC
Madison—KEYS

7:30 P.M.
Madison—J calls IR
D&J—IR leaves SYC
Dell—information retrieval

8:00 P.M.
EVERYONE—PHS lacrosse
Evidence safe (fingers xed)

I let out a long breath as I looked at the plan that we would attempt to pull off just two days from now. It all seemed fairly daunting. And it relied, pretty heavily, on all three of my less-than-reliable coworkers. I had assured everyone that they would agree to help, but secretly wasn't a hundred percent convinced of that. The prom plan had been complicated enough. But with this one, it seemed like there was even more that could go wrong. More locations, people spread out more places, more uncontrollable variables.

"Man," Mark said as he stared up at the screen. He sighed and turned to look at the rest of us. "Is it just me, or does it seem like we're always stealing stuff from this girl?"

"We wouldn't have to, if she'd stop taking things that didn't belong to her," Lisa said firmly. *"C'est simple."*

"I still feel bad about what we're doing to Justin," Schuyler said, shaking her head.

"Don't," Kittson and I said together.

"We're going to turn it off," Turtell assured her. "Most likely," he added, under his breath.

"Do you guys really think this will work?" Dave asked, then yelped in pain as Dell ran the truck into his ankle.

"Sorry," Dell muttered, reversing. "My bad . . ."

I looked back at the screen. In all honesty, I had no idea if we'd be able to pull it off. We'd managed it at the prom, but just barely. And we'd had luck—and a streaker—on our side.

I couldn't be sure we'd have luck on our side again. But I was pretty sure that there would be no semi-naked people involved this time, as the plan was streaker-free. I hoped it would work. Because if we didn't pull it off, Isabel would know what we'd tried to do. And all our futures would be hanging in the balance.

"It has to," I said, leaning back against the couch cushions.

"Okay," Schuyler said, looking up from Dell's laptop. "So I'll save this, right?" She closed out the document, and Dell's desktop filled the TV. Dell turned even paler than usual, dropping the controller and prompting an outraged "Dude!" from Dave.

"That's okay," Dell said, hustling over to the couch and reaching for his laptop. "I'll just take that—"

"What's *Poem for Peyton*?" Kittson asked gleefully, pointing to the Word document on his desktop. Peyton looked up at the screen and rolled her eyes, but I could have sworn I saw her give a tiny smile as she looked away again.

"Nothing," Dell said, flustered, as he wrenched the laptop away from Schuyler and tapped at the keyboard frantically. "Nothing at all. Just . . . um . . . about football. I'm a big fan of, uh, Peyton Manning and the, you know, team."

"The *Colts*," Turtell said, shaking his head.

"Right, them," Dell said, shutting his laptop and looking at his phone. "Wow, look at the time. I had better get going. . . ."

Dell started to pack up his enormous backpack, and this seemed to be the cue that the get-together was breaking up. Everyone stood, gathered up purses and motorcycle helmets and mini monster trucks, and headed out of the pool house.

Once outside in the warm, humid night, Dell turned to us, shouldering his bag. "So I'll check in tomorrow to confirm we're set for Monday," he said. His eyes fell on me, and he sighed. "Well, except for you, Mad. You're really going to need to get another phone before then."

"I know," I said, stifling a sigh. I wasn't sure how this was going to happen, but it needed to. And fast. I turned to Schuyler. "Hey, you know all those Razrs your dad bought for you when you kept throwing your phone out the window?"

"What about them?" she asked. Peyton turned to her, eyebrows raised. "I don't do it anymore!" Schuyler said defensively.

"Do you think I could borrow one?" I asked. "Just for tomorrow and Monday?"

"Sure," Schuyler said. "But you know they don't have internet capability, right?"

"Oh," I said. I would be needing to update my location—and see where my friends were—if this was going to work out. "Well, never mind."

"We'll think of something," Ruth said encouragingly. "Want me to make a list?" I shook my head at that, but couldn't help smiling.

"If there is nothing else," Dell said. "Then *adieu*." He looked around at us, his gaze lingering on Peyton the longest before he headed for Dave's driveway.

"Glen, you got a minute?" Dave asked, taking a few steps toward the edge of the property and the rock wall that overlooked Long Island Sound.

"Sure," Turtell said. He kissed Kittson on the cheek, then headed over to where Dave was waiting. The boys turned their backs on us and Dave began speaking, Turtell leaning close to listen.

"What's that about?" Schuyler asked, looking over at them.

"Who knows?" Peyton asked. "Who cares? Schuyler, shake a leg. Let's motor."

"I should go, too," Ruth said, pulling out her phone and checking the time. "I need to call Andy. He was pretty confused about why I cancelled on him at the last minute."

Schuyler said goodbye to all of us, Peyton did not, and the two of them took off. Ruth took a step closer to me. "Mad," she said in a low voice.

I looked around, but didn't know what the caution was for—Lisa and Kittson seemed to be involved in a discussion about toy trucks and how best to dismantle one. "Ruth," I repeated back to her in the same quiet voice.

She smiled at that, but only fleetingly. "I think we need to be careful," she said, still speaking quietly.

"About Dell?" I asked, and she nodded. "I know," I started. "We've all had issues with him, but I think this time—"

"I've just never known him to do anything without getting something out of it," she said. "I don't think you wake up one morning and suddenly become a different person."

I could see how worried she was. "But then what is he getting out of this?" I asked.

"I don't know," she replied. "And that's what worries me." Her phone beeped with a text, and she looked down at it. "That's Andy again," she said.

"Tell him I say hi," I said. "Actually, don't," I amended. "No need to scare him."

She smiled at me. "TTYL?" she asked.

I felt myself smile back, a real, genuine one, the kind I'd had far too few of over the last few days. "TTYS," I replied. Ruth smiled back and headed for the driveway, texting as she walked.

I turned to Kittson and Lisa and saw that Kittson was in the foot-tapping stage of her impatience dance. "This is ridiculous," she huffed, staring at Turtell and Dave, still deep in conversation. "I didn't come back from the Hamptons so my boyfriend could talk about toy trucks." She flipped her hair and stalked over to the boys.

The phone in Lisa's hand beeped, and she looked down at it and sighed. "Tricia again," she said, shaking her head. "I don't know about her. She's getting kind of clingy and *un peu* annoying."

"What do you mean?" I asked, trying not to seem too happy about this.

"Je ne sais . . ." she said, with a one-armed shoulder shrug. "Just kind of a feeling. But you know what was really weird?" So much of this had been really weird that I had no idea where to begin with that, so I just shook my head. "When Dell was saying goodbye," she said, "it was in French."

"I caught that," I said. "I think you're rubbing off on him."

"Not the language," she said. "The word. He didn't say *au revoir*, which means goodbye. He said *adieu*."

"So?" I asked. I had taken—and somehow passed—Latin last year, so I wasn't sure what Lisa was getting at with her vocabulary lesson.

"Adieu . . ." Lisa paused, her expression troubled. "It means farewell. It's what you say when you don't plan on seeing someone ever again." She looked at me closely. "Mad, are you sure we can trust him?"

CHAPTER 24

Mad about the smoothies.
Location: On A Blender Smoothie Shop. Putnam, CT.

"So!" I said as cheerfully as I was able, looking at my fellow employees and hoping we wouldn't have to go through this a third time. "Is everyone clear on the plan?"

Daryl and John shook their heads as Kavya, from her perch on the counter, sighed loudly. "I'm clear on the *plan*," she said. "I'm just not clear on why I should do this in the first place."

I resisted the urge to wave some carrots at her. "Because it would be really helpful," I said, giving her a big smile. "And we'd really appreciate it." Kavya just folded her arms over her chest. "And," I said quickly,

251

scrambling for something that might convince her, "I'll work Fridays alone for the rest of the summer."

Kavya looked at me for a moment, as though considering this, head tilted to the side. "Fine," she finally agreed. "I'll help you out tomorrow, and then you work Fridays for me for the rest of the summer *and* every other Tuesday."

Since I already worked on Tuesdays, this did not seem to be that much of an imposition on me, and I nodded. "Deal," I said. She hopped off the counter and walked to the back, emerging a moment later with her purse slung over her shoulder, phone already in hand.

"Is it quitting time already?" John asked, looking puzzled. He took out his phone and checked the time.

"No," I said, staring at Kavya. Since the store closed at six, and it was just a little after noon, it was certainly not quitting time. "What's going on?"

Kavya looked up from her phone and sighed. "Madison, I thought this whole plan rests on me being able to seduce this guy."

"You're not actually seducing him, remember?" I said quickly. "You're just getting him to *think* that you are."

"Well, anyway," Kavya said, "if I'm going to do that, I'm going to need to look good."

"You do look good," I said as encouragingly as possible.

Daryl nodded. "Thumbs-up," he said.

"But I'm going to need to look *really* good," she said. "So I'm going to need time off, to relax, get some beauty sleep. . . ." She raised an eyebrow at me. "Unless you'd rather I don't help you out," she said. "I could do that, too."

"It's fine," I said through gritted teeth. I had a suspicion that the rest of the summer might be a series of ultimatums. But since Kavya had never done much work anyway, it wasn't like her contribution was really going to be missed. "I'll see you tomorrow?"

"Sure," she said vaguely as she headed out the door. "Later!" The bell jangled and I just looked out the window for a moment, hoping against everything I knew about her that she would come through for us. Because we were pretty much dead if she didn't.

I took a long sip of my Straw-Mango, hoping that the extra scoop of energy powder I'd mixed in would start kicking in soon. "Okay," I said, turning to Daryl and John. "Let's go over the details again."

Daryl shook his head. "This whole situation, Mad," he said. "The secrets . . . the lies . . . if you'd have watched this spring's episodes of my *telenovela*, you'd have known that they never lead to anything good. You know what Rosa learned last week? *La verdad te hará libre*."

I waited for a translation, but none seemed forthcoming. "What does that mean?" I finally asked.

Daryl smiled at me. "Aren't subtitles great? Check it. It means 'the truth shall set you free.'"

John shook his head. "That's deep, dude."

"She was kidnapped and tied to a chair at the time, though," Daryl added thoughtfully after a minute. "So maybe they meant it literally."

"Maybe," I said, nodding as though this stoner wisdom was sinking in. "It's something to think about. Now, why don't we go over this again?"

****

I pulled into our driveway that night feeling utterly wiped out. It didn't help that when I wasn't going over different aspects of the plan, I was thinking about Nate.

My mind kept circling back to him, like a bruise that wouldn't heal, because I refused to stop poking at it. Mostly, though, I just *missed* him. It was like a physical ache somewhere deep inside, some vital part of me that had been ripped away. Throughout the day, I kept thinking about things that I wanted to say to him, when it would hit me that was no longer an option. It was like my mind was refusing to accept that the reality of the world had fundamentally changed.

So as I headed up our driveway, I was looking forward to a long bath and seeing if I could convince my father to pick up a pizza for dinner again. I parked in the turnaround and headed into the house—and nearly fell on my face as I tripped over the huge, overstuffed duffel that was directly inside the door. T. MACDONALD was stenciled across it. "Oh, no," I groaned. I had a feeling I knew exactly what its presence meant.

"Hey, Mad." I looked up and saw my brother standing in the kitchen doorway, looking several inches taller and entirely too pleased with himself. "You miss me?"

I walked into the kitchen, giving him a slight shove—our version of a hug—as I passed him. I beelined for the fridge, feeling acutely in need of a restorative Diet Dr Pepper. "What are you doing here?" I asked, grabbing a can out of the fridge and gulping it gratefully. "What happened to camp?"

"Camp was good," he said, following me to the fridge, giving me the opportunity to see that he had, in fact, grown enough that he was now officially taller than me. He reached over my head for a Mountain Dew, then slouched over to the kitchen table. "But I was just doing the first session. I go to art camp next week."

I had known this. In the pre-breakup, pre-disaster version of my life, I'd been well aware that Travis's camps were split into two sessions. "Right," I said. "Of course."

"I'm going to need your input on these craft projects I made for Olivia," he said. "Oh, and then for you to mail them for me. Cool?" He pulled out his phone and started typing on it, not waiting for a response. In times past, I absolutely would have said something snarky to him about this. But there just didn't seem to be any point to it now.

"Sure," I said. I turned to head upstairs, and Travis put his phone down on the table and looked at me.

"Uh," he said, then cleared his throat a few times. "Dad said that you, um, stayed in bed for a while last week."

I took just a moment to wonder what my father had been thinking, sharing this information with my former Demon Spawn brother. Even though Travis and I weren't on the outs as much as we traditionally had been, I still didn't want my father arming him with information like this. "Yeah," I said, looking down at my soda can. "But I'm fine now."

"Was it about Nate?" he asked, and I looked over at him, shocked that he would have put this together. He shrugged. "I saw on Constellation that you changed your status."

I felt my bottom lip threatening to tremble, and I bit down hard on it, certainly not about to let myself cry in front of my brother. "Yeah, well," I said when I'd pulled myself together.

"What happened?" Travis asked, taking a sip of Mountain Dew.

"Let's just say it wasn't my idea," I said, fighting to keep my voice steady. "And that if it had been up to me, we wouldn't have broken up."

Travis looked at me for a long moment, then nodded and jumped to his feet. "I'm going for a bike ride now," he said, a little louder than was probably necessary. After all, it was just us in the kitchen.

"Oh," I said. "Um, okay." Travis nodded and, looking oddly determined, headed out of the kitchen. Then he turned back, walked toward me, and before I knew what was happening, gave me a quick, awkward hug.

"Be back soon," he said, stepping away and practically running out the door. I watched him go, slightly bewildered, not sure where this sudden need for exercise had come from. But maybe camp did those kinds of things to you.

I was about to head upstairs when I saw Travis's phone sitting on the kitchen table. I picked it up and turned it over in my hands. It was new; my parents had bought it for Travis for his eighth-grade graduation. Unlike the now-antique box of phones Schuyler's father had bought, this phone certainly had internet capabilities. Which meant that it might be just what I needed.

CHAPTER 25

Song: *Crosses Fingers*/The Secret Handshake
Quote: "Every man is surrounded by a neighborhood of voluntary spies."—Jane Austen

 Young MacDonald Okay, I'm set. Kavya's ready. I'm waiting behind the 1st concession stand.
Location: First Concession Stand, Putnam Beach. Putnam, CT.

 Schuyler We're waiting on the other side. Over and out.
Location: First Concession Stand, Putnam Beach. Putnam, CT.

 Peyton's Place → Schuyler Schuyler, that's a radio term. You really don't need to keep using it.
Location: First Concession Stand, Putnam Beach. Putnam, CT.

 Lord Rothschild Ready & waiting for my cue. Can I use an accent again?
Location: Second Concession Stand, Putnam Beach. Putnam, CT.

 Young MacDonald → Lord Rothschild NO.
Location: First Concession Stand, Putnam Beach. Putnam, CT.

Dave Gold → Lord Rothschild NO.
Location: 84 Shoreline Road. Putnam, CT.

 La Lisa → Lord Rothschild NON.
Location: Putnam Hyatt. Putnam, CT.

 Rue → Lord Rothschild Mark, why would you need an accent? Aren't you just playing yourself?
Location: Stanwich Library. Stanwich, CT.

 Lord Rothschild → Rue Well, technically. But I think accents just make everything more fun, don't you?
Location: Second Concession Stand, Putnam Beach. Putnam, CT.

 Young MacDonald → Rue Stanwich Library??
Location: First Concession Stand, Putnam Beach. Putnam, CT.

 Rue → Young MacDonald Don't worry, I'll be at OAB in time for Phase 2.
Location: Stanwich Library. Stanwich, CT.

 Young MacDonald → Rue No, I meant why are you there?
Location: First Concession Stand, Putnam Beach. Putnam, CT.

 Young MacDonald → Rue Ruth?
Location: First Concession Stand, Putnam Beach. Putnam, CT.

 Mad Hanging out at home & playing my Xbox. Thinking that my sibling needs to bring me home some Doritos later, as a thank you for all that I am doing for them.
Location: 76 Winthrop Road. Putnam, CT.

259

La Lisa → Young MacDonald Okay, this has officially gotten weird.
Location: Putnam Hyatt. Putnam, CT.

 Young MacDonald → La Lisa Tell me about it.
Location: First Concession Stand, Putnam Beach. Putnam, CT.

 Mad For reals, yo.
Location: 76 Winthrop Road. Putnam, CT.

Leaning against the side of the First Concession Stand, I checked the time on my phone and took a deep breath, trying to calm my racing heart and convince myself that we were doing the right thing. Because in just a few minutes, this would begin, and there would be no turning back.

I had been in position for about twenty minutes now, which was really too long to hang around the side of a building without looking suspicious. But luckily, it was the side that faced the parking lot, so I hadn't had to encounter a lot of foot traffic. It was a blazing hot day, and Schuyler had been messaging us all morning to remind us of the importance of applying—and then reapplying—lots of sunblock.

As I felt sweat begin to form at the base of my neck, I checked the time again. We really had to pull this off. Because in addition to all the other reasons we were doing it, I was now seriously in debt to my brother and didn't want it to be for nothing.

It had taken some real persuading to get him to agree to switch phones with me for the day. I had to promise that I wouldn't put anything on there that would confuse or upset Olivia, or make him lose his "street cred" with his friends. And in return, he promised to remain in the house all day, writing depressed journal entries on my computer and updating his status on my phone, so that the location would show up. For getting him to agree to these terms, I had to promise to buy him snacks whenever he wanted for the next week and to drive him and Olivia on one date a month come fall. I had agreed, knowing that at this point, much like poor Rosa on the *telenovela*, my hands were tied.

Once I'd called all my friends and let them know that, for the next day, I would be Travis and he would be me, they had all followed him, and then made their updates private. Since nobody was friends with Isabel, we didn't have to use codes, like we had during the prom, but could communicate openly. With everyone, that is, except Kavya. She'd claimed that it would be *far* too damaging to her social status to be seen joining a less-than-cool social networking site, even for the day, and had refused to rejoin Constellation. So the only way to communicate with her was through calling or texting.

When it was a minute until go time, I texted Kavya.

OUTBOX 1 of 41
To: Kavya
Date: 7/1, 3:59 P.M.

Kavya, are you ready?

I stared down at my phone as I waited for a response, feeling my heart begin to beat a little more quickly when one didn't arrive right away. The "Concession Entrapment" part of the plan, as Peyton had dubbed it, hinged on what she had told us was a collision play. Which meant several things had to happen, all at the same time, in order for this to work. Which meant that if Kavya had gotten distracted by something, the whole thing could be in jeopardy.

A moment later, my phone—technically Travis's, but mine for the day—beeped with a response, and I let out a sigh of relief.

INBOX 1 of 36
From: Kavya
Date: 7/1, 4:00 P.M.

Ready.

I switched to Constellation and updated my status as fast as I could.

Young MacDonald Okay, Smoothie Operator's in place. Mark, Schuyler, Peyton, give it one minute.
Location: First Concession Stand, Putnam Beach. Putnam, CT.

Schuyler You got it. Over and out.
Location: First Concession Stand, Putnam Beach. Putnam, CT.

Lord Rothschild Lock and load.
**Location: Second Concession Stand, Putnam Beach.
Putnam, CT.**

 Peyton's Place Seriously, people, stop this.
**Location: First Concession Stand, Putnam Beach.
Putnam, CT.**

I checked the time, waited thirty more seconds, then texted Kavya back.

OUTBOX 1 of 42
To: Kavya
Date: 7/1, 4:01 P.M.

Go.

I peered around to see if I could see her approaching the concession stand window, but it remained empty. I was just about to text her when my phone beeped again.

INBOX 1 of 37
From: Kavya
Date: 7/1, 4:02 P.M.

You know, you could say "please," Madison.

I looked around and saw that Mark had already started his approach, and there was no time to waste by having a meltdown.

Pretty please, Kavya? ☺

A second later, my phone beeped with a response.

Yes. But only because you asked nicely.

I gripped the phone but resisted the urge to throw it against the wall, mostly because I knew Travis would make me pay for it, and probably also spring for an upgraded model. I peeked around the side of the building as subtly as I was able and saw Kavya, wearing a bikini top and jean shorts, sauntering up to the concession counter. I shook my head. Justin really didn't stand a chance. I spotted Mark arriving from the other side, with what I'm sure he thought was a nonchalant walk but actually just made him look both suspicious and uncoordinated.

I hustled over to where Schuyler and Peyton were waiting, by the back door of the concession stand.

"Okay?" Schuyler whispered. She was wearing her usual warm-weather attire of a hat and long-sleeved shirt, and was looking very overheated as a result.

"I think so," I whispered back as my phone rang with an incoming call from Mark. I pressed the button to answer it, but didn't say hello, just put the phone on speaker, and we huddled around it so we could hear what was going on.

"Heya, Justin," I heard Mark say in what was unmistakably a Boston accent. And not a very good one. Peyton frowned at the phone and I just shook my head, knowing there was nothing we could do about it now. The sound was slightly muffled, and with good reason—we were hearing this through Mark's shirt pocket. "Greetings from the concession stand at the other end of the harbah!"

"Why is Mark talking like that?" Schuyler whispered.

"Because apparently he thought this wasn't complicated enough already," I whispered back to her.

"Uh, hey," we heard Justin reply, as another voice cut in.

"Well. Hi there," Kavya said in a voice that was much breathier—and nicer—than her normal one.

"Hey," Justin said, sounding shocked, but very happy. "You're, um, Kavya, right? From the smoothie place?"

"A man with a good memory," Kavya practically purred, causing Peyton to roll her eyes hugely. "How . . . refreshing."

"Did you need something, Matt?" Justin asked, sounding more distracted than ever.

"Mahk," Mark corrected, his bad accent getting

265

stronger. "We're outta napkins. Can I ask a favah? Could I borrow some of yours?"

"Oh," I heard Justin say. "Um, sure . . . just . . ."

"I could come back later," Kavya said, and even through a phone in a shirt pocket, I could tell that she was pouting. "Since it seems like you're busy now."

"No," Justin said eagerly. "Not at all . . . uh, Mike?"

"Mahk," Mark corrected.

"Right, sorry," Justin said. "Just go on back yourself and take what you need. And I'll help out my lovely customer."

"Did you really used to date him?" Peyton asked me, looking appalled.

"Wicked," Mark said. "Thanks!"

We heard a door slam, and Justin and Kavya talking in voices that were growing fainter. "Mark," I whispered into the phone, looking around. I knew there was only so long the three of us could stand huddled around a phone by the back door, particularly when one of us was wearing the world's largest sun hat, and not be noticed by someone who would want to know what we were doing there.

"Almost theah," Mark said, sounding more and more like a Kennedy. Or an Affleck. "I'm just walking down the corridah."

The back door swung open, and Mark held it for me as I glanced around quickly before stepping inside, Peyton following behind me. I met Schuyler's eye before the door swung shut, and she nodded. She was going to be keeping watch, and texting if there was anyone coming in who might be surprised to find two nonemployees there. "Mark," I hissed, once the door was closed behind us, "what is with the accent?"

"I'm sorry!" he whispered. "I do accents when I get nervous!" He started to walk down the narrow, dark hallway that led to the counter, and gestured for me to follow. He pointed Peyton to a large wooden cabinet, and she opened it. Then he led us to a small row of employee cubbies, all thankfully open and without locks. I scanned them, just hoping that Kavya was working her magic and keeping Justin occupied. "There," Mark whispered, pointing to Justin's black messenger bag.

I took a deep breath and lifted it from the cubby, pausing for just a moment before unzipping it. This felt like it was crossing a line, for me. I was about to steal—or, technically, borrow without permission—someone's personal property. But then I thought of how Isabel had stolen my prom dress and cut it up, how Justin had abused my trust to lure me into Isabel's trap. True, Justin wasn't as bad as she was, but he had thrown his lot in with her, and therefore would be held to the same standards. I unzipped the messenger bag and began rifling through it.

"Fastah," Mark whispered to me, and I shook my head, feeling around in the darkness of Justin's messenger bag.

"That's not actually helping," I said, sorting through what was in the bag. But I wasn't finding what I was looking for. "What if it's on him?" I asked.

"We're not allowed to have them on us when we're

267

working," Mark whispered back, though he didn't sound totally sure of this.

"You update your status from work all the time," I replied, digging through the bag even faster now.

"Yes, but I nevah have any customers!"

I was trying to be fast, and thorough, *and* silent, which was a very challenging combination. I had just about given up when I felt it, at the very bottom of the bag. I closed my hand around it and, smiling, pulled out Justin's phone.

"Thank Gad," Mark murmured.

I had just started to tiptoe back toward the exit when the phone in my hand lit up. ISABEL CALLING, the display read. I froze, hoping that the phone was set on silent mode, but a moment later, "Gotta Be Somebody," by Nickelback, began playing. I hit the button to silence the call immediately, but didn't move, well aware of how quiet everything seemed to have gotten, and how it felt like I could hear my own heart beating. Peyton crept around the corner silently, her arms full of napkin packages. She handed them to Mark, then raised a finger to her lips.

"Hey, Mike?" Justin called, and I glanced down the corridor, trying to estimate how long it would take us to make it out, and realizing with a sinking feeling that if Justin did come back, we wouldn't have enough time to get out unseen.

"Heah!" Mark called, his voice crackling with nervousness.

"Did you hear my phone ring?" Justin asked, and

268

his voice sounded closer than ever. I looked toward the door again desperately, ready to run for it, when I caught Peyton's eye. She shook her head and held up a hand, as though telling me, *wait*.

"No, I sure didn't," Mark called back, sounding more nervous than ever. "I was just . . . ya know. Singing. To myself."

"But—" Justin started, and a moment later, Kavya jumped in.

"So do we have a plan?" she asked. "I'd just love to show you how our . . . equipment works."

I wasn't sure how she had managed to make absolutely everything she was saying sound like a double entendre, but she was pulling it off with aplomb. I had a feeling it had something to do with growing up in L.A.

"That . . . would be great," Justin said, and he must have turned back to her, as his voice grew more muffled.

Mark, his arms full of napkins, nodded toward the front of the concession counter. "Thanks," I whispered. "See you later tonight."

"I'll be theah!" he said, giving me a quick smile before hurrying off.

Peyton jerked her head toward the door, and we hustled down the corridor to the exit. She eased open the door slowly, and we stepped out into the sunlight. It seemed especially bright after the darkness inside, and I blinked, trying to get my eyes to adjust.

"Is everything okay?" Schuyler whispered, looking worried.

I nodded, and held up the phone. "We got it," I said,

and Schuyler let out a sigh of relief. I tucked the phone carefully into my jean shorts pocket.

"So are you set for the yacht club?" Peyton asked, and I nodded, then turned to Schuyler, remembering a crucial component of this plan.

"Did you bring your permit?" I asked. Schuyler reached into her purse and pulled out a small plastic hangtag. I tucked it into the back pocket of my shorts, just hoping that nobody would notice that Judy was not, in fact, a massive SUV.

"And we'll see you back at school tonight," Schuyler said. "Good luck with the smoothie shop. And . . . be as nice to him as possible, okay?"

"He deserves everything that's coming to him," Peyton said dismissively. "I mean, Nickelback? *Really?*"

At that moment, an older man wearing a Putnam Beach Concessions polo and holding a clipboard approached the back door. Schuyler and Peyton broke left, suddenly very engaged in a conversation, and I lifted my phone to my ear, pretending I had a call as I veered right, then doubled back around, heading for my car.

By the time I reached Judy, my phone beeped with a text. I looked down at it and breathed a sigh of relief.

INBOX 1 of 39
From: Kavya
Date: 7/1, 4:15 P.M.

Done! He's coming by OAB tonight at 6:30.

I felt a little guilty twist in my stomach about what was still to come. Stealing—or borrowing—Justin's phone was just the tip of the iceberg. But I pushed that thought away and texted back.

OUTBOX 1 of 44
To: Kavya
Date: 7/1, 4:16 P.M.

Great! THANK YOU. See you then.

I unlocked my car and got in, stashing Shy's permit in my glove compartment and placing Justin's phone on the seat next to me. I put the keys in the ignition but didn't start the car yet. I checked the time and sat there, thinking. I had some time before the next step, but not quite enough time to go home. And I was fairly hot, and had a feeling that if I was going to get through the rest of the day, I was going to need an iced latte. I started my car and steered it out of the parking lot, heading for Stubbs.

CHAPTER 26

 Young MacDonald Phase 1 = successful.
Location: Stubbs Coffee Shop. Putnam, CT.

 **Dave Gold → Young MacDonald, Schuyler, Peyton's
Place, Lord Rothschild** Nicely done, guys.
Location: 84 Shoreline Road. Putnam, CT.

 **King Glen → Young MacDonald, Schuyler, Peyton's
Place, Lord Rothschild** Totally. WTG.
Location: 84 Shoreline Road. Putnam, CT.

 Queen Kittson → King Glen Sweetie, what are you doing
at Dave's?
Location: Nails "R" We. Putnam, CT.

 King Glen → Queen Kittson Just, you know, hanging.
Guy stuff.
Location: 84 Shoreline Road. Putnam, CT.

Dave Gold → Queen Kittson Right. Guy stuff.
Location: 84 Shoreline Road. Putnam, CT.

La Lisa → Queen Kittson And by "guy stuff" they mean "playing with toy cars."
Location: Putnam Hyatt. Putnam, CT.

Mad Toy cars!! Awesome! Can I join?
Location: 76 Winthrop Road. Putnam, CT.

Mad But someone would need to come pick me up.
Location: 76 Winthrop Road. Putnam, CT.

Young MacDonald → Mad MADISON, listen to your... brother and just stay where you are. Okay?

Mad → Young MacDonald LAME. But FINE.

Young MacDonald → Dave Gold, King Glen Everyone, please just ignore . . . Madison.
Location: Stubbs Coffee Shop. Putnam, CT.

Mad → Young MacDonald Okay, just for that, you're going to have to buy me some Skittles. FAMILY SIZED Skittles.
Location: 76 Winthrop Road. Putnam, CT.

I leaned back against my chair at Stubbs and took a long sip of my iced latte. Then I turned on Justin's cell phone, took a deep breath, and pulled up his text menu. I was sorely tempted to look at some of his other texts, but restrained myself, feeling like we were already doing enough, with the phone borrowing and identity fudging. Plus, it had made me feel sick when I'd found out that Isabel had been able to see what I'd been doing on my computer. I didn't want to cross that line with Justin.

I began texting on an unfamiliar phone, trying to sound as much like someone else as possible. Because of these reasons, and the fact that my hands were shaking slightly, it took me longer than I'd expected it to. But I finally finished, reading it over several times before sending.

OUTBOX 1 of 15
To: Isabel
Date: 7/1, 4:32 P.M.

Hi Isabel. I was wondering if maybe we could go out tonight? I wanted to talk to you about . . . us. —Justin

The only problem we might run into here was if she saw or talked to him before I sent this. I pulled out my own phone and sent a message on Constellation, to the two people who were serving as our lookouts.

 Young MacDonald → Jimmy+Liz Hey guys. Has anyone visited the First Concession Stand that I should know about? **Location: Stubbs Coffee Shop. Putnam, CT.**

Jimmy+Liz → Young MacDonald You're all clear. Been watching thru the binoculars all morning. (Jimmy)
Location: South Putnam Beach. Putnam, CT.

 Jimmy+Liz → Young MacDonald AND watching the water, don't worry. I've been alternating. (Jimmy)
Location: South Putnam Beach. Putnam, CT.

 Jimmy+Liz You're so good at multitasking, baby! ☺ (Liz)
Location: North Putnam Beach. Putnam, CT.

 Jimmy+Liz Miss you! (Jimmy)
Location: South Putnam Beach. Putnam, CT.

 Young MacDonald → Jimmy+Liz Okay, thanks, guys.
Location: Stubbs Coffee Shop. Putnam, CT.

 Jimmy+Liz → Young MacDonald And Mad—I mean, Mad's brother—are you going to tell us what's going on? (Liz)
Location: North Putnam Beach. Putnam, CT

 Young MacDonald → Jimmy+Liz Soon! Hopefully.
Location: Stubbs Coffee Shop. Putnam, CT.

So the coast—literally, in this case—was clear. I read the text through one more time and pressed SEND. Then I put the phone back in my bag, so I wouldn't stare at it, just waiting for a response and then respond too quickly. And because what I remembered about Justin's texting style was that he would sometimes wait a long time to get back to you. Isabel would undoubtedly know this, and I didn't want to give her even the slightest indication that I was not, in fact, Justin. I gathered up my things, preparing to head to the smoothie shop, when the bell above the Stubbs door rang. I looked up and saw Connor Atkins stepping inside.

I hadn't seen Connor much since he and Schuyler broke up. The two of them seemed to be mutually ignoring each other in the halls, which was absurd, since they both looked equally miserable and unhappy about the breakup.

Connor took off his sunglasses as he walked inside, meeting my eye. He paused for a moment, clearly not sure what to do, then finally nodded at me. I waved and after hesitating a moment, he walked over to where I was sitting. "Hey, Mad," he said.

"Hi, Connor," I said, very glad that I had just hidden the evidence that I had been guilty of identity theft—or, technically, identity borrowing. Connor was the most by-the-book person that I knew, and he would have undoubtedly felt compelled to report it to Justin, the authorities, and anyone else who he felt might have deserved to know. I smiled at him as brightly as possible, trying to pretend that nothing out of the ordinary was going on. "How's it going?"

"Oh, you know," Connor said with a sigh. He shifted from foot to foot and gestured at the couch across from me. "Mind if I . . . ?" he asked.

"Sure," I said, secretly crossing my fingers that we weren't going to have a long chat, since I didn't have time. As he took his seat on the couch, I wondered with a pang if he had any idea that he had chosen to sit in what was always Schuyler's spot.

Connor sighed again, like even the act of sitting had worn him out, which was so out of character—Connor was a one-man high-energy volunteer squad. I leaned forward and saw that he did *not* look good. He looked tired, defeated, and fairly miserable. Much like I had, actually, post-Nate breakup. If I'd only known, we could have formed a support group or something.

"How's Schuyler?" he asked, clearly trying for nonchalance, but not coming close to pulling it off.

I shook my head, getting annoyed. Nate and I weren't together for an actual reason. But the only reason that Schuyler and Connor weren't together was because Schuyler hadn't been honest with him. And thinking of them both alone, and unhappy without the other, was making me mad.

"Connor," I snapped at him, and he looked at me, surprised.

"Yes?" he asked, a little hesitantly.

"Are you dating Roberta Briggs?" I asked, hoping, for Schuyler's sake, that the answer was no.

Connor frowned at me. "No," he said. "Did someone say that I was?"

"I was just wondering," I said quickly. "Are you dating *anyone*?" It was strange to have to ask this question, since normally, I would have just checked Constellation. But Connor wasn't on it any longer, and so I'd lost that resource.

"No," he said, looking slightly offended by my tone. "Why?"

"Schuyler's miserable," I said bluntly. "She misses you. She wants to get back together, but doesn't think you want that."

Connor just blinked at me, and I had a feeling that I'd thrown him for a loop, since he'd probably just expected to get coffee at Stubbs, not an interrogation about his love life and then relationship advice from me. "But . . ." he started.

"If you want to be together, you should be," I said. "Especially if there's no reason for you to be apart." He nodded slowly, apparently thinking this over. I checked the time on my phone and realized that I had to get going. "Sorry if this is none of my business," I said, shouldering my bag and standing up. "I just . . . thought you should know."

"Right," Connor said, still looking a little dazed. "Um, thanks, Mad."

"See you," I said, hoping that this actually would be the case. I gave him a quick smile and headed out of Stubbs, crossing my fingers that this might have done some good.

I stepped out into the late-afternoon sunlight and hurried over to my car, as I was now running late for Phase 2.

CHAPTER 27

Song: The Drama Summer/The Starting Line
Quote: "A good sacrifice is one that is not necessarily sound but leaves your opponent dazed and confused."—Nigel Short

From: Isabel
Date: 7/1, 4:45 P.M.

I would LOVE that. It's about time! ☺ Dinner?

To: Isabel
Date: 7/1, 5:20 P.M.

Sounds good. Stanwich Yacht Club? 7?—Justin

From: Isabel
Date: 7/1, 5:22 P.M.

Yes, that's perfect. You'll make a reservation?

To: Isabel
Date: 7/1, 5:55 P.M.

Okay. See you soon.—Justin

From: Isabel
Date: 7/1, 5:56 P.M.

Looking forward to it! ☺

Pacing in the back alley behind On A Blender, I checked the time and looked around for the reinforcements that were supposed to be on their way. I could feel my pulse racing. It might have had something to do with the sheer amount of caffeine I'd had today, not to mention the smoothies with extra energy powder I'd made myself when I'd arrived at work. I'd taken over so that Daryl and John could make it to their second job on time, since it was crucial for our plans that they not get fired tonight.

I had closed up as usual at six, except for a few small

differences tonight. I had turned the freezer off, and then had locked the front door and exited through the back, making sure to keep the alley door propped open.

I had been sitting on the milk crate until my nervousness had taken over, and I'd started pacing, constantly checking both phones for any sign of change, and getting more and more anxious.

"Hey!" I turned and saw Dave, followed by Turtell and Ruth, heading down from the street and toward the alley. I felt my face relax into a smile. The cavalry, such as it was, had arrived. My phone beeped, and I looked down at it to see the Constellation update that had just been posted.

Aligned: Young MacDonald, Rue, Dave Gold, Justin, and King Glen
Location: On A Blender. Putnam, CT.

"Hi," Ruth said, hurrying up to me and looking, for some reason, happy. Not that this was a problem; it just wasn't what I had expected. "Sorry we're late."

"Yeah," Dave said, glancing at Ruth and Turtell. "There was . . . traffic. Is she here yet?"

"Not yet," I said. "I've been listening for the front bell, and haven't heard it." I looked at the three of them, wondering if I was missing something. They *all* looked a little too happy, considering what was going on. But maybe I had just lost perspective on what normal happiness looked like, during my swan dive into misery.

"Did Isabel take the bait?" Dave asked, and I nodded.

"She's going to be there at seven," I said. "So Kavya

really needs to show up with him . . ." I checked the time once more. "Now."

"I'm sure she'll be here," Turtell said, pulling out his own phone. "Unless she bailed," he added after a moment.

"Don't say that," I said quickly. As I watched Turtell texting—most likely Kittson—I couldn't help notice that his hands were dirty, like he'd been at work. "Glen," I started, "did you—"

"What?" he asked, sounding uncharacteristically nervous. He glanced over at Dave, and I saw his hands and forearms looked equally grimy.

"What were you guys doing this afternoon?" I asked. The boys looked at each other, and I remembered the earlier Constellation updates. "Was there some mini truck repair going on?" I asked.

"Yes," Dave said immediately. "My truck threw a wheel, and Glen lent his expert advice."

"*Shh,*" Ruth said suddenly, holding up her hand. We all fell silent, and sure enough, I could hear the bell over the door of the smoothie shop jangling faintly, and low voices from inside the shop.

I walked up to the back door and eased it open. I could hear Kavya's voice. She was laughing, and it didn't sound faked, either. "So this is where the smoothies get made," she was saying.

"This is great," Justin said back. He sounded happier, and more relaxed, than I'd heard him in a while. "You're sure it's okay that I'm here?"

"Oh, sure," Kavya said. "We practically don't have a

manager. And if you want to learn more about smoothies, I have to give you the full tour, don't I?" Justin laughed, and I felt a tiny stab of guilt. He clearly thought he was on a great first date. I hoped he wouldn't take it too hard when he found out it wasn't real. "So . . . want to check out the *freezer*?" Kavya asked, projecting the last word much louder than the others.

"Oh. Um, sure," Justin said, and I could hear his smile in his voice as he said it.

"Great. So we're *going to the freezer now*," Kavya practically yelled.

I looked at Turtell, Dave, and Ruth, who nodded. Ruth counted out fifteen seconds, then we began moving. I opened the back door and stepped into the brightly colored smoothie shop. Turtell, Dave, and Ruth followed.

I pointed to where the freezer was, then climbed the two steps and stood outside it. The heavy metal door wasn't totally soundproof—I could hear some low laughter from inside. I took a deep breath and pulled the door open.

Inside, Justin and Kavya were standing very close together as she pointed out the rows of slowly thawing fruit to him. Justin had a slightly dazed smile on his face that fell as he turned and saw me. "Madison?" he asked, sounding baffled. His gaze shifted behind me, to where Ruth, Turtell, and Dave were clustered in the doorway. His expression grew even more confused. Which made sense. If you thought you were going to be making out with a hot girl, to have your ex and three of her friends show up was probably not what was expected. "What's going on?" he asked. "I thought you guys were closed."

"We are," I said. "But we're hoping you wouldn't mind, um, hanging out here for a while."

"Well, no," he said, "because that's what we were doing . . ." his voice trailed off and he glanced at Kavya, who had taken a step away from him, and toward the rest of us. "Weren't we?" he asked.

"Not exactly," she said with a shrug. "Sorry."

Justin looked back at me, comprehension slowly dawning. "Now wait just a second," he said.

"Sorry to burst your bubble," Ruth said. "But did you really believe that, out of nowhere, a cute girl would want to make out with you in a freezer?"

"I would," Dave said immediately.

"Me too," Turtell replied. "When miracles start happening to you, don't ever ask why."

"Guys," I said, shaking my head. I had a feeling this wasn't exactly helping.

"Not that you're not totally hot," Kavya piped up. "Because you are. And under normal circumstances . . . I mean, who knows, right? But Madison promised she'd work for me on Friday and every other Tuesday if I helped her out, and that was an offer I just couldn't refuse."

"But . . ." Justin said, looking flabbergasted, from Kavya to the raspberry section and back to me again, ". . . you can't, like, kidnap me."

"Dude," Turtell said, taking a step inside the freezer and standing next to me. I noticed that his voice had gotten a lot lower, "nobody's kidnapping anyone. You came

284

here of your own free will, walked into the freezer voluntarily, and then the lock happened to malfunction." Turtell cracked his knuckles and raised an eyebrow. "You got me?"

"But . . ." Justin said, looking more confused than ever.

"Sorry about this," I said, and meaning it. Justin had crossed over to the dark side when he'd joined Isabel, but I was sure that nobody liked to spend time in a freezer involuntarily, even if the freezer was turned off. "It'll just be for a little while. It's crucial to the next part of the plan that Isabel think you're about to meet her at the Stanwich Yacht Club."

Justin blinked, and looked around at all of us. "Are you serious?" he asked.

Dave nodded. "Afraid so," he said. "But I promise it will be painless." He looked hard at Turtell, who grumbled but stopped cracking his knuckles.

"We wouldn't do this unless it was necessary," Ruth added. "But people's futures are on the line here."

"So this is actually happening?" Justin asked. He glared at me. "I can't believe you would do something like this, Madison."

"Well, I can't believe you would team up with Isabel to hurt me," I shot back, hearing my voice tremble. "Do you have any idea how hard she's worked to ruin my life? And you *helped* her."

Justin opened his mouth to say something, but nothing came. After a second, he broke our eye contact and looked away, his expression troubled—with more, it seemed, than just why he was being held in a freezer against his will.

Before I could say anything else, I heard the bell over the front door jingle. All of us in the freezer, well, froze. "Kavya," I said, in a much lower volume than I had just been using.

"The door," Kavya said, snapping her fingers. "I knew there was something. I was supposed to lock it again, wasn't I?"

"Hello?" the voice—it sounded vaguely familiar—called from the front of the store. It seemed to be what we needed to snap back into motion again.

"Hey!" Justin yelled. He took a step toward the door, just as Dave and Turtell stepped in front of him, blocking his path. I hustled around the boys, and Ruth and I both stepped out into the hallway. I caught Turtell's eye and he nodded, and I pushed the heavy silver door closed and turned the lock. I could hear muffled voices coming from the freezer, but I hoped that they wouldn't be audible to whoever had decided that they needed a smoothie *right now*.

I looked at Ruth, and she gave me a nod and a tiny, encouraging smile as we walked down to the main counter area—where Tricia, of all people, was waiting.

"Hi," she stammered, staring at me. She glanced at Ruth, and her expression became, for a second, almost as confused as Justin's.

"Um, hi, Tricia," I replied, not quite able to stop myself from looking back to the freezer. Feeling like we really hadn't needed this tonight, I turned back to her, hoping she wouldn't wonder why I was wearing a black tank top and black jeans, and not a T-shirt that read *Blender Bias*. "I'm sorry, but we're actually closed," I said. "I just hadn't . . . um . . . locked the door yet."

"No," she said, still looking lost. Then she cleared her throat and seemed to regroup a little. "I mean, I didn't want a smoothie," she said. "I just saw on Constellation that Ruth and Glen and Dave were all here, and I was in the neighborhood, so I thought I'd drop in."

I glanced at Ruth, who bit her lip. "Yes," I said quickly. "They were just keeping me company while I closed up. And Glen and Dave are, um . . ." I paused for just a second, trying to come up with some reason why their phones had them here but they didn't appear to be physically present.

"In the freezer," Ruth added quickly. "Getting some . . . fruit."

At that moment, the muffled voices from inside the freezer became raised, and Tricia looked back toward it.

"That's them," I said quickly.

Tricia nodded, but her eyes lingered on the freezer for another second before she turned to me. "I didn't expect to see you, Madison," she said, her brow slightly furrowed. "I thought I saw a Constellation update that you were at home. And playing some Grand Theft Auto?"

"Right," I said, my mind racing. "That. Yes. I was. I just love those, you know, video games. But then my coworker got, um, busy, so I had to fill in."

"Well," Tricia said, looking at me for a moment before smiling wide. "I'm so glad that everyone is friends again!

I thought that you'd left us forever! But I guess you're hanging out again?"

"Yes," I said, forcing a smile, hoping she wasn't mad that I hadn't called her to tell her I was now friends with everyone again. "It's kind of a long story. . . ."

Tricia nodded, but she looked around the shop again, like she was trying to find something. "I also thought I saw that Justin Williamson was here," she said in a voice that sounded like it was trying a little too hard to be casual.

I thought with a sudden knot in my stomach about Justin's phone in my pocket, and how it had aligned with everyone else's. I took a breath, thinking about how I could spin this somehow, when Ruth spoke.

"Are you friends with Justin?" she asked Tricia, her eyebrows raised. I looked over at her and saw what I knew all too well as her "scientist expression." She had encountered an anomaly and would not let it go until she discovered the answer. "I'm surprised you know him."

Tricia blinked once, then cleared her throat. "I don't," she said quickly. "I just . . . um . . . think he's cute, so I follow him on Constellation. That's all. Don't tell, okay?" she asked, giving us a smile. "So is he here?"

"No," I said quickly. "I mean, he was, but he just left."

"Oh," she said, nodding. "Got it."

Ruth met my eyes, and we had a moment of non-verbal communication, with her asking me, *How are we going to get rid of Tricia?* and me replying, *I have no idea. But OMFG.*

"Well," I said, glancing down at my phone, all too

aware that time was ticking by, and I really needed to be getting on with Phase 3, "I should probably close up."

"Right!" Tricia said, giving me another smile. "Well, Madcap, I'm just so glad you're back!"

"I know," I said, just as another muffled voice sounded from the freezer. Tricia frowned, looking over at it again, and I took a small step to the right, trying to block her field of vision. "I would have called but things have been . . . crazy," I said.

"I'm sure," she said, looking back to me sympathetically. "Do you want to talk about it?"

"That's okay," I said, keeping a smile on my face, but wondering where this was coming from. I liked Tricia, but we didn't exactly share our deep feelings. I was suddenly starting to understand Lisa's "clingy" comment.

"Well, I just want you to know that if you want to talk about it, Mad—" Tricia started, when the bell above the door jangled again. I looked over and saw Sarah Donner, also dressed all in black, standing in the doorway.

"Sarah?" I asked, unable to fathom what she was doing there.

"Hey," she said, walking toward the counter. "I was just—" She stopped when she saw Tricia, and frowned, as though trying to place her.

Tricia had turned pale when she'd seen Sarah, and seemed to now be looking very fixedly at the ground. "This is Tricia Evans," I said to Sarah, "and that's Sarah Donner."

"Hi," Sarah said, trying to get a closer look at Tricia,

who seemed to be looking anywhere but at Sarah.

"Hey," she murmured. "You know, I've got to get going. Bye, Ruth. See you, Mad." Tricia said this very fast, and still mostly looking at the floor. As I watched, trying to figure out what was happening, she turned and hustled out the door.

I waited until the door had closed behind her and Tricia was out of sight before I turned to Ruth. "Close one," I said.

"Yeah," she agreed, still looking at where Tricia had gone, frowning slightly.

"Hey, guys!" Sarah said, leaning over the counter and giving me a hug, then giving Ruth one. Theater kids hug a *lot*, even, apparently, when school is no longer in session.

"Sarah, what are you doing here?" I asked.

Sarah shook her head dramatically, as was her custom. But I was happy to see that, even after being immersed in a theater camp, she hadn't reverted to wearing overalls and a bandanna. "They were stifling my creative vision at that camp," she said. "And I will not work where my creative vision is being stifled! It's just—"

"No," I said quickly. "I mean, what are you doing *here*?"

"Mark said something was going on tonight," she said. "You know," she said, raising a conspiratorial eyebrow at me, "something on the *down low*. And then I saw on Constellation that Ruth and Glen and Dave had all aligned here, so I thought I'd drop by. I thought you might need my help!"

"That's really nice of you to offer, Sarah," I said, wondering what part of "confidential" and "let's not tell Sarah" Mark had had trouble grasping. "But . . ."

"It's kind of complicated," Ruth finished, glancing at me.

At that moment, more muffled voices came from the freezer. Sarah looked at us, eyebrows raised. I sighed and decided just to tell her, figuring that if Mark had already spilled most of the beans, there was no point in trying to cover up what was happening. "Here's the thing," I said. "Justin Williamson's in the freezer."

It was maybe a mark of how much we'd all been through together that Sarah didn't ask why one of the most popular guys in school was currently in the walk-in freezer. Or if this was a good idea. Or even if the freezer was off. Instead, she just nodded. "Gotcha," she said. "So what's going on? Can I help?"

"Yes," I said, realizing that we needed to prevent more customers from wandering in. "Could you lock the front door?"

"On it," she said, heading toward the door as Ruth and I walked up the stairs to the freezer and unlocked it.

"Madison, you're running late for Phase 3," Ruth said, looking at her watch.

"I know," I said, heading to the freezer, well aware that I had a narrow window of time. I was especially nervous about this part of the plan, since it was contingent on the participation of people who occasionally couldn't remember my name and had irrational phobias about berries.

291

I pulled open the walk-in. Turtell and Dave were clustered by the door, talking intensely about something, and stopped immediately when they saw me. Justin was sitting on the floor by the boxes of energy powders, with Kavya sitting next to him. And even though the freezer was a pretty small space for four people to share, they seemed to be sitting *very* close together.

Justin looked up at me as the door opened. "Can I leave now?" he asked, even though, maybe due to the fact that Kavya was in such close proximity, he made no move to get up.

"Almost," I said. I looked at Dave and Turtell, and tipped my head toward the door. They followed me out, and I looked back at Kavya, who was also making no move to leave the freezer.

"I think I'll stay and keep Justin company," she said, moving even closer and brushing an invisible piece of lint from his shirt. "He's having such a traumatic evening, after all."

I rolled my eyes at that, but couldn't help noticing that Justin no longer looked at all upset about being there. Dave and Turtell stepped outside, and I closed the door behind them. I started to lock it, but Dave shook his head.

"I don't think that's necessary, Mad," he said. "That guy's not going anywhere."

I looked back at the closed freezer door and realized that now I couldn't hear anything—not even any voices. "Really?" I asked, looking back to Dave.

"Oh, yeah," Turtell said as he walked down the

steps. "The makeout vibes in there were crazy. They both totally wanted us to leave. Except, you know, we were locked in."

"Hey, guys!" Sarah said as we all arrived back behind the counter. "I came to help. I hear that there's a operation going on tonight."

"We'll explain," Ruth said quickly, before either of the boys could launch into an explanation. "Mad, you really have to leave."

I checked the time and saw that she was right. "Crap," I muttered, heading for the side door. "I'll text when we're set and you can let Justin out," I said as I hopped over the counter.

"Good luck," Turtell said.

"I second that," Ruth said. "You'll be great."

"Thanks, guys," I said, reaching for the doorknob.

"Mad," Sarah called, and I looked back at her. "That girl who was here," she said, "looked *really* familiar. But I can't place her. And I could have sworn her name wasn't Tricia, either."

"Probably from the prom," I started, as Ruth checked her watch again.

"I'll fill Sarah in," she said. "You have to *go*, Mad."

"Gotcha," I said. "I'll see you guys a little later." Everyone nodded, even Sarah, who had apparently decided she was in on this plan, despite not knowing what it involved. I started to head out the door, but turned back when I realized that none of them were talking. Everyone just smiled at me and waved. I smiled back, and pushed through the door, trying to shake the very odd feeling

I'd just had. It was almost like they'd been waiting for me to leave before telling Sarah what was going on.

But that didn't make any sense. And I didn't have time to try and figure out alternate scenarios now. I speed-walked to Judy, started the engine, and pulled out onto Putnam Avenue, aiming the car toward the Stanwich Yacht Club.

CHAPTER 28

Song: Losing Keys/Jack Johnson
Quote: "Never interrupt your enemy when he is
making a mistake." — Napoleon Bonaparte

 Justin Dinner at the Stanwich Yacht Club. I'm excited.
And also, hungry.
Location: Stanwich Yacht Club. Stanwich, CT.

I swerved into the employee parking lot of the Stanwich
Yacht Club at five minutes to seven, hoping against hope
that Isabel had not already arrived. Thankfully, I hadn't
had any problems getting in, as the TV-watching guard
at the employee entrance had only glanced at Schuyler's
hangtag and waved me through without question.

I put Judy in park and pulled out my phone, ready to
call John, hoping that I hadn't missed the window. But
before I could dial him, the phone rang with an incoming call, from Daryl. I answered, but didn't say anything,
hoping that Daryl would have remembered to put the
phone in his shirt pocket and *not* his pants pocket (there

had been some confusion over this when we'd been going over the plan).

"Welcome to the Stanwich Yacht Club," I heard John say. His voice was slightly muffled, but I could still make out what was being said. "May I take your car?"

Despite the circumstances, I felt myself smile at that, as it seemed like maybe he was getting the lingo of the two jobs mixed up.

"Be careful with it," I heard a familiar voice snap. "The last time I picked it up from valet, there were all these *scratches* on it."

It was unmistakably Isabel. I sank down lower in my seat, as though she could somehow see me, even though the employee parking lot was on the other side of the club from the valet area.

"Bummer," I heard Daryl say, his voice much clearer than John's had been. "Did you park it next to a bush or something?"

"Not scratches from me," Isabel said, and it was like I could practically see her rolling her eyes as she said it. "Scratches from *you*."

"Me?" Daryl asked, sounding surprised. "What did I do?"

"Not you, specifically," Isabel said, and I could hear the frustration rising in her voice. "I meant from the valets in general. So be careful with it. Okay?"

"Okey-doke," Daryl said.

"You got it," John said. Then I heard the sound of doors opening and closing, and the sound of a car moving.

"Guys?" I asked, after there had been silence for a

few seconds and I was pretty sure they were alone.

"Hey, Mad," John said. "You know, that girl is not very nice."

"Tell me about it," I said.

"Well," Daryl started. "First, she was all blaming me for the fact that she parked next to a tree or something, and then—"

"I didn't need you to actually tell me about it," I said, jumping in before Daryl could keep going. "Because I could hear it all, remember?"

"Then why did she ask?" I heard John mutter.

"Guys," I said, getting a little worried that I hadn't seen them yet, "you are coming to the employee parking lot, remember? Not the valet drop?" There was a worrying pause.

"Oh, right," John said after a moment. "Totally. We're heading there now. Just give us a second to, you know, turn around."

"See you in five!" Daryl said, and the line went dead.

I put my phone on the seat next to me, and placed Justin's next to that. I had been worried that Isabel might have called before now to check in, but luckily there hadn't been any communication from her after the final text.

As I watched in my side-view mirror, a low-slung red sports car veered into the employee parking lot and parked in the space next to my driver's side. I rolled down my window, and the passenger-side window rolled down as well.

"Hey, Mad," Daryl whispered. The engine of the car

stopped, and through the window, I could see John hand Daryl the keys. Daryl held them out the passenger-side window, and I reached out and took them.

Heart hammering, I turned on my car's interior light and flipped through the contents of the key ring. There was a leather key fob, the car key, what looked like a house key . . . and a flash drive. I let out a long breath as I looked at it, relief flooding over me. Our whole plan hinged on this flash drive, and I was just glad Ruth had been able to figure out where it most likely was. And that the valets that Stanwich Yacht Club employed were not above being bribed with munchies.

I slipped the flash drive off Isabel's key ring and looked at it. It was silver, and unremarkable. The one I had to substitute for it was slightly smaller, but I was betting on the fact that Isabel wouldn't notice. I threaded the replacement onto the key ring, placing the real one carefully in my purse. I passed the keys back to Daryl, along with a huge bag of Fritos.

"Oh, awesome!" Daryl said. "Thanks, Mad!" Daryl passed the keys to John, but the car didn't start up again.

"Guys?" I asked. I could see John frowning down at the dashboard.

"Just a second," he said. "I think the car might have automatically locked when I took out the keys. And with some of these, the alarms go off because of the smallest things. And it would be uncool if the alarms went off now."

"Yeah," I murmured as my heart began to beat faster.

It would be very uncool if an alarm went off, since Daryl and John were currently on the other side of the country club from the valet drop. I had a feeling if alarms started going off, there might be some questions to answer—not the least of which would be where the Fritos had come from.

"Okay, let me try this," John said. I held my breath, and a moment later, the car started up again, without a problem.

"We're good," Daryl said, giving me a thumbs-up out the window.

John shook his head, but he looked very relieved. "These people with the security. But it makes sense. I mean, you want to protect what's most important to you, right?" I nodded, even though something he had said was starting to ring a bell for me.

"Thanks a million, guys," I said. "See you at work."

"See you!" Daryl called. A moment later, the car roared to life and peeled out of the employee parking lot at what was probably a much faster speed than Isabel would have been comfortable with.

I turned off the interior light and started Judy up, checking the time on my dashboard. I had about fifteen minutes, and I wanted to get as far away from the Stanwich Yacht Club as possible in that time.

****

I had managed to make it to Putnam High School in record time—and, well, by speeding a little. I pulled into the parking lot by the sports fields, put the car in park, and killed my engine. Then, using Justin's phone, I dialed Isabel's number.

"Hi," she said right away, managing to sound equal parts relieved and annoyed. Without waiting for a response, she jumped right in. "Justin, where are you? I saw on Constellation that you're here, so it's ridiculous that you haven't gotten to the restaurant yet. Did you get lost or something? I have just been *waiting* here. Did you not make a reservation? Because they don't have a record of it, and at this point—"

"Sorry," I cut in, and I could hear Isabel draw in a sharp, surprised breath. "Actually, it's Madison. I hate to be the bearer of bad news, but Justin's not going to be able to make it tonight."

"How do you have Justin's phone?" Isabel asked after a moment, her voice clipped.

"It seems," I said, remembering her earlier phrasing, "that he should really learn not to leave his phone lying around when he's at work."

"What do you want, Madison?" Isabel asked, and I could hear a low, simmering anger in her voice.

"I'm going to have to renegotiate the terms of our agreement," I said. "If you wouldn't mind meeting me on the lacrosse field at Putnam High School, I'll explain it all to you." And then, before she could say anything else, I hung up.

CHAPTER 29

Song: Alter The Ending/Dashboard Confessional
Quote: "You have learned something. That always feels at first as if you had lost something."—H. G. Wells

 Young MacDonald Got it. Just arrived back at rendezvous point.
Location: Putnam High School. Putnam, CT.

 Rue Can we open up the freezer?
Location: On A Blender Smoothie Shop. Putnam, CT.

 Young MacDonald Let my people go! And if you could turn off lights & lock up?
Location: Putnam High School. Putnam, CT.

 Rue Of course. SYS.
Location: On A Blender Smoothie Shop. Putnam, CT.

 darylparksthecars Fritos are the best food EVER. I think they should get their own food group. I mean, right?
Location: Stanwich Yacht Club. Stanwich, CT.

As I waited for tech support to arrive, I sat on Judy's back bumper, thinking. Something John had said was reverberating in my head. It touched on a part of this scheme that had been bothering me, just a little, since this whole thing had started.

Dell had told me once, right after my hacking, that he had crazy password protections in place on his computers. And John, in his infinite stoner wisdom, had been right—people do protect the things that were most important to them.

So how had Isabel been able to gain access to Dell's computer—and then take something off it, apparently without him even finding out?

It didn't add up. As Ham had said in our production of *Great Dane: The Musical Tragedy of Hamlet*, something was rotten in the state of Denmark (Kansas).

I pulled out my phone and called Kittson, knowing that the clock was ticking. "What's wrong?" she answered, not bothering with a greeting. Not that I minded—it was that kind of night.

"Maybe nothing," I said, keeping my eyes fixed on the entrance to the parking lot, knowing that Dell was due to arrive any minute. "But are you still at home?"

"I was just heading out," she said. "What do you need?"

"Got your laptop close by?" I asked.

"Of course," she said, and a moment later, I could hear the clacking of keys. "Why?"

"Ready to prove to Dell that you can do what he can't?" I asked. "It's going to have to be fast." I explained

302

as quickly as possible, and as I did, I could hear the sound of keys clacking getting faster and faster. By the time I'd finished, I saw a pair of headlights swinging into the parking lot. "He's here," I said. "I need to go. Is this possible?"

"Of course," she said. "But I'm going to need a few minutes. Stall, okay?"

I watched as the SUV got closer to me, feeling like I'd done the right thing. Because even though he had shown up—when Lisa was sure that he wouldn't—I still wasn't entirely sure we could trust him. "Thanks, Kittson," I said.

"See you soon," she said, and hung up, just as Dell parked his SUV in the space next to Judy.

Dell climbed down from the driver's seat as I got out of my car and walked around to his passenger's side. I opened the passenger-side door and got in the backseat, which was absolutely enormous. And, unlike Judy's much more modest backseat, it would give us room to work.

"Hey," I said as I slammed the door behind me.

"Good evening," Dell said, looking up from where he'd already opened his laptop and shooting me a small, rare smile. "Everything going according to plan?"

"So far," I said. I was slowly becoming aware that the inside of the car smelled overly woodsy, like there was a small pine forest growing in the back. And this car was massive enough that it might have been a possibility. I looked around for an air freshener, but didn't see one. I turned to Dell, realizing that he was the one who

303

smelled like a lumberjack. "Are you wearing cologne?" I asked.

Dell, lit by the light of his computer screen, flushed bright red. "Maybe," he muttered. "Anyway. That's neither here nor there. Did you get it?"

"I did," I said, reaching into my purse and pulling out the flash drive. I opened my palm and showed it to him, but didn't hand it over yet. I couldn't help but notice, though, that his eyes gleamed a little as he looked at it.

"Well?" he asked, reaching out for it. My phone beeped with a text, and I glanced down at it.

INBOX 1 of 40
From: Kittson
Date: 7/1, 7:36 P.M.

I'm in.

I looked up at Dell and handed him the flash drive. "Here," I said. Dell inserted it into his laptop, and a moment later, looked over at me with a smile.

"It's here," he said. "The folders that she gave you, plus the file on Nate."

I let out a long breath. "Anything else?" I asked. Dell looked at me sharply over his laptop, then back down at the screen again.

"No," he said. "Why?"

"Just wondering," I said. "And the Nate file can't be copied, right?"

"I told you that," Dell said, sounding annoyed. "It's

either on the drive or on my desktop, but it can't be both places."

"And it's still on the flash drive?" I asked. Dell nodded. "Great," I said. I held out my hand for it. "Time to destroy the evidence."

Dell raised an eyebrow at me. "Very smart," he said. He typed rapidly for a moment, then handed me the drive. "When's she going to be here?"

I checked the time on my phone. "Probably five minutes," I said. Dell nodded and kept on typing, a small smile on his face. I looked at him closely, and after a moment he seemed to sense this and looked up at me.

"What?" he asked, sounding a little nervous.

"Nothing," I said as I started to slide toward the door. "Are you hanging around?"

"I thought I might," he said. "You know. See if . . . people . . . show up."

I had a feeling that by "people" he meant "Peyton," and that she was the reason that he currently smelled like a redwood forest. My phone rang as I climbed down from Dell's SUV, feeling like I really could have used a ladder, and I answered it as I dropped to the ground. "Hello?" I asked.

"Is this Madison?" the voice, which I recognized as Sarah's, asked. "Because Ruth told me that your brother has your phone, or something, and to call this number . . ."

"It's me," I said. "What's going on?"

"I'm on my way over to the high school," Sarah said, "but I needed to talk to you now. I remembered why that girl Tricia looked so familiar. And I talked to Zach, and he confirmed it."

"Confirmed what?" I asked, feeling myself get increasingly nervous.

"Listen to this," Sarah said. I heard her take a deep breath, and then she told me. As I listened in stunned silence, I had to restrain myself for the second time that day from smashing my brother's cell phone. "I just thought you needed to know," she said when she'd finished.

"Thanks for telling me," I said, a little hollowly. I hung up with Sarah and stared, unseeing, across the fields, leaning back against Judy. I was feeling totally betrayed—once again. My brain started to make half-hearted attempts at a way to deal with this, but I wasn't sure I had the energy anymore.

I was just sick of it. Sick of the fact that this had been happening since *April*. And that, always, it seemed to come down to secrets. Secrets that I'd told to other people, which were then used to hurt and alienate my friends in my hacking. Schuyler's secret that had led to the whole prom debacle and her breakup with Connor. And now, all our secrets—mine, Nate's, my friends'—being held against us as leverage. I hated it, but wasn't sure what could be done about it.

Totally unexpectedly, something Daryl had said came back to me. Maybe these secrets only had this power because they were, in fact, secrets. And maybe Rosa was right, and the truth would set you free.

And just like that, I had an idea.

I thought about what it would mean. It would be a big step, one that would change all our lives massively, and one that I couldn't even have fathomed a few days ago. But there was also something a little exciting about that. Mostly scary, but also the tiniest bit exciting.

I pulled out my phone and updated my status, knowing it would be the last time.

 Young MacDonald ATTENTION EVERYONE. It's time to come clean, ASAP. And then jump ship.
Location: Putnam High School. Putnam, CT.

CHAPTER 30

Song: Better Than Revenge/Taylor Swift
Quote: "I count him braver who overcomes his desires than him who conquers his enemies; for the hardest victory is over self."—Aristotle

By the time the now-familiar sports car pulled into the parking lot, we had assembled on the lacrosse field. Not everyone had been happy about the change we were all making, but everyone had finally been able to see that it was probably the only thing to do, especially once Sarah had explained about the Tricia situation.

The hardest part had probably been the confessions. We'd had to do them fast, which actually made them easier. Schuyler had talked to all of us, Sarah had called Zach, Ruth had called Andy, and Kittson and Turtell had stepped apart from the rest of us and had what looked like an intense conversation. When they rejoined the group, Turtell looked subdued, and Kittson looked like she'd been crying, but they were still holding hands tightly, and she'd given me a small nod when we'd made eye contact.

We were now standing in a lopsided semicircle, everyone present and accounted for, except Dave. Lisa assured me that he was coming, just *un peu un retard*, as he was running an errand. This struck me as strange, and also as terrible planning, but there didn't seem to be anything to do about it now. Dell was standing next to Peyton, and despite the fact that he smelled like the olfactory representation of the Brawny paper towel guy, Peyton wasn't moving away—or even downwind—from him.

Before everyone else had arrived, I had made absolutely sure to destroy Isabel's evidence against Nate. I'd put the flash drive under Judy's back wheel and had run over it until it was nothing but shards of glass and metal, the information forever destroyed. But even so, just in case, I'd collected those shards and thrown them away in three separate trash cans.

"Mad," Mark said to me as Isabel emerged from her car and started walking toward us. "I'm nawt sure I'm going to be able to stap tawking like this." It seemed that Mark's bad accent had decided to make a reappearance.

"It's okay," I said, giving him a quick smile.

"Lovely use of assonance," Sarah gushed. "Can you do a good Will Hunting? Maybe give us a little less Harvard, a little more Southie?"

"Why are you encouraging this?" Peyton asked.

"He's an *actor*," Sarah explained in a this-should-be-obvious voice. "It's part of his *craft*."

"Guys," Turtell said in a low, warning voice.

Isabel was now just a few feet from us. I could see that she was thrown by the sheer number of people standing in front of her. She'd probably expected to just deal with me, not me and my backup. When she reached us, she stood several feet away.

"Well," she said frostily, crossing her arms over her chest. "Looks like the gang's all here." She scanned the group, and I saw her expression change to one of genuine surprise. "Frank?" she asked, sounding stunned. "What are you doing here?"

"Hello, Isabel," he replied, as deadpan as ever. "I just thought I'd help Madison get back what you took from me."

Isabel seemed unnerved by this, and glanced back to her car before focusing on me. "So it seems like you've chosen to break our arrangement, Madison," she said as she glanced around at my friends. "I must say, I'm surprised. I thought you were willing to do *anything* for your friends."

"Oh, I am," I assured her. "But the thing is, they're also willing to do anything for me."

Isabel narrowed her eyes at me, as if trying to figure out what I meant. But after a moment, she just shook her head. "Well, then, you should know that this is going to have consequences. And they're going to be worse than you imagined. I know much more about you and your little gang than was in those folders. And if you think I'm not going to make the information public, you're crazy."

"How did you get that information?" Kittson asked, almost conversationally.

"Funny you should ask," Isabel said, and I could tell she was enjoying this. She pulled out her phone and sent a quick text. A moment later, from the parking lot, the passenger-side door of her car opened. A figure emerged from it and began walking toward us.

It was Tricia.

Even though Sarah had told me who she really was, it was still a little jarring to see her stand next to Isabel. She had lost her perpetually smiling demeanor and her expression was now serious—and a little bit nervous.

"So this is Beatrice," Isabel said, smiling at her, and then turning to us. "My best friend."

Lisa glared at Tricia. "You borrowed my pink shirt last week," she said coldly. "I want it back, and *maintenant*. And *dry-cleaned*."

Isabel seemed a little stunned that this was the reaction to her bombshell. "You're not upset?" she asked, looking around at us and frowning.

"*Oui*, I'm upset," Lisa said scathingly. "It was my favorite pink shirt."

"Sarah told us who you were an hour ago," I said to Tricia. "She recognized you from the prom."

When Sarah had told me, I had remembered that my computer had started acting weird well before I'd inserted Isabel's flash drive. It had started right after I'd clicked on Tricia's mysterious link. And this explained a lot of other things, too—like how she'd seen—and copied—my eyeliner. How Kittson's secret had gotten out. I turned to Isabel and shook my head, appalled. "Seriously, you sent a spy?"

"Not just a spy," Isabel said, clearly trying to regroup. "I had a feeling you wouldn't be able to survive without your precious friends for long. And I wanted to know when that happened so I could make sure to enact the consequences for such actions."

"And what consequences are those?" Schuyler asked, glaring at Isabel.

"Madison should keep you better informed," she said patronizingly. "I have information on all of you that's going to be posted on your Friendverse pages, Constellation feeds, you name it. It's going to be *everywhere*."

"But none of us are friends with you," Kittson said. "Because we all have taste." She looked over at Mark and sighed. "Mostly."

"I was aware of that," Isabel said. "Which is precisely why Tricia was imperative. Because *she's* friends with all of you."

"Good plan," I said, nodding. "Seriously. Mad props. Well thought out, devious, manipulative. You got the trifecta. And it almost worked."

"Almost?" Tricia asked, frowning at me.

"Close," Mark confirmed, "but no cigah."

"There's one major flaw in your plan," I said. I looked around at my friends, and everyone pulled out their phones again. I nodded and pressed SEND on the text to Travis that contained only one word—*Now*. As I watched, everyone hit the button on their own phones.

And just like that, an era was over.

"What flaw would that be?" Isabel asked, smirking.

"You might want to check Tricia's Constellation feed," I said. "Or Status Q, or Friendverse. Because none of us are there anymore."

Isabel narrowed her eyes at me, then held out her hand for Tricia's phone. I looked down at my own feed, still a little unable to believe what I was seeing.

 Mad THIS USER HAS LEFT THIS SITE.

 Rue THIS USER HAS LEFT THIS SITE.

 Queen Kittson THIS USER HAS LEFT THIS SITE.

 Dave Gold THIS USER HAS LEFT THIS SITE.

 King Glen THIS USER HAS LEFT THIS SITE.

La Lisa THIS USER HAS LEFT THIS SITE.

Schuyler THIS USER HAS LEFT THIS SITE.

 Lord Rothschild THIS USER HAS LEFT THIS SITE.

 Peyton's Place THIS USER HAS LEFT THIS SITE.

 Sarah♥Zach THIS USER HAS LEFT THIS SITE.

dudeyouregettingame THIS USER HAS LEFT THIS SITE.

Isabel looked up from her phone, mouth open. "You can't just leave," she said, a little faintly. "I mean . . ."

"You know, it seems we can," Kittson said. "Sorry to disappoint you."

"I still know your secrets," Isabel shot back at Kittson. "Like, have you told your *boyfriend* about what you did in the Hamptons?"

I felt my heart begin to beat faster at that, but Kittson just took a step closer to Glen, and he put his arm around her shoulders. "Of course," she said.

Isabel's jaw dropped, and she looked around, a little desperately. "I can tell you what Schuyler did," she said, clearly grasping at straws. "At boarding school. She . . ."

"I already told them," Schuyler said, her voice clear and confident. She took a tiny step toward Isabel, and I was thrilled to see Isabel take a step back. "And you know what? They didn't care."

"And," Peyton said, taking a step closer as well, "if you ever try and threaten my stepsister again, you are going to be very, very sorry."

Isabel glanced at Tricia, whose mouth had fallen open. Isabel looked back at us, and then gave a few small claps.

"Well, congratulations to the Scooby gang," she said. "So you managed to get around this. So what? This was never what it was about. It was just a bonus." She turned to me, a cold, confident smile on her face. "I hope you can live with the fact that you've just wrecked your boyfriend's life." Her smile widened after she said this. "Oops, I think I mean *ex*-boyfriend, don't I? When I come forward with the information I have on Nate—"

"You don't," Dell said, and Isabel stopped short, frowning at him.

"What do you mean?" she asked.

"I mean you don't have the information," he said, as Isabel shook her head and dug in her purse, pulling out her keys triumphantly.

"I keep it with me at all times," she said. "So there's no way that you've gotten to it."

"You might want to check your flash drive," I said. "I have a feeling you might be surprised."

Isabel turned the flash drive over in her hands and

looked up at me. "How did you do it?" she asked, her voice low and angry.

"You should be nicer to your valets," I said. "They'll sometimes do favors for you."

"If there's nothing else," Ruth said after a moment in which Isabel had simply opened and closed her mouth a few times, as if searching for words to say, "I think we should get going."

"I can still tell them about Nate," Isabel said to me, her voice desperate. "The mascot costume still hasn't been returned. And if I can describe what I saw on the tape, my headmistress will listen to me, and . . ."

I lost whatever Isabel said next. Because a very strange sight was approaching from the parking lot.

A wooden Trojan horse, apparently of its own accord, was wheeling toward us.

CHAPTER 31

Song: Gamble Everything For Love/Ben Lee
Quote: "In a series of events, all of which had been a bit thick, this, in his opinion, achieved the maximum of thickness."—P. G. Wodehouse

The horse was large, almost real-horse size, and made of wood. There were two large wooden wheels at the base, but these weren't even turning. I noticed that there was a metal plate stretched under these, and there seemed to be a second set of wheels moving the horse forward over the grass slowly. As I watched it jerking forward, the tiny motor revving, it struck me that something about it looked very familiar. And just like that, I had a feeling I knew why Dave wasn't with us at the moment.

"What is that?" Schuyler asked. She looked around at us. "Other people see that, right?"

"It's the Hartfield mascot costume," Sarah said. "I recognize it from Zach's yearbook. They're the Trojans."

I now knew why Nate had laughed when we'd been watching *Troy*. A moment later, a second, much bigger realization crashed over me. This was the mascot costume that Nate had helped, um, borrow during the senior prank. And here it was. Did that mean . . . *could* it mean that Nate was somehow involved now? That he knew something about what was happening? A tiny ember of hope flared to life, and I could feel my heart start to beat a little bit faster.

"Where did that come from?" Isabel snapped, as the horse rolled right up to her. "Who is controlling it?"

"And since when is it motorized?" Tricia asked, sounding puzzled.

"Since Dave and I added some Hot Wheelz to it," Turtell said, sounding inordinately proud of himself. "And thanks to a little thing called welding."

As I looked at the horse, I put it together—the reason that both Turtell and Dave had had grease stains on their hands earlier.

"Baby," Kittson said to Turtell, sounding genuinely impressed, "you're so *talented*."

"*Someone* tell me what is happening," Isabel snapped, her voice verging on hysterical.

"Well," Ruth said, after a pause in which it became clear that nobody was going to volunteer for this job, "it looks like you've gotten your mascot costume back. And since it showed up at Putnam, I would say that it pretty much clears anyone from Stanwich, wouldn't you?"

Tricia looked skeptically at the horse, which rolled backward, and then toward her, causing her to yelp and jump away. "Maybe we should go," she said. "This is getting weird."

"No," Isabel said, looking from the horse to all of us. "*NO*. I have worked too hard to just walk away from this."

From the distance of the parking lot, I could hear the faint sound of a car door slamming. After a moment, I heard a second door slam, but couldn't see the actual car, and had no idea who had arrived.

"I mean," Isabel said slowly, "just because the mascot is here doesn't mean anything. It might never make it to Hartfield. It might get accidentally broken on the way. And then Madison's ex-boyfriend wouldn't be off the hook after all."

Ruth glanced toward the parking lot. I looked over as well and saw one figure heading toward us, but wasn't able to make out who it was. "I think you've done enough," she said. "Let it go, Isabel."

"I will *not* let it go," Isabel spat. "Madison humiliated me in front of my entire school, and I am not going to forget it. And you're not going to convince me to." She turned to me and shot me a furious glare. "This is *just* beginning, Madison. Just watch. I am going to find a way to hurt you, and if you don't believe me . . ."

"I don't, actually," a voice said from behind Isabel. I looked and saw that it was Dave, a black controller in his hand.

"And what does that mean?" Isabel asked. She was clearly trying for bravado, but looked undeniably shaken.

Out of the corner of my eye, I saw Sarah take out her phone and start texting.

"Well," Dave said, piloting the horse so it spun

around and wheeled over to arrive by his side, "I think that you're going to agree to walk away from this and leave Madison—and *all* of us—alone. Forever."

"And why would I do that?" Isabel asked, arching an eyebrow, but she sounded much less confident now. It was like she was realizing we had many more people—and a really big horse—on our side, and she just had Tricia. And Tricia, since Dave had shown up, had started edging slowly away from Isabel, like she wanted to distance herself from the whole situation.

"Because of this," Dave said, holding up his phone, which was playing a streaming video. It was jerky and shaking slightly, but it was still clear what it was.

"*It might never make it to Hartfield,*" the Isabel on Dave's phone was saying. "*It might get accidentally broken on the way.*"

"What . . . ?" Isabel said faintly. "How . . . ?"

Dave turned off his phone and patted the horse on the back. "Video," he said. "We've got everything you just said. And in addition to threatening to destroy your own school's mascot costume, you're also on record threatening Madison here, fairly seriously. Which I'm sure your future college prospects wouldn't be too happy to find out about."

"But . . ." Isabel said, looking at the horse, as though trying to figure out just how this had happened.

"It is a *Trojan horse,*" Ruth said. "You'd think you might have been a little more careful."

Isabel glared at me. "Nice, Madison," she said.

I shook my head. "I had no idea any of this was going

to happen," I said. "I'm as surprised as you are." I looked from Dave to Turtell to Ruth, and understood all the secrecy that had been swirling around them earlier. "Which is *very* surprised."

"What can I say," Ruth said, smiling back at me. "It seemed like the best way to handle things."

"Also, don't even think about doing anything to this mascot," Sarah said, holding up her phone. "I've texted Connor Atkins, who's pretty much Dr. Trent's favorite person, and let him know that it's here. And he's making arrangements to have it transported back to Hartfield."

"Connor?" Schuyler asked faintly, grabbing on to Peyton's arm for support. "Really?"

"So what are you planning on doing with that video?" Isabel asked, her voice fainter now, with the first note of genuine fear sounding in it.

"*Rien,*" Lisa said. "Nothing. We're not like *you*. We're not going to blackmail you with this."

Mark turned to her, looking crestfallen. "We're nawt?" he asked.

"Nope," Kittson said. Since I had no idea what my friends' plan was, or what they had discussed, I was as in the dark as he was, and just going along for the ride. "We're not. But." She crossed her arms and glared at Isabel. "We hope that the knowledge that this video exists—in multiple copies, since Dave just sent it to all of us—will help you calm down your vengeful streak whenever you get the urge to try and hurt Madison or any of the rest of us. Because something you should know—it's pretty much the same thing."

I blinked at Kittson, beyond touched, and feeling very strongly that I had the very best friends in the world.

Isabel looked at all of us, a unified group, staring back at her. Her shoulders slumped, and the fight seemed to leave her. "All right," she said quietly. She met my eye and I looked back at her.

There was no more anger in her glare, and, I hoped, no more need for justice in mine. It was just the look of two people who were walking away from a fight. Isabel gave me a small nod, then turned and walked away alone.

****

Once Isabel's headlights disappeared down the road, it was like we all let out a collective breath. Tricia had stayed behind, looking genuinely regretful and tried to apologize. But Lisa had cut her off and told her, in no uncertain terms, *adieu*. Tricia had glanced back at all of us for a moment longer before turning and walking toward Isabel, but not appearing too happy about it, which I could understand. If you'd spent the last few weeks with my friends, and then had to go back to just being friends with Isabel, I could imagine you'd be less than thrilled.

As the last sight of Isabel vanished, everyone began talking again, and we started to make our way back to where our cars were. As Dave steered the horse to the parking lot, Turtell pointed out how he'd attached the wheels and tried to look modest as Kittson gushed. Lisa, Dave, and Schuyler were walking together,

Schuyler fixing (but not chewing) her hair—clearly thinking about Connor. Peyton walked next to Dell, who seemed to be holding forth about something. I caught her eye and we exchanged a quick smile. I hurried past Mark and Sarah—Mark seemed to be complaining, now back to his normal accent, that he was one of the only people kept in the dark about the plan—to catch up to Ruth, who was speed-walking toward the parking lot for some reason.

"Hi," I said. I shook my head. "Wow."

"I know," she said, smiling back at me. "Just your average Monday night, right?"

I laughed at that, and felt relief flood through me. It was *over*. We had done it. "Thank you so much," I said. "Though you guys could have told me."

"It seemed safer this way," she said, eyes still fixed on the parking lot, and I wondered what she was looking for.

"I'm just so glad it's over," I said as we reached the end of the field. "It's been a good night."

"I think it might get better," Ruth said. She looked toward the parking lot, and as I followed her gaze, I realized why I'd heard two car doors slamming when Dave had arrived. It was because he hadn't been alone. There was someone else standing next to his car.

It was Nate.

CHAPTER 32

Song: Breathe In/Hit the Lights
Quote: "True love stories never have endings."
—Richard Bach

My heart started to beat double-time, and I found that it was suddenly getting hard to breathe. Nate was looking at me, and for just a moment, everything else around me—the ten other people and the motorized wooden horse—disappeared. And there was only Nate and me, seeing just each other.

I opened my mouth to say something, but Ruth spoke first. "Glad you made it," she said, smiling at Nate.

"Oui," Lisa agreed, walking up with Schuyler, who gave Nate a wave. "Though I'm afraid you missed the show."

"It was epic, dude," Turtell said. *"Epic."*

"Wait," I said, looking around at my friends, absolutely none of whom seemed surprised to see my ex-boyfriend in the parking lot. "What's happening?"

"We took things into our own hands," Kittson said. "You're welcome."

I looked back at Nate, who still hadn't spoken. He looked at me, and I could feel the charge of the silence between us, filled with all the words we still needed to say.

"So!" Dave said, a little too loudly. "My house? Fifteen?" He glanced at me and Nate. "Or . . . you know, a little longer." He gave me a smile, then clapped Nate on the shoulder.

I took a breath to say something, when Kittson tugged at my arm. "We need to handle the Dell thing," she murmured. I looked over and saw that Dell was standing by his car next to Peyton, looking very happy. I nodded, and looked at Nate once more.

It was killing me not to talk to him, but I did know I had to clear things up with Dell first.

"I'll, um," I said, clearing my throat, feeling my heart pound with nervousness. "Be just a second. If you don't mind waiting?"

Nate gave me one of his slow half smiles and shook his head. "No," he said in a voice that was a little more hoarse than usual. "I don't mind."

Kittson tugged me in the direction of Dell, and it was a good thing she did, because I don't know if, of my own volition, I would have been capable of looking away from Nate.

We headed over to Dell's SUV and arrived as he was giving Peyton a card. "That's all my numbers," he was saying, his words coming out in a tumble. "And all my e-mail addresses. And if you want to get dinner, I can compile a database that breaks restaurants down by rating, or cuisine, or . . ."

"Coffee," Peyton said, tucking his card into her back pocket and putting on her helmet. "I like coffee." She gave him what, for her, was a big smile, and headed over to her Vespa, her cheeks, it seemed, a little pinker than usual.

Dell sighed and leaned back against his car, watching Peyton start her scooter and peel out of the parking lot.

"Dell," I said. He looked over and gave us a vague smile.

"Hey, guys," he said. "Interesting night, right?"

"More like illuminating," Kittson said, her voice crisp. This seemed to snap Dell out of his love haze a little.

"I suppose," he replied, his voice level.

"I was glad to find out why you did this," I said. "Everyone knew you didn't suddenly grow a conscience overnight."

"I don't know what you're talking about," Dell said in a monotone, though his eyes darted nervously between the two of us.

"I'm talking about *Frank Info*," Kittson said. "The third file that was on Isabel's flash drive."

Dell gaped at her for a moment. "And how do you know about that?" he finally managed.

"Because I asked her to monitor your laptop," I said.

Dell's jaw dropped and he stared at Kittson. "You hacked my computer?" he asked incredulously.

Kittson shrugged, clearly trying for modest but not pulling it off. "I told you I was good," she said.

"But . . ." Dell stammered.

I shook my head. "It just didn't make sense that Isabel would have been able to gain access to your computer—especially without you knowing it. Did you leave it out for her at your family reunion?" Dell looked down at the asphalt and shrugged, which was pretty much all the confirmation that I needed. "Is that why this whole thing happened?" I asked, staring at him hard. "Isabel had something you wanted, and you needed to get us to steal it for you?"

Dell shrugged again, and I looked at Kittson, who shook her head. "Well, it didn't work," Kittson said. "I pulled it off your hard drive, and I'm going to put it—whatever it is—on a flash drive and send it back to her. If you want it from her, steal it yourself."

"Or ask her for it," I amended quickly. "There's that option, too."

"But—" Dell started. I raised my eyebrows at him and saw that Kittson did the same. "Never mind," he muttered, backing down, maybe recognizing a losing battle when he saw it.

"See you," Kittson said as she turned on her heel and walked away.

I lifted a hand and waved at him. *"Adieu,"* I said, thinking of Lisa's vocabulary lesson. I had just started to follow her when Dell called out to us.

"It wasn't the only reason," he said. I turned back to him and saw Kittson do the same. "I just . . ." he started.

He looked at us, and then back down at the ground. "I thought that you would need my help," he muttered.

"What do you mean?" I asked, taking a step closer to him.

"I thought," Dell said slowly, like each word was painful to say, "that you would need my help figuring this out. And that you'd forgive me for what happened in the spring. Andmaybewecouldbefriendsagain." He said this last part very quickly, stringing the words together.

I met Kittson's eye, and she narrowed her eyes at Dell before shrugging. "He didn't get it," she said to me in a low voice. "And he actually did help."

I looked at Dell, and finally shrugged as well. "No more secrets," I said to him, and he nodded vigorously.

"Yes," he said. "I mean, no."

"Good," Kittson said, turning to go again. "Party at Dave's if you're coming," she called over her shoulder. She hurried to catch up with Turtell, who was loading the horse into the back of a Jeep I recognized as Connor's. Connor was standing in front of his car, totally ignoring Turtell staggering under the weight of the horse, and talking to Schuyler, who was holding a bouquet of Gerbera daisies and smiling wide, looking happier than I'd seen her in months.

As I got closer to where Nate was waiting, I slowed my pace, even though what I really wanted to do was run to him as fast as I could. But I was trying to get my thoughts together. All around me, cars were pulling out of the parking lot, heading for Dave's. Schuyler got into Connor's Jeep, still smiling radiantly. They were the last to pull out of the parking lot, and then it was empty except for Judy, Nate, and me.

I walked until I was standing right in front of him, feeling like I simultaneously wanted to laugh and cry. It was so good to see him, but it also reminded me how much I'd missed him, and how much had passed between us.

"Hi," I murmured, hearing my voice crack.

"Hi," he said back. He gave me another half smile.

"Nate, I'm so sorry," I said, the words, the ones I'd wanted to say to him from the beginning, rushing out of me. "I didn't want to break up with you, but Isabel was going to release the video of you, and I thought you wouldn't be able to go to Yale, and—"

"I know," Nate said, cutting me off. "Dave told me."

I blinked at him. "He did?"

"And that was after Ruth and Lisa and Schuyler all told me," he said, smiling again. "But I first started to know something was going on after your brother came to see me yesterday."

This was not what I had been expecting to hear. "Travis?" I asked, shocked.

Nate nodded. "He biked up to my house and threatened to beat me up for dumping you," he said.

"He did?" I asked, feeling a surge of affection for my brother, and realizing he had come through on the promise he'd made me after the prom.

"He was very serious about it," Nate said, his smile

329

widening. "He said that you told him our breakup wasn't your idea. Which got me wondering. And so I called Ruth, looking for some answers."

"I'm sorry to have put you through this," I said. "I just . . . didn't see any other way."

"I think . . ." Nate said, and he cleared his throat. "I think it's an amazing thing to do for someone."

I nodded and exhaled, ready to tell him what I should have been brave enough to tell him the second I felt it. Because I could see now that it didn't matter who said it first. But it needed to be said because, as I'd learned, things could end suddenly, and your once wide-open window would slam shut. And it seemed better to take the opportunity when it presented itself, because you never knew how many more there would be.

"Nate," I said, my voice trembling. I didn't know if he'd say it back. But I also knew that it didn't matter. I just had to let him know how I felt. I took a breath. "I love you."

He looked at me in silence for a moment, then broke into a big smile. "I know," he said.

I blinked at him. "You know?" I echoed, confused, as this had not been the reaction I'd been expecting.

"After Travis showed up, I started thinking about your note," he said. He pulled a piece of paper out of his pocket and handed it to me. I unfolded it, and smiled when I saw that it was my letter to him, translated. He'd cracked the code.

Nate,

Does one not tell?   *DON'T*
When a new thought   *WANT*
Takes hold it sticks.   *THIS*

Better let a change kommence,
meaning an initial loss ends doubts.   *BLACKMAILED*

It's   *I*
Letting one version end   *LOVE*
You once understood   *YOU*
Tragically, once's over.   *TOO*

Madison

"A cipher," he said when I looked back up at him. "Nicely done."

"Well," I said, handing the paper back to him, "I learned from the best."

"I thought you might want this back," he said, reaching into the messenger bag that was at his feet and pulling out my wooden tortoise.

"Thank you," I said, feeling my heart pound as I took it from him. He didn't let go right away, but held on to it, reaching out with his other hand to touch my cheek carefully.

I felt myself shiver, and took a step closer to him, my heart pounding harder than ever. I dropped the tortoise in my purse, and Nate reached out and took both of my hands in his.

"How about," Nate said, his voice slightly choked, "we don't do that again?"

I shook my head, smiling, even though I could feel tears in my eyes. "Never," I said. I stepped closer to him, closing the distance left between us.

"That sounds good," he said, smiling down at me. "That sounds *perf.*"

I laughed as I stretched up toward him and Nate tipped his head down to me. When our lips met, it felt almost like our first kiss all over again. But it was more than that. It felt like after a long time wandering, alone, lost . . . it felt like I'd finally come home again.

CHAPTER 33

Song: Summer Hair = Forever Young/The Academy
Is . . .
Quote: "I had the time of my life, fighting dragons with
you."—Taylor Swift

"Got everything?" Nate asked as he killed the engine and I opened the passenger-side door of his truck.

"I think so," I said, peering into my canvas bag. For whatever reason, I had been assigned chips as my bonfire food. My bag was stuffed with them, all the normal varieties, as well as a bag of something called "Yumm Crisps" that my mother had brought back with her from the UK.

"Let's *go*!" Travis yelled. He pounded on the back of my seat with one hand and scrolled through his phone with the other. "Olivia's been here for, like, ten minutes already."

I rolled my eyes but stepped out of Nate's truck, pulling my seat forward so that Travis could get out. My brother had wasted no time in taking full advantage of the snacks—and rides—promised due to our phone swap. But since he was largely to thank for getting Nate and I back together again, I didn't even mind that much.

Travis climbed out, and I shut the door behind him. The night was still warm, the sun just beginning to set. "See you over there," he called behind him, already speed-walking across the sand to his girlfriend.

I met Nate at the front of the truck, and he took my hand in his. But that didn't seem like quite enough for me, so I stretched up and kissed him. Since we had gotten back together, things were very good between us. It wasn't like we'd never been apart—I definitely felt what the separation had done to us. But as it turned out, all the changes were good.

Before, the thought of being without Nate for two days had sent me into a panic. But now, it was, oddly, easier to be separated from him. Not that either of us liked it, but our break had proved that we could be apart from each other and still be okay. It was why I was no longer worried about Nate heading to Yale in the fall. We'd weathered so much already; I was sure we could handle an LDR. Plus, I'd been doing research online, and New Haven was supposed to have Connecticut's best pizza, which was just an added bonus—even though I hadn't yet been able to find out what the pineapple situation was.

Nate and I were just a little more serious about each other now. We'd seen what we stood to lose, and both of us seemed committed to making sure that didn't happen again.

But even though we were back together, I was very conscious about not letting myself get lost in him as I had earlier this summer. I wanted to have more of a balance between Nate and my friends. Sunday night was now, in perpetuity, for my friends. I didn't think it was a possibility, but I wanted to be sure that I would never take them for granted—or put a relationship before them—ever again. And so far, it seemed to be working.

Nate and I broke our kiss, and I traced my finger over his cheek, kissing him once more and then hugging him tight, hearing the chips in my bag crunch as a result.

"So," Nate said as we stepped apart and he took my hand, kissing it once, and then interlacing his fingers with mine, "who's going to be at this shindig?"

"Oh, just the usual suspects," I said as we headed over to the small patch of beach that was ours for the night. I glanced over at the Second Concession Stand and shook my head. "Kavya and Justin were supposed to come by when he finished work," I said with a laugh. "So they'll probably show up around eleven."

I had been a little worried that Justin would be holding a grudge as a result of the freezer detainment, identity theft, and phone stealing. But by the time I talked to him about it, he and Kavya were officially an item, and he seemed so thrilled about this that I wasn't entirely sure that he knew who I was when I was trying to apologize to him.

And since On A Blender had been closed for the last two weeks, Kavya and Justin were getting to spend a lot of time together. I'd been really concerned about the fruit in our freezer thawing, then freezing, and thawing again, and had left an anonymous tip with the health inspection office. So while the "freezer malfunction" was looked into, we were all temporarily jobless. Daryl and John had picked up some extra valet shifts, and Justin had switched concession stands with Mark, solely so he could spend the entire workday customerless and making out with Kavya, who seemed to be adjusting to unemployment just fine. In my jobless interim, I had started helping Ruth with the Volturi, which meant the amount of laundry I had to do had increased threefold. But I got to spend the whole day with my once and current BFF, which made up for all the juice boxes that were constantly being spilled on me.

As Nate and I got closer to the bonfire, I could see that maybe Travis had been right to be hurrying me along, as it seemed like everyone else had already arrived. Travis was standing off to the side of the group with Olivia—who appeared to be sporting several lanyard necklaces.

Ruth and Andy were standing at the edge of the group as he gestured to the sky to point out a constellation—an actual one. Schuyler and Connor, virtually inseparable since getting back together, were holding hands despite the fact that they were both also trying to eat burgers. Dave and Turtell (who had fully embraced Dave's obsession, and was using his mechanic skills to pimp Dave's small rides) were racing their dune buggy mini trucks across the sand while Kittson and Lisa stood apart, laughing about something. Brian

McMahon and Sarah's boyfriend, Zach, were watching the race closely, in a way that made me think that there was a small wager in play. Jimmy and Liz were, as was to be expected, making out furiously on a blanket while, nearby and paying them absolutely no attention, Ginger was carrying on a conversation with Mark and Sarah. John was playing the guitar—badly, I could hear, even from over here—while Daryl tried to roast marshmallows on a stick, seemingly unaware of the fact that the stick—and the marshmallows—had caught fire. Dell was standing slightly apart, talking to Peyton, who, I had noticed, was smiling a lot more lately than she ever seemed to before.

As I looked around, I felt a wave of affection for them all. Now that I knew what it was like to be without them, I knew how much they meant to me—and how lucky I was—in a way I never had before.

Schuyler waved to me and Nate with her burger hand, and Daryl waved with his flaming stick, sending a shower of sparks flying dangerously close to Sarah's hair.

"Shall we?" Nate asked as he squeezed my hand once, then four times, then three times.

I squeezed his hand back, and gave him a smile. "Let's," I said. And hand in hand, we walked across the beach to join my friends.

You've received an invitation to join
THE FINAL WORD
in social networking . . .

Zyzzx

Zyzzx . . . **The Road to Friendship**

MADISON M.

PUTNAM, CT

AGE: 17

SOUNDTRACK: A Story to Tell Your Friends/Every Avenue

QUOTE OF THE DAY: "The final mystery is oneself."
— Oscar Wilde

THIS IS ME: Maker of smoothies.
Girlfriend of Nate.
Drinker of iced lattes. Enjoying the summer.
Suddenly and worryingly addicted to Yumm Crisps.

MADISON M Thinking that I need to have s'mores more often.

 DARYL O Mad, you can say that because your marshmallows didn't explode. I mean, what? There should be a warning on the package, or something.

 JOHN R Do you need me to sign something, dude? I totally will.

 TRAVIS M Thanks for the invite, Mad! I'm, like, the only rising 9th grader to be on here. The Coolness has arrived.

 MADISON M Kavya, is it possible to revoke an invite?

 TRAVIS M Hey!

 KAVYA C Not that I know of. But I can look into it. Or you could. That might be better, actually.

 SCHUYLER W Mad, you and Rue should bring the Volturi by the Club tomorrow. I'm giving a lecture on the importance of sunblock for children!

 RUTH M Not a bad idea, Mad. We've been having trouble getting them to nap lately. . . .

DAVE G My house. Tonight. Davy 500. Around the pool. BE THERE.

 KITTSON P Mad, get Dave to stream it, will you? I want to see from the Hamptons when Glen KICKS HIS BUTT.

 GLEN T Thanks, baby!

 LISA F Madison, Schuyler, et Ruth! Let's meet at Stubbs ASAP. Je pense que it's time for a major, fundamental change. And I'm thinking . . . bangs.

 MADISON M Now? Iced lattes on me.

 RUTH M See you soon!

 SCHUYLER W I'll be there!!

 NATE E Hey gf. Dave's tonight? Pick you up at 7?

 MADISON M Sounds perf. ☺

NATE E Oh, and there was one more thing I wanted to tell you . . .

 NATE E 1

 NATE E 4

 NATE E 3

 MADISON M Right back at you. ♥

 MADISON M logged out.

Follow all the drama of Madison and her friends, both online and off. . . .

Don't miss:

TOP 8

Madison comes home from vacation to find her Friendverse profile hacked! Someone has posted damaging secrets and even broken her up with her boyfriend. Can she fix this mess before her life is ruined?

and

WHAT'S YOUR STATUS?
A TOP 8 NOVEL

When Madison is put in charge of her school's priceless heirloom, it accidentally falls into the wrong hands. Can she and her friends pull off a heist with the help of their status updates?

www.thisisteen.com

To Do List:
Read all the Point books!

♡ 📖 ♡

Abandon
Airhead
Being Nikki
Runaway
By **Meg Cabot**

Wish
Wishful Thinking
By **Alexandra Bullen**

Top 8
What's Your Status?
By **Katie Finn**

Sea Change
The Year My Sister Got Lucky
South Beach
French Kiss
Hollywood Hills
By **Aimee Friedman**

Ruined
By **Paula Morris**

Possessed
Consumed
By **Kate Cann**

Suite Scarlett
Scarlett Fever
By **Maureen Johnson**

The Lonely Hearts Club
Prom and Prejudice
By **Elizabeth Eulberg**

Wherever Nina Lies
By **Lynn Weingarten**

Clarity
By **Kim Harrington**

And Then
Everything Unraveled
And Then I Found
Out the Truth
By **Jennifer Sturman**

Point